Before the Alamo

the

A Tejana's story

Before the Alamo

A Tejana's story

FLORENCE
BYHAM WEINBERG

Maywood House
San Antonio, Texas
2021

Before the Alamo, a Tejana's Story

Maywood House
an imprint of F M Weinberg Co
331 Royal Oaks Drive
San Antonio, TX 78209
www.florenceweinberg.com

Registration Number: TXu 2-264-966

First Edition: July 2021

ISBN 978-1-7374182-9-0

Cover and Book design by Tamian Wood, BeyondDesignBooks.com
Printed in the United States of America

"*Before the Alamo* presents me with unforgettable characters, some based on historical people, and brings a time and place to vivid life. [The slogan] 'Remember the Alamo!' is a historical catchcry that has justified patriotism and pride, but also discrimination, divisiveness, and hate. Here, in a superbly researched book, is the real story."

~ Dr. Bob Rich,
Aussie, psychologist,
and prize-winning author

"This book, *Before the Alamo*, not only presents a gripping story and unforgettable characters, but also, wonder of wonders! a balanced and accurate story of events prior to and in the battle of the Alamo. Read it, enjoy, and learn. I did."

~ Andre Csihas,
Texas court interpreter

Acknowledgements

My warmest thanks to the members of the Daedalus Critique Group, who read and gave advice on style, plot problems, character flaws and other useful comments. They read the entire novel, 25 pages at a time, giving it their closest attention. Bless them for their patience and wisdom!

Dora Guerra, historian of Texas and especially of San Antonio de Béxar, her native city, read the first version of a hundred pages of the novel, and commented tartly, "We don't need another lousy history of Texas! Pay more attention to your characters!"

I took her advice, junked those hundred pages and started again. The results, I believe, are far more satisfactory. Thank you, Dora!

Special thanks are due to Dr. Bruce Winders, Curator and Historian of the Alamo. Before I started writing, he introduced me to the librarians at the Alamo Library and Archive. I had time to complete most of my research there before the State of Texas took over the Alamo Shrine with its grounds and buildings, including the library and all holdings. I also owe my warmest thanks to those librarians, who knew just where to find what I needed.

Dr. Winters' kindness was not limited to that introduction. As perhaps the most knowledgeable person alive about details regarding the Alamo, including its history and post-battle fortunes, he read my finished manuscript and gave me highly valuable information, correcting me and my sources where we had gone astray. The result is a far more accurate portrait of the Hispanic people, founders of Texas and builders of San Antonio. The novel now gives a better idea of their daily habits and interrelations, religion, law-keeping, and most of all their political beliefs. These determined their reactions to the central government, far away in Mexico City, as well as to the influx of Anglo settlers after Stephen F. Austin brought in the first colony of three hundred families in 1821.

For the portrait of Emilia, the protagonist of the story, I mined my memories of Anita, an intrepid and saucy little playmate I once knew in Alamogordo, New Mexico, when I was a child her age.

Author's Note

This novel is set during an extremely eventful period of Texas history. For those readers unfamiliar with it, I strongly recommend reading the brief history that I have included in the Appendix. It outlines Texas history from the beginnings of San Antonio de Béxar in 1718 to 1847, when Texas became a part of the United States.

I also include a list of characters.

Chapter One
January 1814

The wind, keening from the northwest, bore the threat of sleet or snow, causing former Lieutenant Juan Andrés Altamirano to wrap his buckskin jacket tighter. Three days of travel in cold and sloppy weather lay behind, from San Juan Bautista on the Río Grande to San Antonio de Béxar and the small fort called "the Alamo" that had once been a mission.

Ruana, his mare, stumbled and he slowed her to a walk. Like him, she must be exhausted as well as muddy. They had finally reached Potrero Street. He was coming home and had needed but couldn't afford to buy a second horse somewhere along the way from Monclova. He'd made do with just this one. Her gait told him her feet were sore, and he should dismount and lead her to give her some relief, but he was so close to home and so tired. Her head hung low as she plodded along, the bit nearly scraping the ground. Andrés, travel-sore and headachy, lowered his chin to his chest, pulling his sombrero down and his bandana over his nose to protect his face from the relentless wind.

The letter summoning him back from exile crackled as he fingered his breast pocket. *General* Joaquín de Arredondo of the Royalist Army, fighting to put down a massive rebellion for Mexican independence, needed his former lieutenant for a "delicate task."

1

Andrés almost feared to speculate what that might be. The letter had probably caused his midnight nightmare of last year's slauhter at the Medina River, the battlefield not twenty-five miles away. There, after Arredondo's victory, eighteen-hundred men lay dead and unburied—the entire army of independence fighters. Their corpses by now must be reduced to white bones, picked clean by coyotes and carrion birds. He, Andrés, had played his part in the massacre: he'd fired upon friends and neighbors.

After the king's army had left the field of battle and entered and occupied Béxar, Arredondo began a campaign of executing anyone he suspected of sympathizing with the rebels. He discovered that the rest of Andrés's family was on the rebel side. Most of them had escaped to Louisiana, but Andrés was now under suspicion. In a public ceremony, Arredondo tore the insignia off his chest, decommissioning and dismissing him without pay. His life was spared, but he fled to Saltillo in case the general might change his mind.

And now he was coming home. But was it still "home"? The nearer he came, the shorter his breath, and the blood pulsed hard in the arteries in his neck. He and Ruana raised their heads in unison. What was that stench? The wind blowing through the town surely bore the scent of death. Perhaps an earlier whiff had been sufficient to sharpen those hideous images of the field of slaughter at Medina. Ruana snorted and shook her head. She, too, knew that stink.

Andrés straightened, peering from side to side as he began to pass low adobe buildings in the outskirts. There. At the corner of Santa Rosa Street, a lance, its haft buried in the ground, and impaled on the blade a blackened globe. Ruana's plodding steps brought them nearer, and it became clear what that round object really was. A human head. The flesh had been pecked and torn by birds, blackened and dried so it was mostly skull, still retaining its hair and a bit of beard. He urged Ruana past only to find another at the bridge across San Pedro Creek. At this one, he stopped. This severed head was not so advanced in decay. The cold had preserved it. He knew the man. Ambrosio Quintana! He had joked, drunk pulque, and passed the time of day with him. Bile rose bitter in his mouth; he gagged and quickly turned the horse's head away, urging her across the bridge.

The Governor's Palace lay to his right, at the corner of Military Plaza, where he assumed the general would have set up his command post. A large one-story building, it and the *Casas reales*, containing the courthouse at the far side of adjoining Main Plaza, were built of stone. Most other buildings around the squares were adobe, except for the looming stone structure of San Fernando Church standing in the center, dividing the two plazas. The streets and the plaza looked like home and yet seemed more squalid than he remembered. He'd seen more grandiose architecture during his service in the army.

He dismounted and cleaned his clothing as best he could, scraping dried muddy splatters off trousers and boots. He still struggled against his nausea and his hands' uncontrollable shaking as he fingered his six-day growth of beard. He spoke aloud to the mare. "I've come all this way to obey Arredondo's orders, but, damn! There's a good chance my head will end up like the others, all of us scarecrows. Not to scare birds, but to terrorize anyone who even dreams of independence from Spain."

He tied Ruana to the hitching rail and entered the icy antechamber of the palace. A young sergeant hunched at a small desk, obviously a mestizo with dark hair and brown skin, rose with a clatter of boots to challenge him, raised eyebrows and slight smirk betraying his scorn for the drooping and bedraggled figure before him. The curt question seemed addressed to a peon. "Who are you and what's your business here?"

Andrés produced the letter, kept as clean as possible during the trip. "*General* Arredondo summoned me, and I am obeying his orders, *Sargento*."

The sergeant unfolded the letter and read it slowly. "This letter is addressed to *Teniente* Juan Andrés Altamirano. Where is he?"

Andrés drew himself up, took a deep breath and squared his shoulders. "I am he, *Sargento*. I am out of uniform because I traveled incognito. I made it in six days from Monclova to obey the general's orders. You've just read them. Now *you* follow orders, *Sargento*. I must see the general at once!"

His bravado worked. The sergeant gave a quick salute. "*Sí, Señor Teniente*. I'll announce you to *el general*." He vanished through the door to the room beyond the antechamber. Juan Andrés heard the murmur of voices, then a louder "*Sí Señor!*" and the noise of boots swiveling and clacking on the tile floor. The sergeant reappeared. "The *general* will see you now." He gave the lieutenant a curious look, from head to toe, then stepped aside.

Andrés must face the man he considered a monster. Now. Nausea and trembling returned. His feet carried him forward as if on their own, while he concentrated on swallowing the bile in his throat. He passed the threshold, was greeted by the perfume of oak logs burning in the huge fireplace to his left and was enveloped in the blanket of its warmth. He stopped before the vast mahogany desk that had belonged to the governor of Texas Province, stood at attention and saluted. "Former *Teniente* Juan Andrés Altamirano reporting for duty, *Señor General*." He thanked heaven that his voice, at least, had remained steady.

"At ease, *Teniente*."

It seemed his rank had magically been restored. "Please tell me, *Señor General*, why I was recalled."

"You and José Ángel Navarro are the only men left who served in the Royalist Army and know the locals. Both of you come from families of original settlers, so you're familiar with the histories of nearly everyone in Béxar. Your records were good, at least until I dismissed the two of you." He paused to stare at Juan Andrés as if remembering his former service. "But I need your knowledge to assess the characters of several men I have in detention, before I execute them. They claim to be loyal partisans of His Majesty, King Ferdinand. I'm restoring your rank—provisionally, mind you—so long as you serve me well. With two of you working together on the task, there will be less chance of deception."

"*Sí, Señor*. I'll do my best, *Señor General*."

"Good. Report to me at eight tomorrow morning. Meanwhile, get yourself a proper uniform from the quartermaster's supply at the old mission, the Alamo, whatever you call it. You look famished. Here's money to buy food." The general reached out, and a silver peso clattered on the desk. "Dismissed."

"*Sí, Señor General*." Andrés pocketed the coin, saluted again, did a regulation about-face and marched out, conscious of the noise his boots made on the tile, the spurs jingling with every step. He passed the sergeant without a word, feeling the man's stare follow him as he closed the heavy entrance door.

He untied Ruana and, his pulse slowing, muscles relaxing, led her across the dusty and rutted plaza to the pump at the rear of San Fernando Church. The trough, a hollow live oak log, held an inch or two of ice-rimmed water, too little to slake the thirst of the animals passing through. He wielded the pump, splashing more water into the trough, and as Ruana slurped the cold liquid, he filled the dipper hanging there and drank. Once they both had their fill, he led the mare to Rosita's Fonda, a mud and wattle lean-to, half a *jacal* outfitted with *un horno*, an oven, *una parrilla*, a grill, a counter, three tables and chairs, and stools that rocked on the uneven earthen floor. Primitive accommodations, but strategically placed to get business from both plazas, since its back door opened toward Main Plaza, *La Plaza de las Islas*.

Andrés moved closer to the horno for warmth and straddled a stool. "*Hola, Rosita. Un plato de frijoles, chorizo y huevo, por favor.* A plate of beans, sausage and egg, please."

Rosita had not changed since he last saw her. Short and squat with stooped shoulders, her iron-gray hair was pulled back and knotted behind her head. A wide, wrinkled face with black eyes like two holes burnt in a blanket, as his mother used to say.

She stared at his wind-burned, half-bearded face. "Why, you're Juan Andrés Altamirano! I was here and watched the parade where the general tore the insignia off your chest and exiled you. How did you get back? Aren't they looking for you?"

Andrés chuckled. "Yes, they were looking, and they found me. They want me to help Ángel Navarro 'assess the characters' of some prisoners, men I know, so they say. If we're not clever enough to construct a believable character for each one, the unlucky ones get shot as independence sympathizers. At least, that's how I understood what Arredondo just told me."

"You spoke with the general, himself? You're still a Royalist, then?"

"Yes, Rosita. Look, I'm not the only Royalist in town. Ángel, the priests—certainly Father Zambrano—and a bunch of neighbors and friends are still loyal to His Majesty and to the country our fathers came from. At least they were when I left here five months ago."

Rosita wrinkled her nose. "You'd better believe they still are! They'd be long dead if they weren't. Arredondo has been on a rampage of universal slaughter of rebels, all over Texas. Every time they ask me, I swear total loyalty. It's the only way I survive."

"Same with me, I guess. I start my duty tomorrow morning at eight. Meanwhile, I'm to get a uniform from over at the old mission, then..."

"Then, my friend, you'd better go visit María, that Indian servant woman of yours. She just had a new baby."

"A baby?" Andrés hesitated. "Boy or girl?"

"Girl."

"Oh...." He pondered. Last year—early April, was it?—he'd come home on leave after one of the continuing battles against

6

independence fighters in central Mexico. He'd seen too much bloody slaughter by then and anticipated much more to come. When he arrived in Béxar, he found a peaceful and beautiful welcome: the surrounding fields rippled intensely blue with bluebonnets, accented here and there by the orange-red of Indian paintbrushes. Trees, too, were in bloom: redbuds, leafless as yet, but glowing with lavender-pink buds, and in dense groves, mustard yellow banks of the huisache had rejoiced his soul. Yes, it was definitely early April.

His wife, Carmen, was ill, so he'd sought companionship with María, that strange combination of native Otomí Indian and refined Spanish mannerisms. He had desired her secretly for months, ever since he bought her at the illegal slave market in San Juan Bautista, and at last he'd felt free to take her. Four months later, after the Battle of Medina, he was decommissioned and disgraced. María must have been pregnant then, but too early for him to notice—and she'd told him nothing. She had hidden him and aided his escape. His exile after that had lasted almost five months. Four months plus five... that would be time enough.

So he was a father! An unnecessary and unwelcome complication in his life just now. And a girl.... He'd have felt less resentful if it had been a boy. He glanced up and saw Rosita watching him with narrowed eyes.

"Now, don't get ideas, Rosita. How about that plate? And the glass of pulque to go with it."

"Humph!" She turned her back, and he watched her deft arm and shoulder movements as she cracked the eggs and scrambled them together with the sausage on the parrilla. She wrapped it all in tortillas and left them on the grill to heat through, then plunked a tall clay cup of pulque before him. He took several sips.

The toasty-hot food arrived on a glazed pottery plate, interrupting his thoughts. He wolfed it like the starving man he was. "How much do I owe you, Rosita?"

"*Nada*, Andrés. I'm celebrating your safe return. You're one of the few customers left whose head is still on his shoulders."

⌇

Andrés's boots thudded on hard-packed soil at the side of the Altamirano adobe house. María straightened to see him as he rounded the corner. Tall, he thought, for an Indian, slender and graceful despite just giving birth. He sought her face—handsome and almost beautiful—and found it unchanged: large eyes with brown irises fringed by black lashes, cheek bones wide and high, strong chin, voluptuous lips, abundant black hair in one fat braid down her back. She gasped; it was as if she were seeing a ghost. She dropped her basket of freshly dug onions. "Andrés! You're alive! You're in full uniform!" She ran toward him, arms wide.

He received her in his embrace, kissing her, self-conscious and awkward. "Yes, María, I got here this morning, saw Arredondo, then went to the Alamo to get cleaned up and find a new uniform. I'll be starting work again in the morning. Now that I'm decent, I'm here to see you... and, of course, the baby... our baby. Rosita told me. I had no idea you were even expecting."

María blinked back tears. "I thought I'd never see you again. Thank God, our baby is just fine. Healthy and beautiful. It's a miracle, since merely staying alive was next to impossible after you left." She paused to wipe her eyes. "I'm so glad you're back!" She took his hands and gave them a squeeze.

He disengaged them to rub his freshly shaven jaw. "I saw the heads on pikes as I came into town this morning. It's Arredondo, doing what they did with Father Hidalgo's head, too, and the other leaders of the rebellion. I escaped to Saltillo after Arredondo disgraced me because I thought I'd be shot and suffer the same fate."

"I know. Béxar's a ghost town. Those not killed are hiding in Louisiana—like the rest of your family."

"But you are still alive. How is it that you're up, digging onions and running to meet me after just having a baby? No white woman would be up before a week's time."

"I'm a servant, remember? I'm tired and sore, very sore, but my arms and legs still work—and so do I."

"What happened to you while I was gone? To the other women who stayed?"

"First, we were cooped up in La Quinta and forced to grind corn and make tortillas for the army—and forced to do other things..."

"You were raped?"

"I made myself as ugly and dirty as possible. My dark skin kept them away for a while. By the time one of the soldiers took me, I was visibly pregnant. I said it was a Royalist baby. I could see he would take me by force anyway, so I told him I'd favor him if he was gentle with me."

"And? Was he?"

"At least I didn't lose your baby. After that, they left me alone because my belly grew so much. I kept on telling them it was a Royalist baby. And she is."

Andrés pulled her to him, his arm around her shoulders. "I'm so sorry you had to suffer like that. But you did the right thing to save the child. How did you get from La Quinta back here, to my house?"

María stood on tiptoe to kiss Andrés's earlobe, then pushed him away. "When soldiers were billeted in your house—they're still in there—they brought me over here to cook and clean for them. You see," she pointed to the basket on the ground. "I need to get those onions into the kitchen. I'll be cooking *la comida*, the mid-day meal, soon."

"Our child. Where is she? I don't hear any crying."

"She was asleep when I came out to dig the onions. She's well fed." María smiled, glancing down at her enlarged breasts, bound with a colorful shawl knotted over her simple brown shift. "Come with me." She led the way and pulled aside the cowhide door-covering over the entrance to the *jacal*, the one-room hut behind the main house and the freestanding kitchen.

She moved to a straw mattress against one wall and opened the blanket. A tiny but well-formed infant lay, clothed in a clean rag diaper. At the sudden gust of cold air, the baby began to cry. María swept her into her arms, turned her back to Andrés, and began to nurse her. The cries ceased at once. Andrés, suddenly feeling dizzy from too much riding and too little sleep, collapsed in one of the two chairs at the central table. He stretched out his legs and listened to the tiny suckling noises. A wave of nostalgia enveloped him. He remembered those sounds from his childhood, when his mother nursed his younger siblings. When the baby had drunk her fill, María re-tied the shawl before moving the other chair to sit beside him.

Andrés touched the baby's fine, dark hair. "She's beautiful. Only a day old?"

"Almost two days by now. Here. You may hold her."

The baby, her hunger satisfied, lay relaxed in the crook of his arm. Her black eyes seemed fixed on his face. He smiled and stroked her cheek, and she waved an arm with a gurgle.

Andrés felt tempted to fall in love with her, but irritation at the inconvenience held him back: another—unwanted—dependent! His voice was neutral when he raised his eyes. "Of course, you had her baptized. What's her name?"

"She is María Emilia de Jesús Altamirano. I call her Emilia, of course. But no, I haven't had time to baptize her yet. Now that you're here, you can take care of that, surely."

"I need to spend the rest of the afternoon finding out who are the men we're supposed to interview for Arredondo. I probably know them already.... But go tell the priest I'll bring the baby for baptism this evening."

María stood, laid a hand on his shoulder, gave him a one-arm embrace and took the baby back. "First, I must get the fire started and cook *la comida* for your comrades. Perhaps you'll be joining them. It's your house, after all." She stooped to place the child on the mattress, covering her to the chin with the blanket. She straightened to face Andrés. "She *is* your child, you know. She has a right to the bassinette you borrowed from the Veramendis when your wife Carmen was expecting, before she lost the baby. I need to have Emilia with me when I work. She's not safe here all alone when I'm away. Do you know where it is?"

"I think I know where to look, María."

Andrés peered furtively from the corner of Real Street, scanning Main Plaza—the Plaza de Las Islas—a small, blanket-wrapped bundle clasped to his chest. The plaza, generally quiet after sunset, seemed deserted in the twilight. He surveyed the expanse, the earth scored and powdered by wagon and ox-cart wheels, dotted with piles of horse and cow manure, dark against the pale soil. A late sparrow hopped amid that bounty, but no human figure was to be seen: the soldiers billeted in the houses around the square and any remaining Tejano neighbors were doubtless in their homes, eating an evening meal. Candle or lamplight glimmered in the windows of several of the stone and low adobe buildings that surrounded the area. The imposing façade and bell tower of San Fernando Church loomed ahead. Casting a last look around, he scurried across the dusty expanse, crossed the churchyard, and pushed open the tall, carved church door.

Only two candles guttered in the cavernous expanse: the vigil light in its red glass shade near the altar and a single candle at the baptismal font. A movement, blacker than the dark surroundings, told him one of the priests was waiting. A voice greeted him, gravelly from imbibing too much bad tequila.

"Over here, Andrés. You're supposed to have at least one sponsor, but I'll bend the rules this time. That bundle. Is that the child?"

Now Andrés could make out the imposing silhouette of the priest, José Darío Zambrano, tall, broad-shouldered and obese. Andrés had known the man most of his life—domineering and dynamic—an all but irresistible force. "Yes, Padre Zambrano." He cursed his own meek voice as he moved into the wavering circle of candlelight and unwrapped the small blanket. Two shining, black-button eyes stared into his, but the child remained quiet while the priest intoned the beginning of an abbreviated baptismal ceremony.

"The child's name?"

"María Emilia de Jesús Altamirano."

"Emilia. That name means 'rival' or 'excel,' Juan. She'll need surpassing strength and luck if she's to excel in this world."

As Andrés passed the child to him, she began to wave her arms, and one tiny fist collided with the priest's face. His hand went to the left side of his tender bulbous nose, red and shot with dark veins, and wiped a tear from his left eye.

"Aí! As tiny as she is, that stung!" Zambrano's scowl looked uncanny, lit from below by the candle. "She's reminding us she's the child of sin. She's got the Devil in her and barely out of the womb. You'd better weep for your sins, Andrés. Your wife, Carmen, may have been ill or in Louisiana at the time, but you still should have been able to curb your base impulses. I assume María the Indian servant is the mother?"

"*Sí, Padre*, and I wouldn't be so high and mighty if I were you. I believe you've failed to curb several 'base impulses' of your own."

The priest glared but let the insult pass. "Let's get on with this. "...*Ego te baptizo in nomine patris et filii et spiritus sancti.* I baptize you María Emilia Altamirano in the name of the Father, and of the Son, and of the Holy Ghost."

Later, Andrés watched the priest enter his daughter in the baptismal record:

San Fernando church, 1814

No. 188. Jan 24. ALTAMIRANO, María Emilia, a coyota, 1 day old, natural child of Juan Andrés Altamirano and Carmen Losoya. Grandparents, paternal: don Juan Mateo Altamirano and doña Isabel Ruíz. Grandparents maternal: José Losoya and Nicola Dominguez.

Padre Zambrano signed the book.

Startled as he read the inscription, Andrés asked, "Why did you record my wife as this baby's mother? You know whose whelp this is."

"Yes. *Your* whelp and that Indian maid's. But naming your poor wife as mother will save you shame in the future."

As Andrés carried the baby girl back to María, he meditated upon the words of the birth inscription: "María Emilia, a coyota... natural child of Andrés Altamirano and Carmen Losoya." *Coyota*. The term meant different things to different people. Most thought it to be a mixture of African, Indian, and Spanish blood. Padre Zambrano had dubbed the baby girl a *coyota*, even though she was a blend of pure Indian and pure Creole blood—a mestiza. Furthermore, he had written that she was a "natural" child, illegitimate. The priest had condemned her to the lowest social status for the rest of her life. It was a lie, Andrés thought, an unnecessary demotion in an already bad situation.

Now, he must decide what to do with the child. The most convenient—indeed the only solution—was to hand her back to her mother and, even before Carmen, his wife, could return to Béxar from Louisiana, pretend the baby didn't exist. That way, his reputation would be saved. Some people might guess, but few would know for certain. Who looked at the baptismal registry in the church anyway?

María, arms akimbo, met Andrés as he returned, well after dark. "So? How did Padre Zambrano describe her birth? Did he record me as Emilia's mother?"

Andrés, as always, was struck by the incongruity of María's worn work clothes, her classical Otomí features and long, straight black hair, with her straightforward manner, speaking to him as an equal, in perfect, grammatical Spanish.

He passed the baby to her mother before replying. "He wrote that Carmen was the mother. I protested, but he said it would save me embarrassment in the future. He also recorded the baby as a *coyota* and as illegitimate."

"Nasty old man, that Zambrano. Hasn't an ounce of Christian charity, never did. How he ever became a priest, I'll never understand. Total hypocrite. By classifying her a *coyota*, he takes away the advantage he offers by recording your wife as the mother. And calling her 'natural' is a total contradiction. Now, in the Baptismal Records of San Fernando Church, a record that will endure for centuries, you, Juan Andrés Altamirano, of pure European stock, have supposedly produced a *coyota*, a "natural child" on a woman of pure Spanish extraction, Carmen, your wife. A miracle in reverse!" Her sarcasm, stiff features, glaring eyes and rigid posture underscored her words.

He admired her sense of injustice and her analytical ability, but, though reluctant, he was about to hurt her more. He saw no other way. "María, I've been given letters from Carmen that were sent while I was in exile in México. She tells me she is unafraid of Arredondo and will return as soon as possible, perhaps in the spring. She has no idea that you and I have been close—uh, close enough to have a child together. I'm sorry but beginning right now I'll have to pretend that you're just our household servant and Emilia is… well, the child of one of the soldiers during the worst of the occupation."

María whirled, her face distorted with fury. "You cowardly bastard! You class-bound slave! You can't admit your own weaknesses.

That you took me to console yourself for the horrors you'd witnessed during those battles against the insurgents; that's understandable. But now, you can't face the truth—not even for the sake of your own child, not to mention the woman you took advantage of."

The baby, disturbed by her mother's abrupt movements and raised voice, began to cry. María rocked her, but continued, "Just what do you intend to do for us, then? You promised when you bought me that you'd free me in three years. Those years are up. At least let me go so my baby and I can find a refuge somewhere where there's peace and freedom." She dashed away tears with the back of her hand as Emilia's sobs continued.

Intimidated, Andrés stretched his hands toward her as if to quell a volcanic eruption. He spoke over the baby's cries. "María, I'm very fond of you! You consoled me in time of deep trouble. Physically, you attracted me, and I'm not immune to the beauty of a woman. But... but I don't *love* you. If I were to acknowledge you as a... a concubine, it would hurt my legitimate wife deeply. You know how fragile she is. Besides, even if we were to live together, just until she returned, you may be sure that everyone in Béxar would know about it and would report it to my wife the moment she arrived. No, starting right now, I must pretend that you are merely our household servant."

María regained control of her voice and continued to rock the baby gently in her arms, soothing her. But her words struck Andrés like steel darts. "Then I will leave Béxar as soon as I'm strong enough to travel. I was born a free native of this country, the ones you call 'savages' and Indians. By Spanish law, I am not a slave, and yet you and your wife have always treated me as one."

Andrés's face stiffened and the corners of his lips drew down. "You forget that you were *sold* to me. Slave or no slave, I *bought* you. I *own* you and can do with you as I wish."

"Don't forget that I'm the mother of your child. She has the blood of two noble races in her veins. I will do everything to see that she finds a place in this world worthy of her ancestors. And don't forget that I hid you and helped you escape when you were disgraced. You could have been killed by Arredondo's soldiers—your own former comrades. Don't forget how friendly you were with me back then. You have no call to abuse me now."

"Don't *you* forget that *I* am of pure European blood." He tapped his chest. "You speak like a Spaniard, argue like a Spaniard, because you were raised by one. But you are inferior by birth, subject to me in race and in culture."

"Ah, but your people invaded our lands and destroyed the wisdom and accomplishments of our ancestors, which rivaled yours, once. I will take my case to the governor. He will confirm what I say, since the law is on my side."

"You may do as you like, but as long as you live on my property, you are my servant, my slave. I don't think you have much choice; not until Emilia becomes self-sufficient. Where else will you find food and shelter? Think about that!" He stormed out of the *jacal*, flinging the cowhide door-flap to one side as he exited.

Days later, when María had gathered strength and courage enough, she walked the short distance to the Governor's Palace, newly inhabited by *General* Arredondo's appointee, Cristóbal Domínguez. María had been there before, and was unimpressed. It was not as grand as some of the other stone mansions in Béxar, for instance, the Veramendi house, but it far surpassed the Altamiranos' current home.

Today, instead of a soldier in the outer chamber, a secretary, a slender balding man a head shorter than she, occupied the small desk. His officious air belied his stature. "You are María, the Altamiranos' servant, are you not?"

She was not surprised to be recognized. Béxareños were so few these days that everyone knew everyone else.

"Yes, I am María. I wish to see the governor."

"Your business?"

"I have a complaint regarding the terms of my work for Juan Andrés Altamirano."

The secretary pulled a small square of paper from a pile under a stone paperweight on a corner of the desk. He dipped his quill pen in the inkwell and scratched a few words. She could see her name written at the top. He glanced up at her, pointing with his chin, nose in the air, to one side. "You may take your place on the bench with the others. I'll call you when your turn comes."

Four men whom she knew by sight, most of them in homespun work clothes, sat on a long, hand-hewn bench against the white-washed adobe wall. Two twisted their hands, glancing at the others as if nervous, one folded his arms, bent his neck to one side and stared at the floor, while another sat stolid and silent, feet flat, hands with fingers splayed upon his thighs. She nodded at them, and most nodded back, murmuring a greeting. All stared at her with puzzled expressions as if she, a woman and an Indian, had no business petitioning the governor. She pretended to take no notice and, after the men had moved over to make room for her, she took her place at the end of the line. Half an hour later, when her turn came, the secretary called her name and pointed to the door of the governor's office.

The fireplace to her left had warmed the room a bit too much. Giving the whitewashed walls hung with paintings and the black-beamed ceiling a cursory glance, she approached the vast mahogany desk on silent feet.

The governor glanced at the slip of paper the secretary had given him, then smiled and addressed her politely. His stiff, upright posture conveyed unease in this position of authority. "In what way may I help you, María?"

He was, after all, an Arredondo appointee, perhaps a former soldier, and his stiffness gave his large body a military air. She would approach him from that angle. "*Gobernador* Domínguez, *Señor*, since you know my name, you may also remember Juan Andrés Altamirano—a lieutenant in *General* Arredondo's army."

He spoke through a heavy handlebar moustache. "Ah, yes, I have met him. Your city council, the *Ayuntamiento*, is considering him as a future member. He's one of the few citizens still loyal to *su majestad, el rey Fernando*. And what is your reason for consulting me today?"

She took a deep breath. "*Señor Gobernador,* I am being held in the Altamirano household as a slave. I am, however, a full-blooded Indian. Since I was taken as an infant from my family somewhere near Saltillo, it is likely that I come from the Otomí tribe. I have just requested my freedom from servitude to Juan Andrés, who refuses it to me. I believe I know something about the laws of New Spain regarding enslavement of a member of the native peoples. I would like you to confirm my belief that I was born free and therefore am being held in servitude unlawfully."

The governor had listened to her, head on one side, eyebrows raised. "That's quite a mouthful, young woman. Where did you learn to speak Spanish with such eloquence?"

"I was brought up by José de la Peña of Saltillo, *Señor Gobernador*. He treated me like a daughter, taught me all the graces pertaining to a Spanish girl, including how to speak properly and to reason logically."

"And why are you not still there in Saltillo with your adoptive father?"

María hung her head, searching for a formal way, a proper way, of expressing delicate matters. "Sir, once I reached the age of maturity, I fear my physical attractions overcame him. I became his concubine rather than his daughter. When he knew I was pregnant, he *sold* me. This is something I still cannot understand or condone. He sold me to a soldier in Río Grande. I was better educated than that soldier, Señor."

The governor stroked his moustache. "This is a sad story, indeed. How did you get here to Béxar?"

María took a deep breath, twisting her hands before her. "After the miscarriage, I acted half as the soldier's 'daughter,' half as a servant. I was at the market one morning, buying food for dinner that day, when I met a handsome young corporal in uniform. He was Indio like me, and, like me, mannerly and well groomed. We talked about our backgrounds. He also had been adopted by a Spanish family and educated accordingly."

The governor began to play with a letter opener. He set it down across the slip of paper with her name and looked at her with half-lowered eyelids. "I suppose you fell in love with him."

María hesitated, her face becoming uncomfortably warm. She hated revealing all her secrets, but felt compelled to do so. "Yes, *Señor Gobernador,* I fear I did."

"And your second father, patron, whatever, found out?"

"Yes. I made no secret of it. My patron was jealous and flew into a rage. He confiscated all my clothing except for the petticoat I wore under my dress and sold me on the slave market."

"Then Juan Andrés bought you?"

"Yes, but he promised to free me in three years. Those years are up, and he refuses to honor his promise, telling me since he paid for me, he owns me and can dispose of me as he wishes."

Domínguez glanced again at the paper on his desk, picked up the letter opener and began to twirl it. María tensed, fearing it would fall and mar the finish on the mahogany desk. The governor seemed to hesitate. "I've heard that you had a child... only a week or so ago? Whose?"

"Yes, a daughter, María Emilia. Juan Andrés Altamirano is the father."

The governor frowned and shook his head. "Until you said that, no one in Béxar knew whose child she was."

"That is correct, *Señor Gobernador*. Only one person knows beside her father and me: the priest, Padre Zambrano."

"I'm disappointed in Juan Andrés. I'll keep his secret, but I'll wager that even so, her true identity will be known all over town in no time."

"Thank you, Señor. It's for the sake of his wife Carmen, returning soon from Louisiana, that Juan Andrés won't acknowledge my daughter Emilia or free me. What can I do, *Señor*?"

Gobernador Domínguez must have formulated his reply during the last few exchanges. "María, according to the law, you are 'free by nature' by being born a native of this hemisphere. Therefore, all transactions involving you are 'null and fraudulent.' However, since he paid money for you, he has some claim on you. I would advise you to stay in the Altamirano household until your daughter can function on her own."

"But, *Señor Gobernador*, that means Juan Andrés will continue to abuse me as a slave."

"I'll talk to him, María, and counsel him to treat you more leniently—and to allow Emilia the freedom to develop her talents, whatever they may be."

María's face darkened and her eyes flashed. "If I am forced to stay as a servant in the Altamirano household, I insist on being paid for my labor. Without compensation I am still a slave. I cannot raise a child and nourish the two of us on nothing, Señor. I want to make sure that my daughter makes something of herself. I want her to prosper in this world. She can't do that if she, too, is treated like a slave!"

The governor took a deep breath, his mouth slack. He seemed at a loss, and a tiny glow of gratification warmed María's breast. Her strong voice, her argument, and her erect posture had achieved their effect.

Dominguez stuttered. "Very well. I... I'll see to that, too, María. Rest assured."

"And tell Señor Juan Andrés that I'll leave the moment my daughter is self-sufficient, and, if I consider myself exploited, even before that."

"As I said, Señora, I'll make sure he treats you fairly. Now, good day, María."

She left still frustrated but with one small glimmer of light—that was the first time anyone had called her "Señora."

1817

Most of the Tejano families who had fled Arredondo's occupation, including Andrés's close relatives, were waiting for the general's departure before they would feel safe enough to return to Béxar. However, Andrés's wife, Carmen, had defied the usual trend, and returned from Louisiana just before Christmas, 1816. She had suffered three miscarriages, the last one in New Orleans, in August, two years before.

The couple waited eagerly in the dining room as María entered with their breakfast tray. The morning sun sent bands of light to illuminate the heavy, straight-backed Spanish-style chairs, upholstered in black leather, adorned around the frames with round-headed brass nails. The large trestle table would easily seat ten, but was now set for only two. A stray sunbeam lit dust motes in the air, some of which settled on the linen tablecloth.

The *huevos rancheros*, accompanied by frijoles and slices of roast pork with hot, freshly made corn tortillas, wafted delicious aromas when María placed them on the table.

"Ah, María, I pined for real food for so long! Creole food is spicy, but they don't have the same peppers. Nothing tastes quite right." Carmen took her first bite. "Delicious! Just the right amount of chiles. I suppose you grew them in the garden?"

María smiled as she poured hot chocolate to accompany the meal. "*Sí, doña* Carmen. These are our very own peppers, our own eggs, pork from the Jiménez family, and tortillas made with corn I ground myself from last year's crop."

"No wonder it tastes so good."

After the couple had left the table, María cleared away the dishes and washed them. She scrubbed the pans with a rag dipped in sand. She now had a few minutes alone with three-year-old Emilia as the child played on the dirt floor of the *jacal* behind the Altamiranos' adobe house. A straw bed, wide enough for her and the child, occupied one corner of the single room. Their few possessions lay stacked on a hand-hewn table and on a set of two self-standing shelves or hung on pegs. Although used to the penury and squalor of her immediate surroundings, María still resented her circumstances, so different from the way she'd been raised. She darted a sad glance at Emilia, playing happily in the dirt. *She'll have to develop callouses on her soul, if she's to get on in this world.*

Only a few moments of freedom left. María would soon have to gather the laundry and take it in a large basket down to the river behind the Veramendi house a block away, where she had good access to the San Antonio River and a flat shelf-rock to kneel on. Washing clothes this way—beating the clothes with a stick after lathering them with her homemade lye soap—was a skill she'd learned from the servants in neighboring houses. Once the clothes were clean, she'd carry them home and spread them to dry on bushes in the fenced Altamirano yard. The sun would further bleach and dry them. She hoped to finish before midday and get back to the kitchen in good time to prepare *la comida*, served punctually at two. María sighed and rose. There was no escape from the demanding, menial labor that ate up her time.

She made sure to be efficient and resourceful, but despite the governor's instruction, Andrés sometimes treated her harshly, and Carmen, too, snapped at her when she felt weak or ill. Then, as before, they called her *esclava*, slave, instead of her real name. She would be patient until Emilia was older. Then she would leave.

But what of Emilia? Should she take her or leave her? Despite her resentment of the social hierarchy, she felt bound by it. Emilia, after all, through her father, was indirectly kin to the *castizo* aristocracy of Béxar, the Navarro-Ruíz-Veramendi clan. Nearly all the founding inhabitants of Béxar were kin in one way or another. Andrés had told her how once, but she couldn't remember the details. Ángel Navarro's wife Concepción was also sickly like Carmen, and had allowed her sister-in-law, Josefa Veramendi, to raise her eldest child, Juana. Her second baby girl, Chipita, had gone to a cousin, Luz Escalera. Her latest baby, Gertrudis, had been, like Juana, foisted off on the Veramendis. María shook her head. They were handing over babies like bags of flour. She considered Juana and Chipita. They were older than Emilia, but might make good playmates for her, if they would accept her. María, too, might entrust her daughter to the Veramendis when she left.

Freedom beckoned to María with a magnetic pull. But if she abandoned Emilia, even to the Veramendis, her daughter's lot would be a life of servitude. María could not leave until she knew for certain that her daughter was self-sufficient. A heaviness in her chest oppressed her. How could she ever have considered leaving Emilia, precious Emilia, whom she loved with all her being?

She resolved meanwhile to raise this child to succeed. She would learn to speak perfect Castilian and to act according to the good manners of a patrician young woman, the manners she, herself, had been taught. Perhaps Emilia could eventually marry well and make something of herself. María would try her utmost.

The next day, Emilia followed her mother when she went into the kitchen to prepare *la comida*. María gave her a wooden bowl and a handful of frijol beans to play with while she worked. An occasional glance assured her that her child was engrossed in spacing the beans around the bowl upturned on the floor. Until she was already in the dining room, she didn't notice that Emilia toddled behind her as she served the first course.

Emilia stopped and stared at Carmen and Andrés for a long moment, then she made for the handsome man in his uniform. Before he had seen her, she embraced one leg and looked up into his face. She pointed. "Look! Pretty man has hair on his lip." She smiled.

"What? Get away from me!" He gave the child a shove with his leg, and she tumbled onto her bottom, her astonished face crumpling as she began to cry. Andrés turned to María, who had rushed to pick up her daughter and quiet her.

"Get her out of here! I don't want that child loose in this house again."

María's glare transfixed him with arrows of anger and contempt as she marched out with a sobbing Emilia in her arms.

Carmen had watched the scene open-mouthed. Now, she scowled at her husband. "Whatever is wrong with you, Andrés? How dare you treat a child in such a way?"

He lied. "It must be the child of one of Arredondo's soldiers. María was here during the worst of the occupation, you know." He felt a load of guilt descend on his shoulders for defaming María and the child, but he simply could not let his wife know the truth.

Carmen sat stiff and upright, her face rigid with disapproval. "You surely can't blame María for what happened during that terrible time. I'm certain she was raped, poor woman. Be more considerate in the future. I'm disappointed in you!" She rose and left the table.

He sat on, bowed head resting on his hands, elbows on either side of his plate. *Damn María, anyway. She brought that brat in here just to make trouble.* In his heart of hearts, he knew that was also a lie.

Chapter Two
1821

Emilia paused in the middle of Main Plaza to squirt dust between her bare toes, delighting in the silky feel, the funny little geysers of dust. She inhaled mixed odors: cattle, horses, and human sweat from a man passing by with a spade over his shoulder. The driver of a team of oxen shouted for her to move out of the way. Unsurprised, Emilia stepped back, barely avoiding a fresh cow pile on one side and horse droppings on the other. Instead, she'd stepped on a sharp pebble, but she scarcely winced. Her feet were tough and well calloused. Sandals were for Sunday mass only.

Legs of horses trotting past gave her intermittent flashes of farmers' booths around the perimeter of the plaza, busy as usual with shoppers, filled with fresh farm produce—but no Manuela, no Jacinta. Surely, her playmates should be there, in their usual meeting place.

She pictured them, Jacinta—like Emilia, seven, going on eight—was smaller than Emilia and wore her hair in two braids with a part dividing her head into halves. If Jacinta had two braids, why should she, Emilia, have only one down the middle of her back? Mamá had explained, "One takes half the time of two." Manuela, eight already, was too fat and didn't smile enough. You had to work to get her to smile.

Ah! There, by the booth selling ears of fresh corn, she saw Jacinta, one braid in her mouth, her head hanging. What could be the matter? A quick glance in both directions, and she skipped across to the booth.

"¿*Qué pasa,* Jacinta? What's wrong?"

"Manuela's sick."

"Sick? How?"

"She's got a headache and a fever and she's throwing up. They think it might be serious."

"We'd better go and pray for her, Jacinta."

"You go. I'm tired of praying."

The church, the biggest and grandest building in Béxar de San Antonio, raised a tower to the sky across the plaza. Emilia trotted to its garden gate. Beyond it, the flowers, yellow zinnias and purple petunias, drooped in the midday sun, covered with dust and needing a drink. She entered the cool twilight of the church, listening to her soft footfalls as she moved close to the altar rail and knelt in a pew on the right side. Surely, prayers coming from there would be more powerful, would persuade God better, since they came from where the town's hidalgos sat during mass. She bowed her head over clasped hands, but a black shadow made her jump. It left the sacristy and started across the sanctuary. The priest.

Father Zambrano stopped and squinted, raising his hand to shade his eyes. He must be blinded by the light coming from the entrance door. He must be looking for her, kneeling just a few steps away. He made a noise like a growl, descended from the altar and strode to her side, like a great black bird of prey flapping in for a landing.

"You're on the wrong side of the church, brat!" He had her ear, twisted it and pulled.

Emilia batted at his hand. "Ai! Ai!! You're hurting me!" It hurt so much she had to follow him. He pulled up and she stood, then he dragged her, stumbling along while he hauled her across the aisle and shoved her into a pew on the left side of the church.

"*That* is where you belong. Stay there and don't forget this lesson."

Her ear throbbed, and she felt it to see if he had pulled it off. She wiped at her tears, not as much from the pain as for the way she'd been treated.

"But why, Padre Zambrano?"

His angry eyes and red face made him ugly, and the broken veins on his potato-nose showed more than usual. The nose quivered. "Because you're half Indian. A *coyota*! You have no right to use pews reserved for your betters. Your father should have taught you that."

Emilia, still wiping at her tears, managed to choke out, "My f-father?"

He stared down at her, eyebrows raised, red nose still twitching. "Yes, your father, that proud lieutenant, Juan Andrés Altamirano. *¡Pah! ¡Gentuza!* Rabble!" He whirled and stalked to the altar, not looking back.

Emilia could think of nothing to say to God about Manuela after that. Señor Juan Andrés her *father*? The priest must have made some mistake. Her twisted and aching ear and her face, burning red with hurt and shame filled her mind, while the strange business about Señor Juan Andrés faded. She'd ask her mother about that later. For now, hurt became anger. He'd called her "*coyota*, *gentuza*, rabble." Mamá would hear about that, too.

Before she went home, though, she'd walk along the river. Last week, magnificent four-foot stands of wild yellow iris had begun to bloom along the shores. Perhaps they were in full bloom by now, and looking at them would make her feel better.

On the lawn-like slope down to the river, other children were playing a game of some sort in the meadow. Dámaso was among them. Her heart swelled when she saw him. He never treated her like an inferior as her cousins Chipita and Juana did, but listened to her opinions and played hide and seek or ball with her. He was two years older, and she respected his opinions even when they contradicted hers. Today, she preferred to be by herself. She took the path that avoided the slope and wandered beyond it to the riverside.

Once, there were four missions below San Antonio de Valero, now the Alamo, along the river as it flowed southward. They weren't missions any more, she knew that, but the old buildings were still there. She'd never seen them, and no one ever told her how far away they were, but now would be a good time to find out. The Indians maintained the well-beaten path. Converts in years past, they continued to live in huts near the old chapels. They often came into town to buy and sell, and mamá bought the vegetables they sold in booths around Main Plaza. Emilia had run down the river path many times, but always stopped when the trees closed overhead. Today, the gloom of the forest beckoned to her. Perhaps she could reach one of the missions. But first, she paused to absorb the glowing yellow of the grove of iris blossoms hugging the riverbank, petals reaching skyward in the bright sunshine, their long stems swaying among green spear-like leaves.

Pecan, live oak and other broad-leaf trees closed over her head, making a tunnel as she followed the river. Grape vines climbed the trees, loops hanging down like long ropes, tying the trees together in a chaotic, long procession. Beside the path grew grasses, still green despite the dry weather. Emilia paused, listening. The water rippled nearby, a constant background for more subtle noises from the forest: branches creaked as they rubbed together in the breeze, occasional rustling from the underbrush meant a small animal passed that way. Birds hopped and chirped among the branches, a few bright red ones, but mostly mottled brown or white with some black. She continued walking, pausing again when the path became muddy alongside a tall growth of reeds and the air became mustier with the odor of rotting vegetation. She squatted to see if a green frog might perch among the reeds, but today, in this shady spot, the reeds stood alone, sighing and clattering in the breeze.

Rising again, she walked away from the path, straight into the underbrush. She made little noise as she pushed through, but she paused, the back of her neck prickling, her heart pounding, her breath coming short. Something was wrong. Something uncanny was about to happen. Why did she feel like that? A dry twig snapped. Now another crack! She froze. Sunlight in a clearing ahead silhouetted a rider on a yellow horse.

¡Un Indio! She hid behind the nearest tree and peeked around. The rider came closer, heading toward the river. A boy. He wore a brow band with one feather stuck in it, naked except for a loincloth and leggings, a belt around his waist, a scabbard with a big knife like those in the mercantile store. Those leggings protected him from brush and cactus. Riding bareback, he seemed part of the yellowish pony with black legs, mane and tail. A Comanche! What was he doing here? He came closer and she hugged the tree, moving to keep the trunk between herself and the boy. But he stopped the pony and turned his head in her direction. He'd seen her! Without a word, he reined the pony toward her, as she stood frozen in fear.

He spoke to her, the tone of his words a command, but she couldn't understand what he said. She moved a few inches away from the tree and stood straight, arms stiff at her sides, fists clenched, looking up at him. They stared at each other for a full minute before he spoke again, and this time it sounded like a question, so she answered.

"I came for a walk. What are you doing here?"

He cocked his head to one side and replied in a string of those strange words, gesturing with his hands and pointing toward the river.

She nodded, thinking he wanted to give his pony a drink. Then she also pointed toward the river, put her hands together and made a waving motion like water flowing. "You go ahead to the water. I'll go back home now." She pointed to herself, then toward Béxar village.

He dipped his head once.

Emilia took two steps toward the path and looked back at him. He and the pony were unmoving while he watched her a moment longer. Then he nudged his pony forward, toward the river.

She ran all the way to the village, glancing behind her. Was he following? No, he had disappeared, hidden by the stand of reeds.

Emilia halted in Main Plaza, gasping for breath while sweat ran into her eyes, down her face and dripped off her chin. The dust on her arms had turned to mud. She wiped her face with her sleeve and saw mud there, too. She pulled the sleeve of the person nearest her in the bustling plaza.

Still out of breath, she began to tell about the Comanche. "I was in the... woods. And I saw... I saw—"

Galloping hoof-beats clattered in from the west. A man—Pedro Martínez—skidded his horse to a stop near her and shouted in a hoarse voice.

"A massacre! Comanches! Encinal Ranch! Everyone killed! Scalped! Gutted! They raped the women before they slit their bellies open. I saw that from where I hid, God help me! The ranch house was still burning when I left. They took all the horses. Slaughtered all the cattle."

A crowd gathered around him and helped him off his horse.

He spoke again, his voice breaking. "My brother and his wife... all dead...." He broke down and wept.

Tears made new paths through the muddy dust on Emilia's cheeks. The man standing next to her spoke.

"The Béxar militia will go after those Comanches, and of course they'll be risking their lives."

Another man answered, "Yes, but will they find them? They're clever, but how can so few men protect all the ranches and the town, too?"

Emilia wiped her eyes again on her sleeve and thought about the Comanche boy who had almost dared to come into town. Why had he not killed her? That knife of his must surely have been taken from one of the murdered ranch hands. She looked at the two men. Should she try again to tell them about him? If she did and if they believed her, they might go after the boy and kill him. If she didn't, the Comanche would know how close they could get to the town without being seen. That was frightening. She would tell her mother about him. María would believe her and know what to do.

In the garden, María shook the earth off the roots of a clump of weeds she'd just pulled. "*¡Hija!* You're covered with dirt! Where've you been?"

"I took a walk down the river, Mamá, and met a Comanche boy on a yellow pony. I tried to hide, but he saw me."

"*¡Dios mío, hija!* And did you run?"

"Not right away. He said something to me and pointed toward the river. I said something back and made a sign like this," she put her hands together and made the wave motion, "and he rode his pony toward the water. I ran all the way here and Pedro Martínez came in on his horse and said the Comanche had massacred everyone at Encinal Ranch."

"How horrible! They're getting bolder all the time. Did you tell people about the boy?"

"No, Mamá. He didn't kill me, so I didn't want him killed either."

"I'll go report him now. The Comanche might try a raid on the city; we need to set guards."

"I'm sorry, Mamá. I should have told them."

"They probably wouldn't have believed you. The boy would have been gone by the time they got there anyway. But they will believe me, and they'll increase the guards around Béxar."

María told Andrés, who told the Béxar militia as they prepared to track down the raiding party. Later, when the militia returned, the men reported having fought a brief skirmish, killed two warriors and wounded three. They retrieved most of the stolen horses. There was no boy on a yellow pony among the raiders.

There seemed to be no good time to tell María what Padre Zambrano had said.

How could she ask her mother? Her ear, so badly twisted, was still sore to the touch. Padre had told her that her father was Señor Juan Andrés Altamirano, the man she saw every day, the man for whom she and her mother served meals, whose house and garden they kept. Fathers loved their children. They protected them, played with them, bought them new clothes and had nice shoes made for them. But Andrés had always kept his distance and sometimes he'd even been mean.

The whole subject scared her. She wanted to know and yet drew back from knowing the truth. If Andrés was her father, why had her mother hidden it from her all this time? Why did Andrés behave the way he did? That man surely couldn't be her father.

She busied herself in other things, and had just played hide and seek with Dámaso and her usual playmates. As she entered the plaza, she danced her joy in the cool spring day, the sunshine, the blue sky with a few blindingly white cumulus clouds. Across the way, the churchyard glowed with bright, multicolored zinnias and petunias, where two older girls had come to play. In the shadow of the church, Juana and Chipita skipped rope. They had never played with her, but, not intimidated, Emilia decided to approach them. She watched until Juana passed the rope to Chipita, then she stepped forward. "May I have a turn, too?"

The two nicely dressed, pale-skinned girls let the rope drag in the dirt. They stood still and stared at her.

Chipita spoke first. "Go away."

Juana lowered her eyelids and looked down her nose. "Who are you, slave girl, to mess with us and our games?"

"I'm no slave girl!" Emilia stamped her foot. "I want to be friends and jump rope like you."

Juana took up the rope and began to jump, chanting. "Slave girl! Slave girl! Nothing but a slave girl!"

Emilia's voice betrayed her hurt and anger. "Why do you call me a slave girl?"

Chipita explained. "You aren't like us. Your mother is a slave and so are you."

The two sisters again took up the "Slave girl!" chorus as they passed the rope back and forth, skipping to the rhythm of the words. Emilia, tempted to cry but not wanting her tormentors to know, turned her back and walked as straight as she could down the street.

When her mother returned from cleaning the big house, she found her daughter in the *jacal*, curled in a fetal position on the straw mattress.

"What's wrong, *m'hija*? Have you been crying?"

"*Sí*, Mamá. Juana and Chipita won't let me play with them. They called me 'slave girl.' Why, Mamá?"

María sat on one of the two chairs by the table. "Come, hijita, sit here. It's not hard to explain. Years ago now, Señor Juan Andrés paid money for me in San Juan Bautista. He thinks that gives him the right to treat me as his servant. You are my child. That means you are a servant, too. That's why they call you 'slave.' They've heard others call me by that name."

"Paid money for you, Mamá? You mean like a horse or a mule?"

"Yes, just like that. But there's more. You don't see Juana and Chipita playing with your other friends, do you?"

Emilia thought for a while. "No-o-o, I guess not."

"Can you guess why?"

"Because they think they're better than us, I guess."

María nodded. "That's right. And why do you think that would be?"

"They have pretty clothes to wear. And they have more money and live in better houses, too."

"Yes, and one other thing."

"What's that, Mamá?"

"They have paler skin and hair."

A crease appeared between Emilia's eyes. "What difference does that make? A white horse is no better than a brown one."

María laughed in spite of herself. "You're so right, precious! But they *think* they are. Pale-skinned people think they are better than brown-skinned ones."

"But that's not true. Not fair. Can't we just tell them so?"

María shook her head slowly. "I wish it were that simple. But, hijita, have you noticed who sits where in church?"

This gave Emilia the opening she'd been waiting for. "Yes. We're always on the left side; they're always on the right. Mamá, a few days ago, I went into the church to pray for Manuela, because she was sick."

"Yes, and thank God she's well again. And what happened?"

"I knelt on the right side. Father Zambrano came down from the altar and dragged me out of the pew by my ear. It hurt a lot. Still does a little." She raised her hand, felt her ear, and grimaced. "He pushed me into a pew on the other side and told me that people like me had no right to pray on the right side. That was for my 'betters,' he said. Then he called me a *'coyota'* and *'gentuza.'* He said my father should have taught me. And then..." she paused to chew on a fingernail. "Then he said my father is Señor Juan Andrés.... Was he lying?"

María's face turned to stone. She rubbed her bowed forehead with both hands, took a deep breath and reached out to pull Emilia into a tight embrace. Mother and child clung together for a few seconds, then María released her daughter, placing her hands on Emilia's shoulders.

"This is all part of what we were just talking about, *m'hija.* Yes, he is your father. You are the child of his love, a 'natural child.' That means he loved me and showed it by making love to me when he was in terrible danger from *General* Arredondo. I hid him in the *jacal* for three days while I found someone who would give him a good horse that could carry him all the way to Saltillo. He left in the dead of night."

Emilia's eyes were open to the limit as she leaned forward. "The 'child of his love'? Then why is he so mean to us?"

"I'll try to explain. I was pregnant with you—carried you in my belly—during all the months of Arredondo's worst cruelties. After nine months, you were born." She cupped Emilia's chin in her hand, her face radiant with love.

"And then?" Emilia reached up and caressed her mother's cheek.

"Then Andrés came back. Arredondo needed him to judge whether some men were to live or die."

"And did they live?"

"Yes, he and José Angel Navarro convinced the general they were not rebels."

"But my father didn't love you anymore?"

"You were one day old when he came back. He took you to Father Zambrano, who baptized you. Then he brought you back to me and told me he would have nothing more to do with you, and would treat me as a servant."

Emilia's face contorted in grief. "But why, Mamá? Why?"

"It's the world we live in, *m'hija*. Andrés loves us somewhere deep inside, but he can't admit it. You see, he believes a very old lie, that white people are better than anyone else. "

With the heels of her hands, Emilia scrubbed away tears that leaked out despite herself. "I d-don't understand, Mamá."

"Then listen. The white people here mostly come from Spain, where darker-skinned people came from a country to the south, Africa. They kept coming, and white people fought them and finally drove them out. They were considered inferior. Also, any child of a white person and a dark-skinned one was considered inferior too.

When white people from Spain came to the New World, they carried the same feelings against people with dark skin.

"They call themselves *Peninsulares* because Spain is a peninsula. We darker people have another name for those Spaniards: '*Gachupines*.' They have rules like making all the dark-skinned people sit on the left side of the church, in older, rickety pews. Father Zambrano—he's a *Gachupín*—makes sure we keep that separation. It means the Spaniards and their descendants are in a 'better' place than we are. It means we work for them. We are their servants."

Emilia sat silent for a moment, thinking about the situation she'd lived with all her life. "Yes, I know how it is, Mamá. It's not right. But at least we're all together on the left side, and we love each other and play together. But now I know who my father is, what shall I do?"

"Your father thinks his honor lies in keeping you a secret, in not admitting he had a love child with a dark-skinned woman. I know most of the town has already guessed he is your father, but everyone goes along with him because they still believe the old lies. I've kept his secret, and so will you."

"But since there are more of us than of them, maybe, if we stick together, we could persuade them."

María raised her head and gazed into the distance. When she spoke, her voice sounded strange to Emilia, slow and somehow far away. "Some years ago, a priest named Miguel Hidalgo noticed that we are many and they are few. He started to make it right, but it didn't happen then and it hasn't happened yet. Maybe one day." She looked down at her daughter and stroked her hair. "Yes, maybe one day."

Chapter Three
1821

From Potrero Street, *Señor* Francisco Ruíz entered Main Plaza, followed by Juana and Chipita. Emilia, perched on the churchyard wall, knew he had started a school and taught all the children in Béxar for a while, but ultimately, he'd lacked the time and funds, and the school had closed. Now, he still had books in his hands. The trio stopped a few feet away.

Señor Ruíz held out one of the books. "Now Juana, I want you to read pages ten to fifteen in this book, and Chipita," he held out another, "you'll read pages six to twelve in this one."

The girls took the books reluctantly, looking at their shoes.

"Tomorrow," Señor Ruíz continued, "I want each of you to tell me what you've read. Can you do that?"

Chipita's feet were still, but she twisted her body left and right, both hands clutching the book against her body. "Yes, of course I can!"

Juana stretched her neck, her head slanted to one side, and spoke in a grown-up voice. "I hope I'll have the time. Tía Josefa is fitting me for a new dress this afternoon."

Señor Ruíz raised his eyebrows. "Do your best, Juana. You do want to learn your letters, don't you?"

Her voice was indifferent. "I guess so."

The two girls turned and walked toward the Veramendi House, but Señor Ruíz continued in Emilia's direction. She jumped off the wall and fell in step with him. "Señor Ruíz, would you teach me my letters, too?"

He looked at Emilia for a moment before he knew her. "Oh, yes. You're María's girl, aren't you? How old are you now?"

"Yes, I'm Emilia. I'm already seven. Señor Ruíz, please! I want to learn."

Ruíz looked down at her with a half-smile. "*You* want to learn. I wish I had the time...."

"Oh, please, Señor..."

"Child, it already takes more time than I have to teach Juana and Chipita. I'm afraid you'll have to find someone else."

That afternoon, when she told María how much she wanted to learn to read, her mother looked sharply at her daughter. "I wish I could give you opportunities like that."

"Opportunities? What does that mean?"

"It means chances, openings. It's a good word, *m'hija*."

"Then, this Sunday, we'll pray for opportunities."

Emilia loved Andrés's cousin, José Antonio Navarro. Whenever he came to dinner at the Altamirano house, María allowed her to carry the occasional bowl of food to the table.

When he was a boy, José Antonio had broken his left leg in an accident that had permanently crippled him, forcing him to use a cane. One evening, the cane, propped against the back of his chair, slipped to the floor unnoticed. When Antonio stood to move to the salon for more conversation, he tripped on it and lost his balance. Emilia stood next to him, having just come to collect dishes to carry them to the kitchen. She grabbed Antonio's coattail, and her slight weight was enough to keep him upright. She stooped, picked up the fallen cane and handed it to him.

He had always been polite to her, but now he bent down to her level. "Emilia... it is Emilia, isn't it?"

"*Sí, Señor* José Antonio."

"Thank you for saving me. I think I would have fallen if you hadn't been so quick to stand me up again. Who knows what would have happened if I'd hit the floor? I'm very grateful."

"*No hay de qué, Señor.* There's no need to thank me."

Since then, he greeted her with a word or two whenever he saw her and asked her questions—what she thought of Andrés's new horse, or whether she'd seen the magnificent sunset the night before. He never ignored her like the other guests.

Snatches of dinner conversations told her that the Altamiranos respected and looked up to him, young as he was, as an authority on things happening outside of Béxar. Surely, he was somehow connected with those mysterious "letters."

Emilia had spent most of the time during Mass on Sunday praying that sweet Jesus find someone who would teach her. On Monday, she returned to the church to pray. The nave lay in twilight, barely lit by the vigil candle in its red glass shade as she crossed the hard-packed dirt floor between the rows of pews and contemplated the eight-foot wooden crucifix. Poor dear Jesus! His glass eyes gazed at her with infinite compassion. He was a powerful presence, painted in living colors, the blood flowing down his arms from the nail wounds in his hands and down along his wounded side. Everyone she knew venerated the crucifix, "*El Señor de los Milagros*, the Lord of miracles."

She knelt reverently and crossed herself, then raised her clasped hands toward the figure on the cross. "Dear Jesus, please tell Señor José Antonio to teach me my letters. I know he likes me and I love him. You always help widows and orphans and the poor, and I'm poor and my papá doesn't love me. I know you do many miracles, so please put it into Señor José Antonio's heart to teach me. Amen."

Filled with confidence, Emilia rose and trotted across Main Plaza and around the corner of Potrero and Soledad streets to José Antonio's place. No one answered the door, but the latch lifted to her touch, and the door opened a crack. She called. Maybe José Antonio or his wife Margarita were in the back. She gave the door a push and tiptoed in, listening. Finally, going from room to room and finding no one home, she was on her way out when a creak and a rustle alerted her. She followed the noise.

Antonio sat at a compact desk in his office, a small room off the salon, lined with shelves filled with heavy tomes, otherwise furnished with two wooden chairs and a table, piled high with papers. He bent his head over a sheaf of papers sewn together in one corner with thread. The page he was looking at was covered with black marks, fancy black marks that whirled and curled and ran down the page in two columns.

She stood a minute, looking at the paper and waited for him to notice her, but he was too busy staring at those black marks, running his finger down the left side of the page. Finally, she cleared her throat.

He straightened, startled. "Emilia! *Hijita*! You surprised me!" He stood, came around the desk and stooped to be face-to-face. "What is it, my dear? Is something wrong?"

"No, Señor José Antonio. Nothing's wrong." She took him by the sleeve and peered gravely into his warm brown eyes. "I want to learn my letters like Juana and Chipita."

"Your letters, child! Have you asked my Uncle Ruíz?"

Emilia nodded. "Yes. He doesn't have time."

Antonio straightened, his long face pensive. "And your papá?"

"He never has time for me, nor for mamá, either—except work for us."

Almost everyone in Béxar took it for granted that Emilia was Andrés's illegitimate daughter, even though her father seemed determined not to acknowledge her. The resemblance was too strong: the long oval face, the straight, narrow nose, the firm chin, the wave in the forelock of her dark brown hair—she was clearly an Altamirano.

Jose Antonio had found the proof only by accident. While checking the birth records at San Fernando Church for a case the *Ayuntamiento* was involved with, he had run across the entry. Clearly, his cousin once had relations with María, the maid, even though the record gave Carmen as the mother. He'd made that discovery two years ago—back in 1819.

He'd never discussed the matter with his cousin, since it was clear Andrés wanted to keep it quiet, even though the whole town knew. María and Emilia were treated as servants, fed and housed, but he'd never given them any thought beyond knowing that. However, now that he considered the matter, he recognized that Emilia was one more cousin—to his uncle Francisco Ruíz, to him and his brother Ángel, to Juana, Gertrudis and Chipita—to nearly everyone who counted in Béxar.

He lowered himself into the chair before the desk. Now he was again on her level. "I don't have much spare time, either, hijita, but I can teach you a few things about 'letters.'" He pulled a clean sheet of paper from a drawer. "Come closer to the desk, my dear."

"*Sí, Señor* José Antonio."

Emilia leaned in close to follow his hand as he printed the alphabet in capital and small letters, pronouncing each one as he went. They went through the list twice. He then pulled off the shelf a copy of *Recopilación de las Leyes de los Reinos de las Indias, Compendium of the Laws of the Kingdoms of the Indies,* a law book issued in 1512, revised in 1680, 1772, 1791 and latest in 1805, the edition Antonio proudly owned. He showed her how the letters looked in print. She was able to pick out the capital and small letters in the print version with few mistakes.

He closed the volume of the *Recopilación* and replaced it on the shelf, and turned to Emilia. "Come back tomorrow, and I'll show you what all the letters look like when they are written with a pen. See the document I was reading?"

"*Sí, Señor* José Antonio."

"It's an inventory, a list of all the goods we have in the store, and it's written in the letters you learned today, but in a slightly different form that makes them easier to write with a pen."

She pored over the document for a few moments and pointed. "There is a 'T'. There's an 'O'. When can I come tomorrow, Señor?"

"If we're going to work together, Emilia, you should stop calling me 'Señor'. Call me '*Tío*', uncle. It's much nicer." He stood to signal that the lesson was over.

"Oh, thank you, *S*—, uh, Tío. I will."

"And come back in the morning, as soon as your chores are done."

Emilia hugged her cousin's legs and skipped out of the office, leaving Antonio's heart warmed and his mind astonished at Emilia's eagerness to learn.

Emilia caught her mother in the kitchen, preparing *la comida*. "Mamá, I went to visit Tío José Antonio—"

"Why do you call him '*Tío*,' *m'hija*?"

"He asked me to. And I asked him please to teach me my letters, and he began."

María sat on a kitchen stool and thought for a moment. "Did you pray in church yesterday for someone to teach you your letters?"

"Yes, mamá. I prayed very hard. I prayed again this morning."

"Then God answered your prayers—and gave you someone, a fine man, who will teach you well. I trust Señor José Antonio. When will you go back?"

"He said tomorrow morning."

Emilia found a sharp piece of flint-rock and spent an hour carving all the letters she could remember into the hard-packed dirt floor of the *jacal*, delighted when she remembered, impatient with herself when she didn't. The next day, after her lesson, she corrected her mistakes and added the letters she had forgotten. A large segment of the *jacal* floor became a slate for her studies, and her mother stepped carefully so as not to blur or destroy her daughter's work. María had never seen her child as joyful as she was these days, now that she was learning—so rapidly!—and working with a good man who would give her the masculine attention she needed. A sad gap in the girl's life had been filled, and perhaps she could make something of herself after all. María began to sing.

Two weeks later, Andrés noticed the joyful activity lately in the *jacal* and kitchen and saw Emilia carrying a pamphlet to her mother, asking that she explain a word in it. He called the girl over. "Emilia, is someone teaching you to read?"

"Yes, Señor, someone is teaching me."

"Who might that be?"

Emilia felt shy and uncertain how she should react, but came and stood by her father's side. "Señor José Antonio Navarro is teaching me."

"Why not Francisco Ruíz?"

"He said he didn't have time."

"Odd. José Antonio is twice as busy as Francisco."

Emilia didn't know how to reply to that, but remained silent.

"Ah well, never mind. You may come to me with words you don't understand, if you wish."

Emilia looked up into his eyes in amazement. "Truly? Thank you, Señor Juan Andrés, I will."

He turned and walked away, feeling proud of his generosity, but wary of coming too close to this child. Emilia walked away, wondering if he really meant what he'd said.

Antonio would have preferred to be a lawyer, but time, money and opportunity were lacking. Instead, he studied the law on his own at every quiet moment and worked many hours each week in the family's mercantile store located in the main Navarro home on the corner of Real Street and Main Plaza.

When *General* Arredondo departed Texas, leaving it to a series of governors, he also left behind certain restrictions. For fear of an attempted takeover by the rapidly expanding United States, there would be no further trade with New Orleans, the closest source of necessities like gunpowder and ammunition. All trade must come from Veracruz, through Saltillo or Monclova. However, Antonio, his brother Ángel and Martín Veramendi knew the mercantile store could not survive the waiting time, the cost, and the uncertainty of the fourteen-hundred mile overland trip from southeastern Mexico. Merchants from New Orleans met buyers from Béxar in La Bahia, and contraband trade continued.

Governor Antonio María Martínez had at first taken a more lenient attitude toward the contraband activities the Veramendis and Navarros were forced to carry on. Illicit activity had continued under the discreet cover of darkness, but by now it had become bold, wagonloads of illegal goods arriving in broad daylight. Too bold. Governor Martínez warned the *contrabandistas*, and now decided to discipline them.

Antonio pulled his watch from his vest pocket. Eleven o'clock and still thirty miles to go. They should make it to Béxar before dark and get the heavy wagonload of merchandise unpacked, goods safely stored away before nightfall. He shivered, although the morning temperature must be well into the nineties. He peered in all directions. Ridges on three sides, a copse of stunted live oak trees on his left. He laid a hand on his carbine just as he saw movement among the trees.

With high-pitched, ululating war-cries, they burst out of cover, four painted Comanche warriors, and the first arrow struck the canvas wagon cover inches from Antonio's head.

He shouted at the two escorting riders on either side of the wagon and urged the horses into a gallop. He crouched, aimed and fired at the foremost Comanche, and, simultaneously, the escort on his left fired his musket. The foremost warrior screamed, clutched at his chest, and rolled off his horse. One of their bullets had struck home.

Antonio drew his pistols. Three warriors left. Arrows rained upon them, and the horse behind the left lead was struck in the shoulder. Its scream added to the pandemonium. The escort on his right dropped slightly behind the wagon and took his first shot. Another warrior, wounded in the arm. Perhaps they could make it yet.

Then from the ridge, coming toward them at a dead run, two soldiers launched their horses off the rise, firing on the warriors. The closest Comanche gave an order, and he and the two remaining men veered their horses away from the wagon, coming to a halt beyond firing range, among the live oaks. Meanwhile, the soldiers had joined the wagon and its two escorts.

Gregorio Esparza, one of the soldiers, demanded the driver's name even before the team and wagon had come to a halt. "Who are you, and what goods are you bringing in this wagon?"

Antonio laughed and answered in short bursts as he caught his breath. "Gregorio, you know who I am. Thank God you got here in time. The attack had barely begun. We'd have been dead by now. The wagon would be on its way to the tribe. You know me. I'm José Antonio Navarro. These goods are for our store."

The younger of the two soldiers, Gerónimo Nava, spoke up. "You've been trading in contraband goods for months. Governor Martínez is finally fed up. You're under arrest."

Antonio gave no reply, but descended from the wagon and hurried to tend the wounded horse. Blood had run down and covered the left front leg, coloring the white stocking crimson. Antonio stroked and talked to the horse, then began carefully backing the arrow out, holding the bit with one hand to keep the animal from rearing.

"It's a clean flesh wound, still bleeding. That'll flush out anything the arrow carried in with it. I'll flush it some more with salt water when we get in." He turned to the closest escort. "Lucio, bring your horse and we'll put him to work with the other three until we get home. We'll lead this horse behind the wagon. You climb up and ride with me on the wagon."

The cavalcade arrived in Béxar just before dark. The soldiers allowed Antonio to treat the wounded horse and then they locked one of their most prominent citizens in a room in the presidio. The room, formerly for storage, had been used for some time when there was need for a jail cell. The high window to the outside was already barred, as was the window in the door, so all that was needed was a strong lock on the door.

Antonio was duly convicted and sentenced to two years' imprisonment. Meanwhile, Ángel Navarro and Martín Veramendi carried on with contraband trading, but only in the dark. After all, the store had to be kept going, and the people did not hesitate to buy, since they needed tobacco, gunpowder, weapons, sugar, cloth, crockery, pots and pans, harness parts, seed stock, and much more.

When Emilia learned that her tío José Antonio was in jail, she went at once to find out why. Shocked, she couldn't understand what she considered an outrage, and her heart felt heavy. *How*

could *they lock my tío* in jail? Isn't that only for drunkards and people who steal things? She decided to ask whoever was minding the store. Today, it was Martín Veramendi. "Señor Martín, why is José Antonio in jail?"

Veramendi, busy weighing up a sack of frijoles, cocked his head on one side. "Because he got caught, Emilia."

"At what?"

He laid his index finger across his lips and turned back to the customer. "That'll be 20 centavos, Señora Jiménez."

The woman looked down at Emilia and gave her a wink. Then she turned back to Martín and became all business. "*Aquí los tiene.* Here they are." She counted out 20 centavos, took the sack of beans, and walked out without comment.

Emilia persisted, now that there were no more customers in the store. "Caught at what?"

Veramendi sighed. "It's like this. Ever since the Battle of Medina, we've only been allowed to buy goods through Saltillo or Monclova. But a lot of what we need comes from New Orleans, so we have to buy from there anyway."

Emilia looked around her, pointing at a bolt of cloth that lay on a nearby table. "This cloth comes from New Orleans, doesn't it? Señora Luz told me so."

Martín squatted to be on Emilia's level. "Yes, you're right. Ever since you were a tiny baby, we've been sending wagons to La Bahía, where we meet merchants from New Orleans. All that time, our trading was illegal. Until recently, we left here and came back at night. Only lately did we decide to send the wagons in daylight."

"What difference did that make?"

Veramendi laughed a little. "Apparently, daylight made it more illegal. Governor Martínez had to arrest one of us to prove to the authorities in México that we were obeying the law."

Emilia pouted. "And poor Tío José Antonio was the one." She folded her arms and thrust out her jaw. "It's not fair! All of you—

Señor José Ángel, too—were in on it. Why not take turns in jail?"

Veramendi laughed a little more. "That's not how the law works, Emilia. Anyway, he says jail is just fine; it gives him more time to read and study."

Another customer came in, asking for a replacement for a rusty bit. He held up a bridle to show Martín, who patted Emilia on the head and went to show the man the variety of bits in the store.

Emilia returned to the *jacal* behind Andrés's house. She picked up the book Tío José Antonio had lent her, tucked it under her arm and crossed Military Plaza to the presidio, where the jail cell was located. She found a soldier posted before the door. She stood looking up at him for a moment, but since he ignored her, she tapped him on the arm.

"Señor Soldado, I need to visit Tío José Antonio, who is in this cell."

"Why, niñita, do you wish to see him?"

She held up the book. "Because he is teaching me to read." She could tell the soldier liked her. Maybe he had a little girl, too.

He took the book and leafed through it. "I see nothing dangerous here, niñita." He paused, thinking. "Surely, there's no harm in you visiting with your uncle. You may go in." He opened the door and stood aside.

Emilia entered the cell with a feeling of foreboding. Underfoot were the usual rose-colored saltillo tiles, but the small room was dimly lit by the one window opposite the door and the room smelled musty. There was a cot against the wall, a table with a tin basin and ewer of water, but no chair. Antonio sat on a built-in, stone-and-adobe bench at the far side of the cell. Despite the depressing circumstances, her mood lightened when she saw him. He held a book in the single sunbeam that came from the barred window. He turned when the door opened, and a broad smile creased his face.

"Ah, Emilia! Welcome! How nice of you to come! How did you get in?"

"I asked, Tío. The soldier said he saw no harm in it. I came for my reading lesson."

"Well, well! I guess I now have plenty of time to teach you your letters."

When her lesson was done, Emilia turned to her "uncle." "Tío, how do you stand being in here all day long?"

"That is thanks to the divine gift of reading, Emilia. While you read, your mind carries you away to any place you read about. Sea voyages, Spanish castles, a cabin in a pine forest. When I've taught you to read, you'll know what I mean."

"But you've only got one book."

"Maybe my friends will lend me others." Antonio sounded doubtful.

"If you tell me who has them, I'll bring them to you."

"That would be splendid!" He thought for a moment, chin on fist, elbow on knee. "There's Erasmo Seguín and my uncle Francisco Ruíz. That would be a start."

"I'll ask them, then."

"Wonderful! That will help to keep my mind occupied while I'm stuck in here." He gave Emilia a big hug.

Her face became radiant. "You are the kindest man in the whole world!" Without waiting for a reaction, she skipped to the jail door, rapped and was let out.

Antonio wiped moisture from his eyes. *That little sprite has more humanity and determination than any child I know. Teaching her is a joy. I'll do what I can to help her overcome her bad situation and make something of herself.*

His imprisonment lased a year and 23 days, by which time, Emilia's education had taken a giant leap forward. She was able to read any or all of the many books and documents she brought him.

Chapter Four
1821

Antonio, aware that Emilia was a cousin and had his, Ruíz's, and Veramendi's blood running in her veins as well as God knew what native tribe's, decided one day that, instead of discussing something she had read, he would take her with him to a meeting of the Ayuntamiento. He of course asked the Alcalde's permission to bring a child into the session as an observer. He glanced down at the girl, knowing she could easily follow and learn from this mundane, simple, typical case. *This will give Emilia a taste of what the Ayuntamiento normally does.*

His brother, now *Alcalde* José Ángel, raised his eyebrows and hesitated, clasping and unclasping his hands. He looked around the table at the assembled *regidores*. "Señores, José Antonio has a proposal. He asks if this eight-year-old child may be allowed to sit in on our current hearing of the *Ayuntamiento* as part of her education. Do I hear any objection?"

When Antonio appeared with Emilia, *Regidor* Andrés seemed to shrink in his chair. At the question, he leaned back hard enough to move the chair two inches. She saw him at once, noted his reaction and lowered her eyes. She would not look at him again.

Two other *regidores* raised their hands. One of them spoke, unrecognized. "*¡Sí!* I object strenuously. I—"

Ángel raised a hand. "Very well. José Antonio, would you please escort Emilia out of the room while we debate your request?"

Antonio motioned to Emilia, and the two left the room. He took her into the kitchen, a small room with a stove, a few pots and pans, a counter with a sink and shelves on the wall. "Stay here, Emilia, until those two reprobates have had their say."

Emilia wanted to ask what "reprobates" meant, but too late; her tío had already left the room. She could hear men's voices rising in argument, but couldn't quite hear what they were saying, so she crept into the hall, stopping when she could hear every word.

A loud voice spoke. "...and I don't want a low-born brat like her to distract us from our proper business. I won't countenance having trash like that spying in this council chamber."

A second voice: "Yes, and she's female. Serious decisions are reserved to the men of the community only."

The words "low-born brat" and "trash" pierced her like arrows. Her eyes grew moist, and she wiped them on her sleeve. Maybe she should go home now.

She had paid scant attention to Ángel's words to the two men, though she knew he was calming tempers. Now, however, her tío José Antonio began speaking. Emilia knew his voice by heart. He sounded quiet but firm. "First of all, Emilia won't be spying—she's too young. And if we were to look into the ancestry of a number of our own members who claim pure Spanish descent, we might find more than one dark face among those forefathers. Emilia can read far better than anyone her age, perhaps as well as the average adult. She's eager to learn more about the workings of her city. I see no possible harm in letting her sit in on the upcoming short session."

A loud rapping sound followed: Bang! Bang! Bang! "Order in the chamber!" Tío's brother, the *Alcalde,* spoke up. "Señores, I'm putting this to a vote. A majority decision will rule. Those in favor of allowing this female child, Emilia, to sit in on our current hearing, please raise your hands."

Silence ensued. Ángel's voice came again. "Was that a yes, Andrés...? Good. Then all but two in favor. Very well, Antonio, call the girl back in here."

Emilia scurried back to the kitchen, but Antonio saw the tail of her skirt disappearing around the doorframe. He knew she'd overheard the debate.

"Hijita, the vast majority, ten of us, think your visit will be a good thing. You may come in and listen to the proceedings. But be quiet as a mouse."

His words made her feel a bit better; she had allies among the *regidores*, although her father was not firmly on her side. "Yes, Tío, of course I'll be very, very quiet."

Her voice was faint, and he knew she'd been ready to cry at the cruel words she'd heard.

"Pay no attention to those two men, Emilia. You're better than them any day." He stroked her hair. "Come along, then."

She had no time to brood, but followed him into the conference room. The *regidores* were seated except for the *Alcalde*, Ángel, who gave his brother a nod and turned back to business. He rapped the table with his mallet to signal the beginning of the formal meeting. Emilia met the eyes of most of the men, but three would not look at her.

She would steer clear of them in the future if she could.

The *Ayuntamiento* must decide a civil case that afternoon: a less pressing but nonetheless vital matter of water thievery from the main water canal that supplied the *vecinos,* the neighbors, on the east side of town. Water was scarce in Béxar. Yes, the San Antonio River flowed through the town, but land only a few yards away could be parched without irrigation. A network of *acequias*, irrigation ditches, brought water from upstream to all the surrounding valley. The system involved a pattern of floodgates that could be opened on designated days to supply water to each plot of irrigated land.

That day, the complaint involved one man opening a floodgate on another man's day. Emilia listened until she was nearly asleep, when Antonio proved that one of the men had made an honest mistake, and now there could be peace between them.

She smiled at her tutor's deft handling of the case, and again looked at each of the twelve members of the *Ayuntamiento*. She knew them all, at least by sight, even the ones who had voted against her presence. Her hurt feelings remained, but she felt privileged at having been allowed to watch real city business being conducted.

There were occasional cases—like the one earlier that day—of greater urgency, such as when one of the men of the home guard had been maimed or killed in an accident or by the Apache or the Comanche. Urgent discussion identified the fighting abilities of available citizens. The *Ayuntamiento* summoned candidates for questioning and evaluated them for service, civic duty, in the Béxar militia. This was where her father, Señor Juan Andrés, shone as a military advisor and judge of aptitudes.

Early that morning, they had dealt with the serious matter of appointing José Manuel de la Cruz to the home guard, replacing a man who had died in a freak accident while tracking Comanches after a raid. Emilia admired the eighteen-year-old José Manuel. He was tall, had mid-brown curly hair, and was a superb rider. His horse, a palomino gelding, arched its neck and pranced sidewise when Manuel paused to greet someone in the street.

She'd spoken to him as she entered the *Casas reales* that morning. That was before Antonio told her Manuel had been chosen for the home guard. "*Buenos días, Señor de la Cruz.*"

He slanted his head to one side and paused, smiling. "*Buen día a tí, Señorita.*" He mounted his horse, touching his sombrero as he trotted away. Emilia clutched her hands to her bosom, a pang of longing piercing her. "Someday I'll marry him."

❧

As Emilia left the meeting room and descended the outside steps, Dámaso Jiménez rounded the corner. He held up an object that flashed in the late afternoon sunlight. "*¡Mira, Emilia!* Look! A present from my papá for my birthday!" She trotted to Dámaso's side to admire his new folding knife.

He jerked his head toward San Fernando Church. "Come. Let's sit on the wall. Here's the knife. See? It's the best all-around folding knife in the store." He laid it in Emilia's palm.

She admired the blades, large and small, and the mother-of-pearl handle. "It's beautiful, Dámaso. I'm sorry I didn't know it was your birthday. How old are you now?"

"I'm twelve." He puffed out his chest and pocketed the knife, then withdrew something else from a separate pocket. "I'm making something with it that I want you to see."

"What's that, Dámaso?

"*Espera.* Wait. I'll show you in a minute."

They hoisted themselves upon the waist-high stone wall, then Dámaso pulled a lump of wood from a cloth bag. "It's mesquite wood. Very hard, but it holds its shape." He handed the lump to her. A head and shoulders had already emerged from the amorphous chunk.

"Oh! It's a wolf! It's going to be a wolf!" Emilia eyed it closer. Dámaso had modeled the head with ears pointed forward, eyes focused as if on a distant prey, even the nose carefully delineated. The mouth was slightly open, with the side of the tongue and base of the teeth also indicated. He had even incised tiny lines to indicate fur. "Oh, Dámaso! I think it's wonderful! You are a true artist."

Dámaso leaned toward her and met her eyes, his tone serious. "You can read and write. That's special. I'm a wood sculptor. That's special, too. So, we're even."

Emilia nodded, feeling a strange tingling, buzzing sensation that left her breathless. She laid her hand on his arm. "Yes. We are even. But I can teach you to write, at least to sign your name. Would you like that?"

Dámaso had not withdrawn his arm. He looked doubtful, though. "I don't think I'm that clever."

Emilia smiled and shook her head at him. "If you can carve like that, you can easily learn to hold a pen and write with it."

"Then yes, I'd love to learn to sign my name." He glanced up behind him at the church tower. "Have you ever been up there with the bells?"

Emilia's eyebrows rose. "No. Why?"

"You can see everything from up there: what people are doing in town—even things they want to keep secret, sometimes. You can know who's coming into town from any direction before anyone else sees them. I go up there when I'm not working for my papá. You want to go?"

"Oh, yes!" She scooted off the wall.

He led the way into the nave. On the right side, a door in the wall of a small chapel opened onto a tight spiral of stairs, lit by windows every ten feet or so. The stairs were hewn in the trunks of huge live oak trees. They climbed thirty feet, came out on the level floor in the belfry and were almost blinded in the bright light of day. The bells hung directly overhead, and waist-high walls prevented falling. Dámaso went to one wall, Emilia to another.

She pointed at the Alamo. "Oh! You can see the old mission from here, plain as day!"

"Yes, the whole town. There goes Señora Escalera on her way to the store."

Emilia ran from side to side until she had taken in everything. Dámaso watched her, smiling with an owner's pride. He squinted and shaded his eyes with his hand. "Over here, Emilia. Someone's riding up Potrero Street. Have a look!"

They leaned over the parapet, peering at the tiny figure in the distance that resolved itself into a dusty rider on a tired horse. A stranger rode into Main Plaza and stopped a local man leading a team of oxen. His words drifted up to them.

"Where's the *Alcalde* of this town?"

They couldn't quite make out the local man's answer, but saw him point at the *Casas reales*. The stranger turned and as he began to lead his horse in that direction, someone appeared at the door.

Emilia nudged Dámaso. "It's Señor José Antonio."

The stranger went straight toward him, his tired horse kicking up the powdery dust with every step. He removed his hat, wiped his brow with his sleeve and spoke. The two youngsters couldn't make out his question, but Antonio's reply was partly audible.

"No, I'm not the *Alcalde*...."

The stranger turned and the children's sharp ears caught a few words. "I've... news.... Tell...."

Antonio stood for a moment staring at the exhausted rider and his horse. "Wait...." He wheeled and mounted the step with the help of his cane, then disappeared behind the entrance door.

Seconds later, Ángel appeared at the door, spoke to the stranger, and sent a messenger-boy across the plaza to the church. Emilia and Dámaso jumped in surprise when the church bells began to swing and then clang the pattern for assembly. They clapped their hands over their ears, thrust their fingers into their ear-holes, but the noise penetrated their hands, vibrating their whole bodies. They needed to retreat, but needed even more to see and hear what would happen next. Over and over the bells rang the pattern, sometimes with errors in the rhythm. Obviously, the priest was excited. When people began pouring into the plaza, gathering around the city hall door, the bells stopped swinging and the two children heaved great signs of relief.

From so far above the people looked like dolls. Some waved their arms and seemed frightened; all were shouting at each other, and the word "Comanche" drifted up through the shouts and the babble. People jostled each other, pushing for a better place.

Meanwhile, Ángel waited on the step until enough people had gathered. Then he moved forward and raised his hand. His words, almost shouted, came up to them clearly, even over the ringing in their ears that the bell clanging had left behind.

"We're free! Free from Spanish rule! The message came to Saltillo from Mexico City late last month and just reached us by this messenger. Friends, the day is here so many of us have hoped for, gave their lives for! Our *Peninsulares* and *Creollos* have declared Mexico independent of Spain's chains and her tyranny. New Spain has already formed its own government!"

A whoop of joy startled Emilia and a few hats flew into the air toward them. A ripple like fish in the river moved the crowd as those nearest the *Casas reales* turned to tell their neighbors behind them. In seconds, the whole crowd was dancing, cheering, waving and tossing hats.

Dámaso pointed. Look! There's fat old Señor Uribe dancing with that skinny widow Sánchez. See his belly bouncing?" Their laughter joined the general racket.

Ángel continued, and the crowd quieted, again with a ripple of movement, front to back. "Tomorrow, we'll celebrate, my friends, with a work-free day and in the evening, with a fandango in Señora Bustamante's house," he pointed diagonally across the plaza to the house to the left of San Fernando Church. "In a few days, we will have a ceremony, swearing our loyalty to the new government, a government of and for our own blessed land: of México and for México!"

A man standing directly below them, whom Emilia knew only by sight, spoke to his neighbor, and Emilia's keen ears caught his words. "Look who's talking. He fought for Arredondo. He probably shot some of our freedom fighters, himself, the hypocrite!"

A wave of shame for the *Alcalde* heated Emilia's face, even though her mother, María, had explained long ago about Ángel and her own father, Andrés. As eldest sons of military fathers, they had followed in their fathers' footsteps: at the time, the honorable thing to do. Emilia understood... partly. She could feel her mother's sympathy for the Loyalists, and an ache of pity mixed with shame as she watched Ángel proclaim Mexico's independence from Spain.

Since Antonio had brought Emilia once to observe the *Ayuntamiento*, he brought her repeatedly, until no one seemed disturbed by her presence. With his and the *Alcalde*'s permission, she even began to serve hot chocolate for a mid-afternoon break, and then added tarts and cookies, *pan-dulces, biscochos, galletas* and such. Andrés, who served as *regidor* or when not in that office as military advisor for the militia, avoided contact with Emilia as much as possible, except for murmuring "gracias" when she served him hot chocolate. María provided the refreshments, knowing that her daughter was fully skilled enough to serve as a waitress, and she, too, could profit from knowing what was being discussed by the city fathers. The quickest way for Emilia to be accepted among the *regidores* was to feed them delicacies. If her presence became "normal," opportunities for her betterment would surely follow.

Like most Béxareños, Emilia missed nothing new or odd in the town. Lately, she had noticed several pale strangers, usually accompanied by the Baron de Bastrop or by Erasmo Seguín. After Mass on Sunday morning, she caught up with Juan Seguín, Erasmo's son, and tugged at his sleeve.

"Who are those strangers, Señor Juan?" She pointed to them,

standing near the altar railing with his father and hers. "They must be important from the way you and the Baron are treating them."

"Well, good morning to you, too, Emilia! Two of them are escorts, whose names I don't recall. The important one, the one in the middle, is Stephen F. Austin. He hopes to bring 300 families from the southern United States into Texas. They intend to create a colony and help us fight the Comanche."

Emilia considered for a moment. "That's a good thing... I think. There are too few of us. They'll be a big help... I hope."

Juan laughed. "You're right there. My father reckons there are only about three thousand Tejanos in the entire province." He glanced at his father and Señor Austin. "I need to speak to my father. Come along. Maybe you'll learn something."

Emilia eagerly followed Juan through the crowd leaving the church. Emilia carefully maneuvered so that the Baron and Erasmo Seguín stood between her and Andrés. Erasmo turned to his son as he approached. "Señor Austin, you remember my son, Juan."

Austin nodded. "Of course." He turned to Emilia. "And who is this young lady?"

Juan placed his hands on her shoulders. "Her name is Emilia Altamirano. She's an unofficial member of our *Ayuntamiento*—serves us hot chocolate and galletas at merienda time, runs errands, and probably knows more about our business than we do." He chuckled.

Austin made a little bow. "Pleased to meet you, Señorita Emilia."

She curtsied. "Likewise, Señor Austin." As she stood, she caught a glimpse of her father's worried face, the only one not smiling.

Erasmo, looking slightly annoyed at the interruption, waved a hand. "But to get back to business..." He moved to close the circle around Austin.

Emilia, knowing she had been dismissed, slipped away.

Chapter Five

1827

Four years after the independence announcement, Mexico's new Constitution of 1824 combined underpopulated Texas with the state of Coahuila to form "Coahuila y Texas," and moved the new state capital to Saltillo. Béxar, however, remained an important city, and nine months after Spain finally recognized Mexico by treaty, the Ayuntamiento designated a *comisión municipal* led by a mayordomo to plan the first formal celebration of Mexican Independence Day from Spain. The celebration would begin on 15 September with a torchlight parade, a cannonade, and the ringing of church bells. The following day—the actual anniversary of the *Grito de Dolores*, Padre Miguel Hidalgo's call to independence—would begin with a solemn Te Deum Mass, sung by Padre Refugio de la Garza accompanied by the best voices in the village. There would be speeches, a reenactment of the "Grito," then, at night there would be a grand baile—a fandango to include everyone in Béxar.

The prospect both thrilled and excited Emilia but posed a problem. She had no *traje típico*, no dancing dress worthy of the occasion. In fact, she had no fine dresses at all. And yet, she could not, would not miss the dance. After all, she was thirteen, and knew that other girls her age would be there, dressed in glorious costumes.

As soon as her serving duties ended, cups and plates washed and stacked in their places, she walked to the Veramendi Palace, where the Veramendi-Navarro Mercantile Store had relocated. The interior seemed dark after the bright sunshine outside, and Emilia paused just inside, momentarily blinded. Then she saw Señora Veramendi. "*Buenas tardes, Señora Josefa*, I have a big favor to ask."

"Hola, Emilia! A big favor? What might that be?"

"There will be a fandango a week from today to celebrate the Grito. Everyone is invited. 'Everyone' includes me. I want to go to the dance, but I have nothing to wear. Does Juana have a dancing dress she has outgrown? Or do you have an extra one I could alter?"

"*Pobrecita!* No, Juana's dresses went to Chipita. As for me, I don't dance often enough to own more than one *traje típica*. But let me see..."

She disappeared into the darker recesses where cloth was stored. She returned with a core, a short length of black cloth still wound around it. She unwound the cloth and measured it in ells, holding the edge of the cloth to her nose and stretching out her arm. She repeated that three times. "Yes, this might make a full enough dancing skirt for you, *m'hija*. There's too little cloth to sell to any grown woman, so I'll give it to you as a present. You'll need to find a white blouse to go with it, though."

"*¡Oh, Mil gracias, Señora!* You're the answer to my dream! But where can I find a white blouse? It has to have lace on it, doesn't it?"

"Yes, if you're dancing. Ask if you can serve at a refreshment table. That way, you're guaranteed a place at the *baile*. And if you're only serving, any white blouse would do." Señora Josefa folded the cloth and passed it to Emilia, who hugged it to her bosom.

She found her mother sitting on a bench in the shade, darning holes in the heels and toes of Andrés's socks.

"Mamá! Look what Señora Josefa gave me!"

"What is it, *m'hija*? I can't tell—it's just a black square."

"It's cloth for my dancing skirt, Mamá. I'm going to the fandango on September sixteenth."

María shook out the cloth. "It's a long stretch from this piece of cloth to a dancing dress, Preciosa. And where will you find a blouse? A cummerbund?"

"Someone must have cast-offs, Mamá. I only know I must go to the dance."

María refolded the cloth and tucked it under her arm. "I'll ask Carmen if she can help."

She was sure of one thing, that Carmen Altamirano would not dance the fandango. She might sit alongside and watch, but she hadn't the stamina to join the dance. María entered the house.

Carmen lay on a sofa in the salon, musing about María and her daughter. She had watched Emilia grow into an attractive, slender girl of marriageable age. The more Emilia grew, the more suspiciously familiar features she noticed. As time passed, Carmen became convinced the child was Andrés's and at some time during her absence he had made love to María. Did she blame him? Yes, if true, then he'd been unfaithful to his vows. No, he'd been under a lot of pressure back then, and she'd already fled to Louisiana. His utter silence since then on the subject of María and her child told Carmen he didn't want anyone, not even his wife, to know Emilia was his daughter. Despite everything, she bore the two servants no ill will. What had happened had been her husband's doing. He was a different person now.

Since her return, she'd been too sickly to care for his needs. She wondered why he was so harsh and uncaring toward María and the girl. His attitude was contagious. Emilia's young cousins, Juana and Chipita, were scornful of her and treated her badly. They had sensed those attitudes in her husband and were quick to imitate them.

But, here came María, uninvited, interrupting her thoughts, seeming about to ask something. "Yes, María?"

"Señora Carmen, Emilia has just learned there'll be a grand ball on September sixteenth to celebrate the Grito. She's eager to attend. Josefa Veramendi gave her three ells of black cloth for a skirt, but she has no white blouse or sash. Do you have any extra blouses she might wear?"

"I do have a white blouse that would be suitable for a fandango and a red cummerbund. But they're fairly new. Oh, well, if I do go to the dance, it'll be purely to watch. I'll just wear my Sunday silk dress…. Just a minute."

She beckoned María to follow her and, in the bedroom, opened the second wardrobe drawer. After lifting a couple of garments and setting them aside, she exclaimed, "Here's the red cummerbund, and here's the blouse I had in mind. You can adjust them temporarily to fit her." She handed both to María. "And if you need needle and thread to do the sewing, I have a sewing box here, too, in the top drawer." She pulled out the box and set it on top of the garments in María's arms. "Now, get along with you. I expect Emilia will want to try on the blouse and cummerbund the minute she sees you."

María's voice, altered by Carmen's generosity, conveyed more than her words. "Señora Carmen, you have no idea how much this means to Emilia and me. A thousand thanks!"

All of Béxar crowded the twilight-dim plazas on September fifteenth, the first day of the fiesta. Torches lit the streets, and the young men of the village paraded in their finest costumes, tight black pants with flared legs sporting conchos of silver, embroidered vests over white shirts with puffy sleeves, ornate spurs jingling on highly polished boots. Their horses pranced and cavorted under their burnished saddles adorned with silver trim, fancy bridles clinking as they danced. Groups of young men played the guitar as they rode and harmonized, singing traditional Spanish ballads.

Emilia, still dressed in her everyday smock, waited in the shadows for José Manuel de la Cruz on his palomino charger. Here he came in the middle of the procession, playing a guitar and singing in a fine tenor:

La más bella niña de nuestro lugar
hoy viuda y sola y ayer por casar,
viendo que sus ojos a la guerra van,
a su madre dice que escucha su mal:
Dejadme llorar, orillas del mar.

The loveliest maiden of our countryside
today widowed and lonely and yesterday's bride,
seeing that her eyes had gone to the war,
says to her mother who attends to her grief:
Just leave me to weep by the side of the sea.

The plaintive tune, the words, fit the situation of the many widows in Béxar so well that Emilia's eyes filled with tears. Such was *General* Arredondo's doing, slaughtering the husbands and lovers of the women, then, like her mother, enslaving and abusing them. Not only did she love José Manuel for his splendor on his prancing palomino, she loved him for his choice of ballads. What a tribute to the suffering half of the population, still alone and destitute thirteen years after the atrocities!

The sixteenth, the second day of the fiesta: all day had been a whirlwind of spectacle, speeches, plays, free refreshments and general celebration. Cannon roared until midnight, then the church bells clanged for at least an hour. During the day, most of the vecinos, the neighborhood Tejanos, had behaved themselves admirably, even the town drunks. However, a few among the Anglo-American strangers, who had begun appearing in Béxar around the time when Stephen Austin had first come to Béxar, became drunk and disorderly, especially toward evening. They staggered, shouting in their foreign language, swearing, spitting, clutching at the breasts or buttocks of any women passing by, and guffawing loudly at the shrieks of indignation they provoked.

Emilia returned home before sunset to don the finery Josefa and Carmen had contributed and her mother María had sewn. She bathed, washed her hair with yucca root so it shone like silk, rubbed herself with lavender, and donned the white blouse with its intricate lace down the front, altered with darts back and front to fit her perfectly, the full black skirt that María had made, and the crimson silk cummerbund, also altered to fit her tiny waist. María made final adjustments and tucked a bright yellow flower in her daughter's hair. She escorted Emilia as far as Señora Busta-mante's house next to San Fernando Church on Main Plaza.

It was still early, but servers needed to be at their stations to get the tables with their refreshments ready for a later onslaught. María embraced and kissed Emilia. "Be sure to ask Antonia or some other older person to chaperone you back home."

"*Sí, mamá.*"

"*Vete, m'hija,* have fun, but be careful."

Emilia, welcomed by the serving staff and shown her station, had been surprised to find Dámaso Jiménez among the servers. She maintained a warm friendship with him and treasured the wolf figure he'd carved out of mesquite wood he'd given her years ago. It was so true to life she almost expected it to move, and it occupied pride of place atop the bookshelf in the *jacal.*

His station was several tables away, but he waved to her as she took her place, and his smile told her he'd noticed her finery. On the other side of the hall, the musicians took their places and, after tuning their instruments, struck up the first fandango. A few dancers, accomplished ones, began swirling on the dance floor, while a sparse audience watched and clapped in time to the rhythm. The mood became less formal and intimidating by the third fandango, and since demand for refreshments was still low, Dámaso appeared by Emilia's side.

"Would you care to dance this one with me, *Hermosa*?"

Pleased that he had called her 'beautiful,' Emilia smiled at him, aware her dimples would enhance her beauty. "I would be pleased, *Guapo*, Handsome, but I've never danced the fandango, only watched."

Dámaso, just turned sixteen, had learned the dance steps well enough to be confident. "I will teach you, Emilia, don't be shy!" He took her hand and escorted her onto the floor where a dozen other couples were already dancing.

She looked up at his face, marveling that he'd grown so tall. She called him "handsome" by reflex, but realized he truly was good looking, A lock of brown hair drooped over his forehead; fine brows arched over large, luminous eyes bordered with heavy lashes. His mouth, slightly open, revealed a flash of white teeth, and he had a cleft chin. A tingle traveled up her spine as she focused on his lips, full enough to invite kissing. She blushed, remembering her jealousy when she saw Chipita succumbing to that same impulse. What was between them by now?

She came to herself in time to pay attention to Dámaso's fandango lessons. Hesitant at first, by the time the dance was over, she knew the steps and was confident she could now dance with any partner. But as they returned to their posts behind the refreshment tables, her only wish was to dance with Dámaso again.

Before he left her, he executed a perfect bow. "A thousand thanks for a delightful dance, Señorita."

She demurely curtsied in reply. "You are most welcome, Señor; the dance with you was... was... enchanting." She pondered what she had said as she poured lemonade into several empty cups. She'd heard a man say it earlier to his partner. Was it too forward, too 'masculine,' for her to say? It did express her mood perfectly. She felt light as air, filled with joy. The dance and her partner had indeed enchanted her. *I wonder if the dance affects everyone this way, or if this is what love feels like.*

A peal of laughter at one side of the hall called her attention to the spectators. A knot of Anglo-Americans must have come to the hall to watch rather than to dance. Among them she recognized Stephen Austin. The colony of three hundred families from the United States he'd brought into Texas four years ago was a success. She'd met him casually when he first came to Béxar. She'd heard good things about him since, and by now everyone considered him something of a celebrity. She started when she realized he was looking right at her. He was coming her way!

"*Buenas noches,* Señorita," he began in fluent Spanish, "If I remember correctly, it's Emilia, isn't it?"

She was astonished that he remembered her. "You have an amazing memory, Señor Austin. Yes, I am still Emilia. And you've learned to speak Spanish so well!"

He tapped his chest. "I'm fully *Mejicano* by now. You've grown to be a beautiful young woman! But since you are graciously serving refreshments, I'd be grateful for a glass of lemonade. It's dreadfully hot in here."

"Of course, Señor Austin." She quickly passed him a clay cup full. "Here you are."

He took his first sip. "Delicious! Where do the lemons come from? Surely, you didn't import them for the celebration."

"No, Señor, we grow them. Several of our orchards have both lemon and orange trees, and also limes."

Suddenly, near the entrance door, she heard shouting and an exchange of blows. A young man, a brown-haired, red-bearded Anglo and a stranger, shabbily dressed, clutched the shirtfront of a Tejano, a man she knew only by sight. The Tejano clearly wanted nothing further to do with the fist fight. The bearded man released the shirt with his right hand but still clutched it in his left. He drew back his fist to punch his victim again, while continuing to abuse the man verbally. The Tejano raised his open hands to ward off the coming blow.

Austin gulped the rest of his lemonade and beckoned two burly companions. They crossed the intervening space in five strides. One of Austin's men approached the bearded man from the rear. Wrapping his arm around his neck, he jerked him back. The other man passed his belt around the man's chest, pinning his arms.

Austin, meanwhile, apologized to the Tejano, who rubbed his jaw.

"I deeply apologize for this man's outrageous behavior. But what caused him to attack you?"

"I'm afraid I provoked him. I told him we don't welcome drunk and disorderly people inside the dance hall. He told me he'd teach me who was drunk and disorderly."

"And he punched you to prove he wasn't disorderly?" Austin's face creased in a wry smile. He continued more seriously. "I hope he didn't hurt you badly, although you're rubbing your jaw. I think liquor is forbidden in the hall, isn't it?"

"I'm just bruised, nothing serious. As to your question, yes. Padre Refugio made sure that we sell no hard liquor here, only fruit juices, beer and wine."

"Your priest is quite right, too. Even beer and wine are risky enough. Too many of my people have brought their own liquor. If you're sure you're all right, I'll take care of this one." He turned to the bearded fellow, now standing like a lamb between Austin's two bodyguards. "Boys, get him outside."

The four men exited the hall. Emilia, consumed with curiosity, set down her pitcher of lemonade and followed. Stephen Austin talked quietly to the bearded one. The man must be in his twenties or early thirties, she thought, since the small area of his face not hidden by his beard looked youthful. But despite Señor Austin's quiet reasoning, he burst out in curses and name-calling. Emilia understood the words "Mexican bastards," "pure Indians," and "animals." Austin continued, his voice becoming harder, sterner. She had lost the thread and turned to a fellow Tejano leaning against the doorjamb. "What is Señor Austin saying?"

"That they—the Anglos—are living in Mexico and under Mexican law. If they don't behave, we Tejanos could throw them out of Texas. He's warning that man."

"Good for Señor Austin. He respects us and speaks our language well."

"Yes, his settlers are well disciplined on the whole. It's the ones not under his governance who are causing the trouble. More *piratas* like that one are coming every day, trying to grab land. *Filibusteros* they call them."

"What's that man's name?" Somehow, naming him became important for her.

"I heard Señor Austin call him Jedediah Crow. Crow... that means *cuervo*, you know."

"Then he's well named." Emilia turned to reenter the dance hall, but heard the Filibuster say something. She glanced back. He pointed at her, a sneer on his face, mouthing something unintelligible. He must be speaking about her—she was the only woman in sight. She quickly went inside, troubled by the entire scene.

The musicians were taking a break, so she was urgently needed at the serving table, swamped with customers. For the next quarter hour, she had no time to think about what she'd just witnessed. Then the musicians took their places again, preparing for the next fandango.

Chipita detached herself from the crowd waiting for the dance to begin. She looked slender and charming in her dancing dress, her hair piled on top of her head, artful curls drooping over her forehead, the whole bound with red ribbon. She stopped before Dámaso.

"I saw how patiently you taught Emilia to dance the fandango. Would you dance with me? I'll be a lot less trouble." She darted a spiteful glance in Emilia's direction.

Dámaso's eyebrows rose and his mouth drooped. "Me? You want to dance with me?"

The server next to him elbowed him in the ribs. "Go ahead, Dámaso, I'll cover for you."

Dámaso stuttered, "Oh, ah, I... I'd be delighted, Señorita Chipita."

The music began, and he whirled her onto the dance floor. Emilia shrugged. She knew what sort of game Chipita was playing and had full confidence in Dámaso. The hall had begun to cool as the night advanced. Emilia watched the two dancing for a moment, but then began to admire the blaze of color in the room. Banners adorned the walls. A few women wore crimson or leaf-green skirts, brilliant accents among the swirl of black skirts like her own. Nearly every dancer, both male and female, wore colorful silk and satin sashes or cummerbunds that gleamed and flashed in all colors of the rainbow. As Emilia followed their whirling movements, they dazzled and nearly dizzied her.

One of the best dancers was Rafael de la Garza, who, all evening, had danced with one woman after another, seeming never to tire. At last, he caught her eye. Emilia smiled and applauded, never dreaming he would approach her, but he did.

"Emilia, is this your first time dancing? I saw you with Dámaso early in the evening"

"Yes it is, Rafael. He taught me the fandango. I'm so excited!"

"Then may I have this dance, Señorita?"

The guitarists began to strum a lively tune—a jota. Emilia, intimidated, cried out, "Oh, Rafael, I don't know this dance!"

"Ah! I wasn't expecting this, Emilia. Well, just follow me. I'll teach you; don't be nervous."

He grasped her hand and led her onto the dance floor. Many other couples joined them. The cadence was breathtakingly fast, but Emilia adjusted and began to advance, stepping lightly, hopping on every other beat and kicking her left foot then her right as Rafael directed her. Soon, they were twirling around each other, continuing the skip-hop-kick rhythm. Emilia's glossy dark brown hair, neatly tucked into a French roll at the back of her head, came loose until it lay on her shoulders. She felt a little wild, and could tell from the way Rafael looked at her, that he found her attractive. As she twirled, the banners, reds, blues and greens of the costumes, the faces and hair blended into a kaleidoscope of continuous color, intoxicating and exciting.

"Thank heaven I've drunk no wine," she thought. When the music ended, she clasped Rafael's hand, paused to regain her balance, thanked him, made a little curtsy and moved toward the serving tables once more. She was proud that she had learned the dance steps so quickly, but the magic of her first dance, the one with Dámaso, came back to her with force. He was watching her from his table. She moved her head sidewise toward Rafael then gave Dámaso a smile and a slight shrug of the shoulders. He nodded in understanding, smiling in return as if reassured.

Doña Antonia, supervising their table, laid a hand on her shoulder. "Emilia, hijita, you're very young and it's getting late. Let me find someone to escort you home."

"Bueno, doña Antonia, I'm tired enough to sleep on my feet. Oh, look! There's José Manuel de la Cruz. Could you ask him to walk home with us?"

Antonia gave Emilia an amused glance, bustled over to José Manuel and exchanged a few words with him. He turned toward Emilia and nodded.

"I'll be honored to escort you, Señorita Emilia." He took her arm.

"Not without a chaperone, *Señor de la Cruz*!" Antonia took Emilia's other arm, and together the trio exited the hall.

José Manuel squeezed Emilia's hand. "You looked beautiful dancing the jota with Rafael, Emilia."

"Thank you, Manuel. And you sang a beautiful ballad last night. It made me cry."

Antonia agreed. "Yes, I heard it too. It's truly moving. Who composed it?"

"It's very old. Written by a Spaniard named Luís de Góngora about one of the wars 'way back. Three hundred years ago, I think."

Emilia paused and looked into his eyes. "But he had such understanding and pity for the widow. Most men would write about heroic deeds and forget about the cost."

"That's why I sang it. We Tejanos know the cost of war."

Chapter Six
1827

Emilia stood still after thanking Antonia, reviewing the evening she had just spent. José Manuel de la Cruz, the young man Emilia had dreamed about as a younger girl, who the night before had brought tears to her eyes with his beautiful ballad, had just walked her home. Every woman in the hall envied her when Rafael de la Garza danced with her. Both men were attractive; most women would jump at the chance to marry one or the other. José Manuel had the wavy brown hair she'd always admired. But their images faded as she recalled the evening. The one that eclipsed the others was that of Dámaso Jiménez.

Dámaso... the very name held magic for her. His image filled her entire being and accompanied her as she slipped into the *jacal*. She stood just inside the door, recreating the dance they'd had together, floating in dreamy joy, remembering every touch, every colorful moment.

Her mother, reclining on the straw bed, watched her in silence for a while, then, "*Bueno, m'hija*, how was the fandango?"

"Mmmmm?"

"Emilia! Are you all right?"

"Oh, yes, yes.... Mamá... what do you know about the Jiménez family?"

María raised an eyebrow. "Which Jiménez family? Why?"

Emilia made her voice casual. "Oh, Dámaso's family. He taught me to dance the fandango, you see."

María's lips widened just a fraction. Emilia recognized that faint smile; her mother was amused at her. Emilia knew she could never hide her true feelings, no matter how cleverly she thought to disguise them. But there was sympathy in that smile. Perhaps María was remembering a first love of her own.

"Ah, *m'hija*, they are poor like us, but not quite so poor. Papá Jiménez and Dámaso raise cattle and sell them to the Navarro brothers and Martín Veramendi, who sell them in La Bahía. There are three more children in the family, two girls and a boy a year younger than you—you know him, Pedro. One girl is already married and gone to La Bahía with her husband; the other girl is four or five. They're good, honest people, as far as I know."

"Ah...."

"Well, then, tell me about the dance!"

Emilia shook herself mentally and strained to recall all the details of the evening. She gave a glowing report of the dances first, then a blow-by blow account of the drama, the fight between a Tejano neighbor and one of the strange-speaking newcomers, and how Stephen Austin had settled the matter. "He was very strict with that Anglo, Mamá. Señor Austin tries to be one of us, but his people are too different. How can they learn our ways when they don't want to? How can we learn theirs when they are so rough, so impolite? They frighten me, Mamá."

"They frighten me, too, *m'hija*. More of them come every day."

"In the *Ayuntamiento*, I hear that many come without property rights and they simply choose a site and build there. They are lawless. We need more settlers in Texas, but not that kind."

Another shipment of goods from La Bahía and New Orleans had arrived during the night, and Emilia was needed in the Mercantile Store, to help arrange the goods. As she entered the door, her father arrived from the direction of the *Casas reales*.

She took a step back. "*Ah! ¡Señor Juan Andrés! Pase Usted primero*. You go first."

He looked at her for a long moment as if noticing her for the first time, although he saw her often at the *Ayuntamiento*. ""You're seeing Dámaso Jiménez, aren't you?"

Emilia's eyebrows rose. "Yes, from time to time. Why?"

"I think he's a decent boy, but be careful."

He brushed past her and entered the store, bought a twist of tobacco and exited without another word, while Emilia stood watching next to the cloth display. *Just what's got into Señor Juan Andrés? He suddenly begins to act like a father.* After a moment she shrugged her shoulders and began to concentrate on the new merchandise.

A bolt of silk taffeta from Barcelona, a dark forest green, glittered with highlights like sunlight filtering through a thicket of live oak trees. Another bolt of the same cloth almost glowed in the dark, yellow-orange like a leaping flame. Next, she found a fancy box that contained delicate French lace handkerchiefs. She imagined Juana or Chipita pulling one of these out of a black satin reticule. She shook her head; such things had no place in María's and her *jacal*. There were bolts of Irish cloth in many colors, too, to be used for more practical purposes. Ángel's voice brought her attention to the entrance of the store. Hired men were rolling barrels through the door.

"Careful with that brandy, boys, we don't want to lose a drop!"

Simón, one of the workers, replied. "No, Señor! I'd lick that right off the floor."

Ángel laughed. "Just be gentle with them and there'll be no leaks. There are four barrels of gin, too. We'll have to stack the barrels—barely enough room in here. Over by the foodstuffs, boys."

Simón paused, thinking. "Better build a ramp to roll the barrels up. We'll bust a gut if we try to lift them."

"Good idea. Emilia, there are four twenty-pound bags of coffee beans in the wagon out there. See if you can carry those in here. The sooner the customers smell that aroma the quicker it'll sell."

"*Sí, Señor.*" She tore herself away from contemplating the taffeta and went out to the waiting wagon. "Manuel," she called up to a worker standing astride a crate, "Where are the bags of coffee beans?"

"I don't know yet, Emilia." He looked around. "Oh yes, over there in the corner of the wagon. Four of them. I'll hand one down to you." He lifted the first relatively light burden and leaned over to place it in her arms. "Yes, and it looks like that small box is full of little stuff." He lifted out a small, flat case and opened it. "Oh, yes! The ladies will like this. Pretty necklaces, beads of all colors. Look!" He handed the case down.

Emilia balanced the coffee beans on the wagon wheel and feasted her eyes on the jewelry, several necklaces laid out on a bed of black velvet. They were made of glass beads, but beautifully assorted and strung, one a choker made of pale green, oblong, opaque glass beads, separated by glittering diamond-cut spheres; another a string of wine red, transparent beads in graduated sizes, with a cameo at the center and a gold lobster-claw clasp. She longed for that one, but suppressed the feeling. She would never enjoy such luxury. She closed the box and tucked it under her arm, then hefted the bag of coffee and returned to Ángel. He had cleared a space for the coffee and helped her set it down. "That'll perfume this place in no time!"

She opened the box she had tucked under her arm. "Here's a box of necklaces. Where does it go?"

He took a quick peek. "Ah yes. This should go under glass. I think I chose well. We don't want any of these to slip away while we're not looking." He took the box to Señora Josefa, who was arranging small items: combs, sewing supplies—needles, thread, and thimbles—and now she added the necklaces, glittering on their bed of black velvet in the new glass display case they had succeeded in bringing from New Orleans some weeks earlier.

Emilia looked around the store, taking mental inventory. It had everything. A section for the type of goods she had just been admiring, another section for foods the Béxareños couldn't grow for themselves, such as cinnamon and other spices Señor Navarro had brought this morning—she could smell their pungent perfumes along with the fragrance of the coffee beans. Cones of sugar marched along the counter. Another section had hardware of all types including a locked, glass-fronted cabinet with guns of all shapes and makes. Beside it stood the sturdy, banded barrels of gunpowder.

Manuel and Simón had just brought in a heavy wooden box they placed next to the foodstuff-counter. She smelled that, too, from where she stood. Tobacco. She saw that the weight had been inked on the side of the box: one hundred thirty pounds! That would sell faster, maybe, than the liquor. All the men wanted tobacco, including the Indians coming in from the missions where they still lived, even though the friars were long gone.

A shadow fell across her as she stood admiring the abundance of goods. Emilia glanced up. That same bearded stranger blocked the sunlight from the door. He looked even more disreputable in full daylight than he had last night when he'd disturbed the fandango. He'd been ogling her, she felt it. His eyes shifted to the wooden crate of tobacco, and he turned his face aside to spit a brown stream. He spoke to her, something she understood from the tone of voice and the expressions on the face rather than the words.

"Why hello again, missy! You're a ripe one, ain't you?"

Ángel's voice came from behind her, speaking English. "May I help you with something, Sir?"

Emilia stepped to one side so Ángel could confront the man directly.

The man's eyelids drooped. "Naw. Just passin' by." He tipped his head to one side and looked her over with a smirk. "See ya 'round, Sweetie." He ambled away, insolence showing in every movement. Ángel apparently hadn't noticed anything amiss, but turned back to unpacking and arranging the merchandise.

1828

The morning session at the *Ayuntamiento* had adjourned, and the *regidores* had dispersed to their homes for the midday meal. Emilia, now free until four o'clock, when the Council would reconvene, strolled toward Rosita's Fonda, kicking at dried cow chips and horse droppings as she crossed the plaza. She should return to the Altamirano house to help María with *la comida* for Carmen and Andrés, but María could cope by herself, and Emilia had no need of a full meal, or a siesta afterward, for that matter. A slice of roast pork and beans would be just right, and perhaps a stroll by the river.

Rosita had retired a few years ago, and her daughter Gabriela now ran the tiny business. Some customers missed Rosita with her cynical and humorous observations of local behavior, but Emilia thought Gabriela a better cook. She would learn cynicism in time, but perhaps not her mother's humor. Gabi's was a solemn soul.

Emilia entered the shadowy lean-to with its aromas of roast meat, chile, sausage and onions and waited for her eyes to adjust to the sudden darkness. A single client, Roberto Morelos, sat on one of the wobbly stools before the wooden slab that was the counter.

"*Hola, Emilia.* What's happening in the Council these days?"

Emilia scooted onto a stool, arranging her skirts and leaving an empty seat between them. "*Lo normal, Roberto,* land and water disputes, loose animals, Comanches now and then..."

He nodded, swabbed his clay plate with a bit of tortilla, popped it in his mouth and dismounted from the stool. "*Bueno,* if everything's so normal, I'm off. See you." He ducked out of the *jacal* and left the two women alone.

"¿Gabriela, How are you? I see you have roast beef today. I'll have two tortillas with scrambled eggs, a slice of the roast and frijoles and a side of those pickled jalapeños you make. Oh, and a cup of pulque, please."

"I'm well, Emilia." Gabriela faced her, planting her fists on her hips. "You've really come up in the world if people are asking you what's going on in the *Ayuntamiento*. Where's your money coming from?"

Emilia, taken aback, raised her eyebrows. "I make a few centavos when I help out at the mercantile store. Enough, anyway, for beef and beans, a couple of jalapeños and a pulque. Why do you ask?"

Gabriela looked at her feet, her face turning a shade darker. "It's just that it seems so strange that María's daughter is hobnobbing with Béxar's finest. I mean..."

"I don't 'hobnob,' Gabi. When the *Ayuntamiento* is in session, I serve them hot chocolate and galletas in the afternoons and sometimes in the mornings. I check whether they have water to drink. I don't see them otherwise unless Andrés and Carmen invite them over for dinner. Then I serve them at table."

"But I've noticed how they speak to you. Like the way they talk to each other."

"That's because José Antonio Navarro taught me to read, and I understand what they're talking about in there—and they know it. I've been serving them since before you took over this fonda, Gabi. Then, too, José Antonio treats me almost like kinfolk, so they follow his lead, I suppose. Do people gossip about that?"

"I've heard a remark or two. I've wondered, myself."

"There's not much I can do about any of that, Gabi. I try to mind my own business."

Gabriela turned to the stove to fill two tortillas with thin slices of beef and frijoles. She fished two jalapeños out of an olla, arranged everything on a clay plate and plopped it in front of Emilia. "Why aren't you married? At fourteen, you're plenty old enough."

Emilia stared, shaking her head. "What's got into you, Gabi? I'm not married because nobody has asked me. I'm not the best prospect, as you very well know. If a man wanted me, it would be to clean his house, cook, and have his babies. I'd be a slave, even worse off than my mother. I'm in no hurry to get caught in a life like that."

"Then you'll be a spinster. That's no life either." Gabriela plunked a cup of pulque next to the plate, then turned her back.

Emilia took the first bite of roast and egg. "Mmmm. Delicious.... I really haven't given marriage much thought. If I'm not worried about it, you shouldn't bother your head with it either."

"Humph!" Gabriela began scrubbing the parrilla and the conversation ended.

What bug had bitten Gabi? Envy, perhaps, of Emilia's relatively easy existence, helping her mother with housework and gardening, serving the village leaders merienda, 'hobnobbing' with them, and working in the store. Gabriela had married an older man about four months earlier, and wasn't that a slight bulge under her apron? Pregnant. Yes, Gabi's life must be very much the one she'd described a moment ago. The thought depressed her. She finished quickly and slipped off the stool. "How much do I owe you, Gabriela?"

"*Cincuenta centavos, por favor.*"

Emilia counted out the money and turned to go. "*Hasta luego, Gabi.* Take care."

"Adios, Emilia."

The day's session at the *Ayuntamiento* finished, Emilia decided to stroll about before returning home. She took the direction of the bridge between Béxar and the old mission, the Alamo. Someone was fishing from the bridge, someone she didn't recognize. As she approached, she could see he was an Anglo, a young man with a bucket at his feet. At the sound of her first footfall on the bridge, he turned with a start. He'd been brooding over the line in the water.

"*¡O! ¡Me asustó!* Oh! You startled me!"

She was surprised that he spoke in Spanish. A quick appraisal revealed a slender man only four inches taller than she, blond hair, blue eyes, handsome in a very Anglo way. "I'm sorry. Have you caught anything?"

"Just a small catfish and a medium-sized sunfish. They're bony, but better than nothing."

Abruptly, the line bobbed and grew taut, and the young man pulled it in. A good-sized catfish, at least a foot long, thrashed at the end of the line, its scales flashing in the sunlight. He stunned it, then put it in the bucket with the other fish. "Excuse me. I'm Charles McCray, from Stephen Austin's colony." He wiped his hand on his trousers before stretching it out to shake hers.

She took his without hesitation. "I'm Emilia Altamirano and I live close by. What brings you to Béxar, Señor McCray?"

"I'm down here to buy a saddle. My father and I are camping outside town, just to the north, and these fish will make a good supper tonight."

"Aha! I can help with that. Come with me and I'll dig a couple of potatoes for you. You can roast them on the coals. Did you bring salt with you?"

"Yes, my father has it. Precious stuff, salt."

They walked in silence back toward town and the Altamirano property. Emilia felt relaxed with this fellow, even though he stole glances at her often enough. They turned in at the house and Emilia reached to open the gate, but Charles was quicker. He opened it with a mock flourish. "Enter your domain, Señorita!"

"*Mil gracias, Señor.*" She passed through, affecting a haughty air, and they both laughed.

Emilia quickly found the spade, went to the potato patch and in a few seconds had dug two hefty potatoes. She brushed the dirt off them and handed them over. "These should complete that *cena* tonight. They and the fish should make a fine meal."

Charles accepted the potatoes with a huge grin. "They're probably more than we can eat. Thank you so much!" He wiped the potatoes still cleaner on this trouser leg, then placed them with the fish in the bucket. "What does your father do, Emilia?"

"It's complicated. He had military duties until we got our independence, then he became advisor to the militia that protects Béxar from the Comanches. He goes out sometimes on expeditions with them. Every other term or so, he serves as a member of the City Council."

"An important man in Béxar, then."

"Yes, a firstborn son of the original settlers."

"And your mother?"

Emilia knew he was fishing for the reason for her dark complexion. Should she tell him the unvarnished truth? Well, why not? He was a total stranger, had no role in the community, and might as well understand something of how things worked in this new land he'd come to colonize. The pause was becoming long enough to be embarrassing. She took a deep breath.

"My mother is the household maid, a pureblood Otomí Indian. She and my father got together when Béxar was under attack, his wife had taken refuge in New Orleans, and he was in danger of losing his life. My mother sheltered him; probably saved him. I'm the out-of-wedlock daughter." Her face burned, but she resolutely looked Charles in the eye.

His face grew red as well. He met her gaze only for a moment then looked away. "Oh... ah... I see." The silence grew thunderous, then, at last, "My father says things like that happen in Europe quite often." He picked up the bucket but didn't move to leave. "And what do *you* do, Emilia?"

She barked a short laugh, the question was so unexpected. "I learned to read and write early on, so was considered worthy to serve mid-morning and mid-afternoon snacks to the City Council, the *Ayuntamiento*. Now that I'm old enough, they use me to run other errands while they're in session, to fetch books and records that may be in one or another councilman's house. And, of course, I help my mother keep this house and garden in order, and I work in the mercantile store."

"You're a very unusual young lady. How old are you?"

The frankness of this conversation stunned her. "I'll be fifteen in January. Why? How old are you?"

"I'm nineteen and hope to be a doctor one day. Our colony has a very fine physician, who has accepted me as his assistant. You speak like someone much older, and so eloquent. I've learned enough Spanish to know that you speak perfect Castilian."

Emilia nodded, thinking of María, her grace, her knowledge and abilities. "My mother was taken from her tribe as an infant and raised as a Spanish young lady. She is quite cultured—more than my father, strange to say. She has shared all I can absorb of her knowledge of Spanish society. And then, I spend much time with the city fathers."

"There's no ring on your finger. Most Mexican girls your age are married with children by now."

She thought of her earlier confrontation with Gabriela. "I suppose I'm an oddity. And, nobody has asked me, so here I am, happy enough."

"Please excuse my directness. I hope I haven't embarrassed you. People tell me I shouldn't ask such straightforward questions."

Emilia gave him a slight smile. "If you're going to be a doctor, you need to practice doing that, I suppose."

He gave her a broad smile in return and thrust out his hand. "I hope I'll be seeing you whenever I'm back in Béxar. I'll certainly try."

She shook his hand with a firm grip. "Good. We'll talk more next time."

He turned and vanished around the side of the house without looking back. Emilia stood, leaning on the spade, both hands on its handle. She didn't know what to make of the young Anglo. He was unlike anyone she'd ever met, but not unattractive and certainly not repulsive. She returned the spade to its place against the back wall of the kitchen. Ah well, she'd probably never meet him again.

She could hear María in the kitchen. "Mamá, I just had the oddest encounter!"

"Wash your hands. There's the towel. Dry these dishes. What encounter was that?"

Emilia told her mother all about Charles McCray.

"He sounds like one Anglo I could like and respect, *m'hija*."

"Maybe, Mamá. But I'll bet he'll never bother to see me again."

"Don't be so sure, you might be just what he's looking for."

"Don't be silly, Mamá. Oh, I did give him two nice, big potatoes. I hope you don't mind."

"We have a good crop this year, *m'hija*, we won't miss them."

Early November, 1828

Sometime in the middle of the night, mother and daughter were awakened by a gunshot followed by shouting and running feet. A lurid, flickering light came through the single window, and a strong smell of smoke. Together, they threw on some clothes and went outside. It took Emilia a moment in the confusion to understand what was happening. The roar, the leaping stabs of light, the snapping and crackling told her that something massive was burning. Two men ran by in the street, and one of them looked like Antonio Fuentes. Then María pointed at a second man. "That's Andrés Nava, I'm sure!" She and Emilia rounded the house and saw what was burning: San Fernando Church!

María grabbed the mop bucket from the kitchen and Emilia took the harvesting pail from the garden and they joined the people running toward the fire. A line of people stood along the acequia, dipping buckets, filling them with water and then passing them down. A few people stood on the other side of the irrigation canal, passing empty buckets back down the line so they could be filled again. They kept up a steady stream of water hurled at the fire, but it was already totally out of control. Emilia gasped at a huge flambeau of fire leaping out of the topmost window of the bell tower. The live oak spiral staircase was burning! The memory of her climb to the top with Dámaso flashed through her mind as she passed another full bucket and another. She knew then there was no hope. All the water in the river would be too little to quench that fire now.

Dawn came. The city's center lay in ruins. Its heart had been consumed. The *Ayuntamiento* went to work at once to see if they could raise enough money to begin a reconstruction. The pride of Béxar could not be left to lie in ashes for long. Even before they knew if any such funds could be found, the *Alcalde* had organized teams of workers to clear the rubble, to save what they could.

The fire had been discovered early enough that the church records, most of the statues, vestments, sacred vessels and other furnishings were saved. The bells were still intact, but no one knew if the heat had made them brittle or had spoiled their tone. Three or four blackened segments of pews were left—unusable of course—but otherwise, the church lay in ashes. The workmen piled the square limestones in neat rows along the still-standing foundations and partial walls. The masons would use them to begin the new structure.

Emilia felt an uncanny sense of foreboding, as if the calamity had been a sign from God that more misery would soon come upon her city. She tried to rid herself of such nonsense. After all, the precious statue of *el Cristo de los milagros*, to whom she still prayed, had been saved along with the other statues. And fortunately, no lives had been lost in the fire. The town looked dreary and unkempt without the imposing church, its heart and center. Would it ever recover?

She also wondered about her own tiny place in this small world. María continually pressed her to do her best, to make her way in the world, to amount to something. Perhaps, somehow, her mother was living through her. Strange thought about a woman so strong and self-assured. But right now, amid the ashes, Emilia fought depression.

Her mood lightened as money came in—what she considered a fortune, the Altamiranos contributing their mite also —and the citizens lined up to contribute their labor. Finally, on September 15, 1830, two years later, the town celebrated the nearly-completed church and the twentieth anniversary of the Grito de Dolores was celebrated in a Solemn High Mass sung by Padre Refugio de la Garza.

Chapter Seven
1830

Emilia crossed Main Plaza on her way home after tidying the Ayuntamiento meeting room. Someone had just repainted the mercantile store sign. That reminded her: she needed to buy something for her mamá, whose birthday was early next month, a month of beauty and joy, when warm days brought mountain laurel and redbud trees into bloom. These would be followed by fields of bluebonnets and Indian paintbrushes. She rejoiced in the rebirth of beauty and the return of green leaves on the red oaks and the elms, the perfect time to celebrate her beloved mother's birth.

She didn't know precisely when her mother was born. María had been taken from her Otomí parents in their ranchería near Saltillo when she was a few weeks old. Her stepfather had told her they took her early in May, so she must have been born early in April, her favorite month. She chose April fourth as a likely birth date. It was now the 28th of March.

Emilia fingered the cloth money-bag containing fifty centavos Señora Josefina had given her for assisting with table service at a recent Veramendi dinner party. That much, in her estimation, made her wealthy. She entered the mercantile store. The money would buy something useful—a platter large enough to hold a roast, perhaps? A long fork with a wooden handle for taking meat off the parrilla? But her mother needed something to raise her spirits far more than she needed kitchen utensils—something pretty, something frivolous.

One of the settlers stood next to the knife counter, eyeing the knives used for butchering, chopping, paring, and the like. She gave him a quick glance as she passed, seeing a youngish man with a drooping mustache but no beard. She recognized him, Jedediah Crow—the drunk and disorderly man Stephen Austin had ousted from the ball three years ago, only now he'd shaved off his beard. He'd been in the store a few times since then, and had spoken to her in English, words she had only understood from their sinister, suggestive tone. She felt uneasy and moved away.

She paused at the counter where feminine "fripperies" were displayed and pored over the rolls of ribbon. Intense, bright colors: reds, greens, golds, and the lavender of lilac blossoms. Any one of them would look beautiful in María's coal black hair, but they were too impractical. Her mamá might tie her hair back with one of those, but hard work would spoil it in a day, especially if she wore it in summer. Emilia knew the store had just received a fresh shipment of cloth and went to check on the new fabrics. The bolts of cloth for women's clothing stood together on a large table, propped nearly upright against a wooden crate, so they could be seen at eye level. A bolt of muslin caught her eye, a pale blue background, printed with tiny, multicolored butterflies in a haphazard pattern. It reminded her of breezy fall days during butterfly migration. She'd buy some of that.

Jedediah Crow continued to stare at the knife display as a female customer passed behind his back. He cut his eyes to the left, watching her. He'd seen her before. Probably poor, dressed in a plain gray dress, gathered at the waist with a cloth belt. He watched her hips sway as she approached the center of the store. She wore sandals, and trim ankles peeked out as her long skirt swished from side to side. A pretty thing, what folks hereabouts called a *mestiza*. She turned her body as she looked over the cloth on a table, standing for a moment in profile, then facing him, her eyes on the bolts of cloth before her. Glossy, brown wavy hair, an oval face, high cheek bones. Big brown eyes with heavy, long dark lashes. Full lips—*must be a good kisser. Cute little tits. Prob'ly 'bout 17. Bet she's good in bed. Lots of practice... brothers... father... the boys next door. These Messkins don't have no morals nohow. Bunch of heathen Cath'lics.*

He reached to the back of the display case and shoved at the sliding door. No lock. Good. He picked out a knife, the kind that would do for just about anything, and tested the edge on his thumbnail. The girl was just buying some of that cloth. He strolled over to the clerk.

Emilia pointed at the bolt of butterfly cloth. "Señora Chávez, how much is the new muslin cloth per vara?"

"Thirty centavos, *m'hija.*"

"And how much would one need to make a blouse?"

"Two varas should do it."

Emilia felt in her little cloth money bag. Yes, she did have ten centavos left from buying the last groceries. "Very well, Señora Chávez, I'd like two varas of the butterfly muslin, please."

The clerk of the day measured off two varas, marked the spot and cut a notch in the side of the cloth. She then ripped it across, cut the selvage, and folded the two varas into a small square, tying it with string. "Here you are, Emilia. It will make a pretty blouse for you."

"Oh, it's not for me, it's for Mamá. Her birthday's coming soon."

"Who's going to sew it?"

"I thought I'd let her do it herself. I'm good at writing and reading and figures, but I'm no good at sewing." She felt something brush her back.

⁓

Jedediah came up behind her, stretched out his hand holding one of the knives, and brushed his elbow against her. He wanted her to know he was there.

"I thought I'd take this one along for the missus." He spoke in English.

Señora Chávez's face showed a flash of disapproval. Her reply was in Spanish. "Oh, Señor, you shouldn't have taken it out of the showcase. I could have done that for you."

He understood something of what she'd said. "Oh. I didn't know. *Yo no sabe...*" he stuttered in Spanish.

The girl didn't look at him and pretended not to notice his presence. She left the store, her purchase under her arm. His eyes followed the sway of her hips.

The clerk brought his attention back to the transaction. "No harm done. That one costs..." she bent her head to consult a price list, then held out her hand. "That'll be one peso fifty, please."

He dug in his pants pocket and counted out the coins. "Does the knife come with a scabbard? A cover?" He cupped his hands around the knife like a clam shell to illustrate.

"Oh, *¡Sí!* Yes, I believe it does, but it costs twenty-five centavos extra."

That's fine, Ma'am. I'll take it." She understood him and went to the knife display and checked the lower shelf. "Yes, here's a nice tan leather scabbard. It hangs on your belt." She held it up.

He nodded and repeated, "That's fine, Ma'am. Here's the centavos." He spilled them onto her palm.

She counted them and nodded. "Good day, Señor."

He nodded back, while unbuckling his belt and hanging the knife on his left side. He hurried out. He didn't want that girl to get too far away.

Out in the street, he looked for her. No movement anywhere. *These Messkins are critters of habit; they all must be having dinner right now. What's that girl doing out, then?* He caught movement down the street. Someone still in Military Plaza. He walked in that direction.

Emilia had noticed a new horse in the corral on the south side of Military Plaza. Even though the sun had set some time ago, and she should be home by now to help with the evening meal, she couldn't resist having a look at the newcomer. Feeling a moment of unease, she shivered and glanced around. Not a soul moved in the whole wide plaza. She'd take a quick look and then hurry on home.

She climbed the log corral fence. The new horse, a bay gelding, stood with his head slung over a neighboring horse's back. The breeze blew her skirt to one side as her head and shoulders cleared the top of the fence. The sudden movements startled the horses. The new gelding snorted and reared and the other two shied. Emilia admired the new bay; he had the conformation of a stallion: a strong, muscled neck, a broad chest and powerful haunches. He stared at her, shook his head, pawed and snorted.

Smiling, she met the horse's gaze. "You're a spirited one, aren't you?"

A footfall behind her preceded a gruff voice and an arm around her waist. He had understood her words. "I'll bet you're a spirited one, too. Aren't you, my girl?"

She understood only the arm's grip, and twisted to see the man. The one who'd just bought a knife! "What are—? Stop! Let me go!"

Instead, he hauled her off the fence, despite her frightened efforts to hold onto the top rail. She let go, struck him with her left fist and clawed at his face with her right hand. He cursed as blood began to come to the surface of the scratches and made a one-handed grab for her arms as she began to yell, "*Socorro! Socorro!*"

Still holding her with one big hand, he set her on her feet long enough to punch her in the mouth. "Shut up or I'll kill you."

She crouched, one hand over her bleeding mouth and nose, and tried to dart away, only to feel him seize the back of her skirt and haul her back. This time, he slapped her, back and forth across the face, with all his strength. Drops of blood from her nose flew in both directions.

Emilia, momentarily stunned, sagged toward the ground. He took advantage of that, lifted her and carried her, face down like a rag doll, to the nearest dark recess. There, he threw her on her back in the dust. With a foot on her chest, he took time to unbutton his worn buckskin pants. He also took the new knife from its scabbard.

"Don't know why you're resisting, missy. You must've been laid hundreds of times by now, a Messkin girl your age!"

Emilia, dizzy from the blows, understood nothing of what he said, but the knife made his intentions clear. Even if he cut her, she was determined to resist. *He's going to rape me. I've heard enough about that. Will he knife me first and rape my dead body while it's still warm? I've heard that's done, too. My only hope is to hurt him somehow.*

She bent both legs and kicked at his knees, hoping to unbalance him. Instead, he grabbed one leg, twisting it violently to the side. She yelped in pain from the stress on knee and hip. He pulled her skirt above her thighs and allowed his full weight to drop on top of her. She rocked from side to side and heaved her body, but he far outweighed her; she wondered if he even felt her movements. His left arm pinned her right, his right hand fumbled and tore at her underclothes and then assisted his entry. At the tearing pain, she screamed again for help, trying to scratch him with her left hand. She was rewarded with another double slap to the face. The laceration and the slap added to the pain of something hard and relentless, pounding inside her body. She moaned in horror.

Jedediah continued thrusting until, within a few short minutes, he reached a climax. He lay inert for a few moments and then slowly stood. "God damn you, bitch! You've tore my face and got my pants all bloody! Well, damn my eyes! You gave me some trouble gettin' in. I think I got a virgin after all!" His new knife lay beside her, glimmering in the twilight where he had dropped it while he satisfied himself. He stooped and retrieved it, carefully inserting it in its scabbard and strode away, buttoning himself as he went.

Emilia, who understood none of his words, trembled in fury, pain and loathing, listening to his footfalls. Gasping in pain, she took stock of her injuries, then rolled over and pushed herself to her hands and knees, pulling her skirt over her lower body, still bleeding. Home seemed very far away. *How can I get all the way there in this condition? Why did no one come to help me? Will I faint on the way?* After a moment, standing, Emilia felt more blood sliding down her legs. Her teeth had cut her lips on the inside, and she spat blood upon the ground. Her nose still oozed blood that found its way into her mouth and she spat again. Pulling up her skirt to blot her face, she saw, even in the darkness, that it was covered in dark, bloody mud—her blood—mixed with the dust where she'd lain. *I can't wipe my face with that.*

The piece of cloth! Where could that be? She staggered out of the dark recess toward the corral fence. There lay the little fold of cloth, pale in the dusky light. She bent to retrieve it, shook off the dust, untied the string and blotted her face, then pressed it between her legs to stop the continuing blood-flow. *I may not make it all the way, but I can't stay here.* The enormity of what had happened overwhelmed her. *What am I to do now? What did I do to attract that monster?* Gritting her teeth, she limped along, her sprained knee and hip slowing her.

~

María waited in vain for Emilia to arrive and help with the evening meal and the cleanup chores afterwards. Now, angrily scrubbing a pot, she wondered what could be keeping her daughter.

"*Mamá! Mamá!*"

She heard the calls and a desperate note in her daughter's voice. She dropped the pot and rushed outside. The light from the open door revealed a shocking sight.

¡M'hija! ¡Dios mío! ¿Qué pasó? Oh my God! What happened?

Emilia's mouth pained her as she spoke. "Mamá, a man hurt me." She stood trembling, not daring to run into her mother's arms for fear of coating her with blood. A wave of relief swept over her to see her strong, capable mother, and at last the tears came, making tracks through the blood and grime on her swollen cheeks, dripping on the collar of her dress.

María embraced her daughter's shoulders, guiding her inside, kissing her again and again. She began speaking, hardly aware of what she was saying. "Come in the kitchen, Precious. I need to wash off the blood and dirt—see what's wrong." Her next words conveyed her fury. "Who was it?"

"A s-settler, M-mamá. I know his name. He's Jedediah Crow, and he threatened me with the knife he bought while I was in the mercantile store this afternoon."

Her face and body stiff with visible fury, María's words were nonetheless gentle. "Sit here, *m'hija*. I'll get clean clothes...." Emilia sat gingerly, while María ran to the *jacal* and snatched another dress from a shelf. Back in seconds, she saw a bloody, wadded bundle of cloth in Emilia's hands. "What's that, *m'hija?*"

"Oh, Mamá! It was a present for you—for your birthday... and now it's ruined." Emilia leaned her cheek on her shoulder and began to sob.

María gently took the cloth. "Thank you, Precious. Maybe I can save it. But first, I'll tend to you."

The kitchen, a separate building, had no window overlooking the house. María closed and bolted the door. She filled a tub with water from the kitchen reservoir, then helped Emilia peel herself out of the bloody dress, camisole, and torn underwear.

"Stand in the tub, *m'hija* and I'll wash you." With a cloth in her gentle hands, she cleaned Emilia's face until she could see the bruises.

"He hit me in the mouth with his fist. My teeth cut my lips."

"I can tell, Precious. He hit your nose, too, but I don't think it's broken."

The sponge bath continued until María reached Emilia's privates. "You're still bleeding a little. Torn. Swollen. Bruised." She fetched a clean cloth and warm water she'd been heating. "Here, darling, wash yourself."

Emilia, calmer by now, took the cloth, but paused. "I'm ruined, now, Mamá. No man would ever want to marry me after this."

María stroked her daughter's hair. "I know about this, *m'hija*. We'll talk later, when you've had a chance to rest."

Emilia, now clean and changed, lay on her straw bed in the *jacal*, her mournful eyes fixed upon her mother.

María, seated nearby, watched her in the candlelight. "Rest, my dearest. You may not be able to sleep, but you need to relax. Healing will come in time. I know. Don't be afraid of anything. I'm here." She began a song that had lulled Emilia to sleep when she was a baby. Emilia closed her eyes. María, her voice husky and low, sang all the familiar lullabies she could remember, until she saw her daughter's chest rising in a slow, regular rhythm, asleep at last.

María kept a candlelight vigil over her daughter that night, in case she awoke and was afraid in the darkness. Sometime between midnight and dawn, Emilia woke, abruptly sat up with a sharp intake of breath, looking wild-eyed around her. Her expression of fear and horror changed when she saw María, still sitting by her side.

"Oh, Mamá! I had such a hideous dream...." She paused. "But it's no dream. It's real, isn't it? How can I go on living?"

"Precious, my darling, I understand completely."

"How can you? You're just saying that to make me feel better."

"No, *m'hija*, I'm saying it because I went through the same thing."

"But how can that be, Mamá?

"Both of us have been raped, Preciosa. In my case, it was not by a stranger you may never see again, but by the man who had raised me and treated me like his very own daughter. I was raped by the 'father' I'd loved and trusted. I felt it as a total betrayal. And I had to go on living with him."

Emilia reached out to take her mother's hand. "Oh, Mamá. I'm so sorry! Did he hurt you?"

"When I resisted him, yes. He slapped me and forced himself on me. I was hurt like you, but the ache in my heart was worse."

"But you kept on going... living..."

"Yes. But he couldn't live with what he'd done. *He* had sinned against *me*, but he turned against me and considered me somehow diminished, spoiled, rotten, worthless. Not long afterwards, he sold me to an acquaintance of his."

"That's so awful! How did you go on?"

"We women endure hardships. We last, *m'hija*. I did and so will you. Your body will heal, and if, in God's mercy, you are not with child, you will go on with your life, too. You are not disgraced; you did nothing wrong but were attacked and wounded by a wild beast. There were no witnesses, were there?"

"I don't think so. I called for help but nobody came."

"Think of it this way, *m'hija*. You are in a far better position than I was. You're worse hurt physically, but I was shamed publicly, betrayed and reviled by people I had come to love. With no witnesses, we can say that you... Where *were* you, Emilia?"

"I'd climbed the log fence around the horse corral in Military Plaza. I wanted to see the new horse."

"Then say that you slipped, and before you could catch yourself, you had fallen, smashed your face against one of the logs, and twisted your leg when you landed. That settler won't be going among our people to brag about what he did. No one need know what happened. And now, my sweet, let's get some sleep before we have to get up and make *desayuno*."

María crawled into bed next to her daughter, and the two women embraced and even slept a little before an early sunbeam forced them to open their eyes.

Chapter Eight
1830

María explained to the Altamiranos that Emilia had slipped off the corral fence and banged herself up badly. They accepted the story without question. She also told it with some added flourishes to Antonio. He came to visit her and entered the jacal for the first time. Emilia was lying on her straw mattress, reading. Her face, still puffy, showed variations of red and deep purple, while her lips remained swollen from the cuts inside.

"Hola, Emilia. *Dios mío*, you look like someone beat you up!"

"Yes, the knot on that log really hurt me when I crashed down against it. At least, my nose isn't broken and I lost no teeth. Some are loose, though."

He tipped his head to one side, considering her injuries. After an uncomfortable pause, he gave some advice. "You need to be careful eating and give your teeth time to heal. They'll get firm again. What about other injuries?"

"I landed badly and twisted my leg. Both my hip and knee are sore."

"We'll miss you at the *Ayuntamiento* meetings. Come back as soon as you feel well and strong again." He looked around the room, his eyes lingering on the bookcase, filled with Emilia's books. "I'm surprised that Juan Andrés hasn't housed you better than this. Maybe Ángel, Martín and I can put our heads together to think what to do." He stood. "Well, I'd better get over to the *Casas reales*; the meeting has probably begun. I'll come back later to see if you need anything."

Emilia's attempted smile ended in a grimace of pain. "Thank you, Tío José Antonio."

María, sitting quietly in the background, stood to accompany him the few steps to the door. "You're very kind. If we think of something we need, we'll let you know." After pausing to make sure he was out of earshot, she turned to Emilia. "Well, I think our explanation of your injuries convinced him. He will spread the word about how it happened."

"I hope so, Mamá."

"Who was minding the store yesterday when you were there?"

"It was Señora Chávez. "

"Pilar?"

"Yes, Pilar. Why do you want to know?"

"Just curious. I need to know everything that happened to you yesterday, to have a mental picture."

"Oh..." Emilia didn't quite understand, but accepted her mother's explanation.

The church bell rang once for one o'clock, and María left the *jacal* to prepare *la comida* for the Altamiranos. "Precious, I'll bring your food as soon as I've served Carmen and Andrés."

"I'm not hungry, Mamá."

"You must eat, *m'hija*, so you'll get well and strong again."

Emilia attempted a crooked smile for her mother, then laid her head back on the pillow. María was right; she needed rest and quiet, and perhaps some food, too.

Her chores done, María hurried to the mercantile store, hoping she'd find it still open before siesta time when it closed from two to four o'clock. She was relieved that Pilar was still there, serving a line of four customers. Odd that they were not taking the usual siesta, and had kept Pilar from observing the usual store hours.

María suppressed her toe-tapping as customers one and two were served, then realized she was wringing her hands, waiting for number three to finish. After the fourth customer had left with a pound of coffee beans, Pilar raised her eyes to María. "Whew! I'll have a short siesta this afternoon!"

"I'll not keep you long, Pilar. Just a question. Do you know anything about an Anglo named Jedediah Crow? Emilia says he was in here yesterday afternoon."

"Oh, him. He's a rough character. He's the one who started a fight at our first Independence Day ball. Stephen Austin settled his hash."

"Ah, yes. I remember Emilia telling about him. She was right there when it happened. Do you know anything else about him?"

"I heard he moved here from Nacogdoches and squatted on a piece of land that's not far off the Béxar-Gonzales road. Built a cabin, has a couple of horses, a cow and a mule."

"You know a lot, Pilar! Is he married?"

"Yes, has a baby girl—wife's still a girl herself. They tell me she's pregnant again."

"Thank you, Pilar! I surely did come to the right source. I'll leave you to your siesta. *Hasta luego*."

Pilar stood behind the counter with a puzzled frown as María left the store.

As she strode purposefully toward home, María planned her next move. *Andrés keeps his tack for the horses, his guns and his work and hunting clothes in the antechamber at the back of the house, just across from the kitchen. I'll borrow a few things.*

She was not certain how it could be done, but she had one purpose: to take revenge for her daughter's rape. Entering the *jacal* silent as a cat, she found Emilia asleep after eating the mid-day meal.

She picked up the empty dishes, relieved that her daughter had eaten well despite her cut lips and loose teeth. After carrying the dishes to the kitchen, she returned to comb her hair into a single tight braid, tying it with string behind her head.

Thank God my second "father" taught me to ride, hunt and shoot a variety of guns. At the time, I wondered why bother with all that, but maybe it was all meant for a crisis—like now. She entered the back door of the house and slipped into the antechamber. Working fast, she chose Andrés' most disreputable work clothes, his well-worn but clean flintlock shotgun and found the hunting pouch with patches and balls and a powder horn with loose powder. She slipped the gun into the saddle-scabbard, then carried saddle and blanket, bridle, clothing, hunting pouch and all into the kitchen, where, in a few short minutes, she transformed herself into a youngish and handsome Indian warrior. She hid her dress and petticoat in the cabinet behind the dishes.

Andrés kept two riding horses in the paddock near the house, and she chose the tamer of the two, a dappled gray named Choto. She saddled him and was soon on her way toward the road to Gonzales. They moved at a quick trot and an occasional lope where the road was level. Whenever they crested a knoll, María halted Choto, stood in the saddle and surveyed the land in all directions. She'd begun to wonder if Pilar had misled her when, about a quarter mile off the road, she saw a thin spiral of smoke. It was the only movement in the great, empty expanse other than a red-tailed hawk making circles above her and the occasional rustle of leaves on nearby trees. That had to be it—there was surely not another soul between Béxar and Gonzales besides herself.

She approached diagonally, avoiding a more a direct entry, where Crow would no doubt have beaten a trail. She and Choto forced their way through thick shrubs, avoiding yucca and clumps of nopal. Close but not too close to the cabin, she dismounted and hobbled the horse. He could graze but could not wander far.

She approached the cabin, first at a crouch, then on her belly. She heard the clink of a harness and a male voice before she saw him. There he was, not fifty yards away. He had hitched his mule to a plow and was breaking soil, apparently for a garden plot in front of the house. *A bit late for plowing,* she thought. *But no, there'll be no garden; I'm going to kill him.*

She wormed her way to the thorn bush on her left, for a clearer line of sight. Propped on her elbows, she brought the stock of the loaded gun to her shoulder and her finger found the trigger. Just then, a movement at the cabin distracted her. A woman exited the front door, a toddler riding her left hip and a canteen in her right hand. She appeared to be fourteen or fifteen—younger than Emilia. *Dear Lord, she's just a little slip of a thing, and looks to be six months along in her next pregnancy.* María watched her as she waded through the freshly turned furrows toward her husband. When he saw her, he halted the mule and met her halfway. She reached up to him, caressed his cheek, and handed him the canteen. He took a long swig, handed it back and gave her a hug. They stood together, while he pointed in several directions, no doubt explaining how big the garden would be and what he planned to plant where. The girl-wife nodded, lifted the toddler toward him and he took her, held her up and, pointing around as he'd done earlier, talked to the child, whose eyes never left his face, a little hand upon his cheek. He passed her back, and his wife settled the infant on her right hip, gave him the canteen and pointed at the plow. He turned and hung it on a plow handle. They were talking the whole time, but María couldn't hear what they were saying.

She shook her head. *If I kill him, the wife'll be desperate out here all alone. Could starve. Killing him would mean killing three more people: the wife, the toddler and the unborn child....* María laid the gun down. *I can't do it. I'll spare him for her sake. But if he's good to her, why was he so hateful toward my daughter? Why attack her? Rape her?* She covered her face in her hands, thinking. *It's the color of Emilia's skin. She's dark skinned, therefore subhuman, a thing to be used and exploited. I could kill him for that. But I won't. Killing him would pull me down to his level. All right, I'll spare him for the sake of his wife and babies.*

She waited until the girl-wife returned to the cabin and Jedediah continued his plowing. Repeating her movements in reverse, she returned to Choto and rode. Her feelings as she trotted and loped westward were mixed. *I've failed in my mission. I didn't avenge the terrible damage to my daughter, my precious girl. But I've done the merciful thing, the Christian thing. Three people have a chance to grow up, and who knows how much good they might do in this world? That man has a dark side—very dark. But he has some good in him, too. None of us are simple, I guess. I'll leave it to Heaven to judge him.*

She'd left Béxar around two thirty and was back just before six. She left Choto in the paddock and went through the kitchen and retrieved her dress, then on into the antechamber. Footsteps and voices came to her through the house wall. Carmen and Andrés were moving around and talking, but María could detect no sound of alarm. Andrés hadn't been in the antechamber. She hung the saddle on the wall peg and replaced the gun on its rack. The hunting pouch and powder horn she hung on antler horns mounted on the wall, just as she'd found them. She quickly changed into her dress and returned the work clothes more or less as they'd hung before. She hurried to the paddock to brush and walk Choto until he was dry and rested. She went to check on Emilia.

Her daughter, propped on pillows, held a book in her hands. "Where have you been, Mamá? I've been awake for at least an hour."

"Oh, I went over to chat with Pilar Chávez, then took a little jaunt out in the countryside to think things over. Nothing especially new, though." She hadn't lied, had she?

Emilia nodded, grunted, and went back to her reading.

Chapter Nine
1830

Dámaso came to see Emilia two days later. He called at the door of the jacal and waited until María invited him in. He pushed aside the cowhide door-flap and paused in the interior semi-darkness for his eyes to adjust. He now saw the two women seated at the table in the middle of the room. His strained voice and halting words betrayed nervousness. "Hola, María. Emilia, I heard you'd hurt yourself; that you fell. H-how are you?"

"I'm better, Dámaso. Come, sit over here."

María rose from the table. "Here, take my chair. I need to get busy cleaning the big house. I'll let you two chat in private."

Emilia's external bruises were already less painful; her lips were healing rapidly. However, internally, she still felt torn and sore, and her sprained hip and knee made walking difficult. The garish colors of the bruises also told their tale. It would probably take two weeks for them to disappear. She beckoned Dámaso to sit in the chair María had just vacated.

He stood for a moment staring before he sat beside her, placing a small cloth bag on the table. "*Dios mío*, Emilia, you look like someone who's been in a fight—and lost!"

"You heard how it happened, didn't you?"

"Yes, but it looks like you were dropped off a cliff, not just slipped on that corral fence."

"It was a bad situation." She summarized the fictitious fall and looked away. "Let's talk about something else."

Dámaso gave a low whistle, shook his head, and remained silent for a moment. Then, "You remember that wolf I carved out of mesquite wood years ago?"

"Yes. I'm still amazed at your skill. You're a true artist. Look. It's there on top the bookshelf." She pointed.

He beamed. "Oh! I'm so glad you kept it! Well, I carved another one. I made it for you." He carefully extracted the carving from the cloth bag. "Here. See, it's much better than the first one. I've carved horses and deer, too, and one bear, but I know you liked the wolf."

Emilia examined the tiny statue. This time, the wolf sat, front legs propping him upright, tail curved around his haunches. He was panting and his tongue lolled out the side of his mouth. "Oh, he's precious! His eyes look happy, and his fur is just right. You even have it parted down his spine. I love it, Dámaso!" She kissed the top of the wolf's head.

Dámaso's grin almost split his face. "I'm so glad you like it. And I hope the next kiss is for me."

Emilia tipped her head. "Not for a while. Maybe one of these days. You see, my teeth cut the inside of my lips when I fell. They're still sore and a bit swollen. Maybe you can tell."

He sighed. "Maybe just a bit. I'll be patient."

"You never asked me to kiss you before."

"Um... I guess it's because we have such a good time together I never think of it."

"I saw you kiss Chipita, though."

"When?"

"Years ago now. Are you two still kissing?"

"Noooo.... She dropped me all those years ago. Said she wanted to marry a creollo, not a mestizo."

"You asked her to marry you?"

"No, that was her fancy. I didn't like her *that* much." He paused and laid his hand on top of Emilia's. "I like *you* that much."

She removed her hand and picked up the wolf carving. "Why? Because I'm a mestiza?"

"No. Because you're Emilia."

Emilia took a sharp breath and stared at the carving in her hands. "And I like *you* that much, because you're Dámaso."

"Then maybe we should do something about that. A few months ago, Papá and I captured eight wild horses. From that day to last Monday, I tamed and trained them. They were beautiful: one sorrel, two grays, one black, two bays and one buckskin. We took them to La Bahia and sold them Wednesday. My share of the profit was almost enough to buy a gold ring... for you, Emilia. I'm saving my money..." He trailed off.

Emilia looked down and sideways, away from him, her pulse beating palpably in her throat. She keenly wanted to say "Yes!" to this indirect proposal of marriage, but she couldn't—not in her present condition. Not after what had happened. Not if she was pregnant. She turned back to him and took his hand. "Dámaso, I've loved you for a long time, ever since that ball when you taught me the fandango. But I... I can't think of marriage right now. I might never marry. Perhaps I can tell you why one day... but not now." She faltered to a stop when she saw his face, reflecting his hurt and disappointment.

"But why? Am I not good enough?"

"Oh yes! You're more than good enough. You're generous, honest, handsome, kind, talented. We get along so well. This has to do with me, only with me. Just give me some time, that's all."

He stood, his face now showing puzzlement and perhaps anger. "All right, I'll give you time. It's you I want.... Just don't expect me to wait forever." He moved to the door, then turned. "*Adios, Emilia.*"

The door flap fell in place behind him, and she heard his receding footsteps. In the silence that followed, she heard the echo of his words, "Just don't expect me to wait forever." She'd lost her virginity, her innocence. Must she lose Dámaso too?

María found her still sitting at the table, head bowed and supported with one hand while she gently held the wolf carving in the other.

"That didn't take long, *m'hija*. I see he gave you a present." Emilia handed her the wolf. María turned it this way and that. "This is amazing—a perfect likeness on so small a scale! The man has talent. How old is he now?"

"He's eighteen. He said he carved the wolf for me."

"I'd say he's sweet on you, Preciosa. But why did he leave so soon?"

"He wanted to know about the 'fall,' and I lied to him like we're lying to everyone. He had a hard time believing I could do so much damage in a fall like that. I had to exaggerate…. Then, he told me he's saving up money to buy me a gold ring. That's as good as asking me to marry him. I said I'd need more time. I said maybe I'd never marry, but to give me time."

"And he? What did he say? How did he seem?"

"He was shocked, I think. Hurt. Disappointed. He said he'd give me time, but not to expect him to wait forever. He just turned and walked out. He did pause to say 'adios' before he went through the door."

"He'll take time to think things over. He's not going to run out immediately to look for another wife prospect."

"But will he wait long enough? If I'm pregnant, my plans for marrying are over—forever."

"If he truly loves you, he'll wait. If he doesn't, you'll know he wasn't serious in the first place. As for what to do if you're pregnant, we'll talk about that when—and if—the time comes."

"*Talking* about it might wait. But I can't imagine not *thinking* about it."

María embraced her daughter. "Yes, the situation is bleak. But if Dámaso is man enough, he might marry you and raise the child as his own. Only time will tell."

"Yes, any way you look at it, time, waiting, is my only choice. But how can I stand it?"

Emilia waited until her lips were healed and her bruises faded. Rest and youth had helped her sprained joints so that, after ten days, she hardly limped and then not at all. After two weeks, she returned to the *Ayuntamiento* with special pan-dulces baked by María. The *regidores* were delighted to see her, happy with the sweets, but concerned that she seemed subdued, almost moody, somehow not in the moment as she always had been before.

The weeks passed slowly and Emilia counted the days, speaking to her mother but to no one else beyond what was strictly necessary. Her period was late, and María counselled a distraught daughter, telling her that her internal injuries might have caused the delay. Then finally, six days later, the blood came.

"Mamá, let's go thank God for showing me mercy."

The two women entered the church and knelt close to the front, on the left side of the nave. Emilia closed her eyes and, addressing Our Lady of Guadalupe, thanked her fervently for interceding on her behalf with sweet, merciful Jesus. María had finished praying minutes before, and sat back in the pew.

A black-robed figure left the sacristy, descended the altar steps and entered the second row of pews. He knelt and began to pray. María touched Emilia's elbow and whispered. "Padre Refugio is here. Why don't you talk to him? He might give you better guidance than I can. He's a kind, sympathetic priest, not like Padre Zambrano used to be."

Emilia raised one eyebrow. "Mamá, do you think it's a good idea to tell *anyone* what happened to me? I don't expect understanding, especially from a priest."

"Well, it won't hurt to go find out. Tell him under the seal of the confessional. Then, no matter what he thinks, he can't reveal anything."

Emilia rose still looking at her mother, a crease of worry between her brows.

Her mother patted her hand. "Go ahead, *m'hija*. It might give you some consolation."

Approaching the priest with slow, reluctant steps, Emilia waited a few inches behind his row of pews for him to finish his prayer. Padre Refugio, a man of medium height and build, had a short neck, and a shock of straight, black hair growing low over his forehead. He had sensed her approach and after a moment raised his head and looked at her. "Is there something I can do for you, Emilia?"

"*Sí, Padre*. Do you have time to hear my confession?"

"Always. Come into the confessional, my child." His dark brown eyes appeared to smile at her, and his gentle, baritone voice soothed and gave her confidence. He rose, lifted the kneeler into its place, and led the way to the booth on the left of the nave. He entered first and seated himself on the bench in the inner chamber. Emilia knelt in the outer chamber and closed the door.

"In the name of the Father, and of the Son, and of the Holy Ghost." She crossed herself. "Bless me Padre, for I have sinned," she began. "My last confession was two months ago, and I've had a dreadful experience lately that has caused me to doubt the goodness of God."

The priest remained silent for a few seconds. "That is indeed a terrible thing. What could have shocked you so terribly as to cause you to doubt God?"

She began telling her story obliquely, about a man named Jedediah Crow who, three years ago, had almost caused a riot at the fandango.

"Yes. I remember the incident. Go on."

"He was cursing us Mejicanos, and as Señor Austin took him away, he said something to me."

"What did he say?"

"I knew even less English then than I do now. It was something dirty, I think."

Refugio cleared his throat. "Then you must have enticed him in your traje típico, your party dress."

Emilia drew back from the grille in surprise. "But Padre, we were all in party dresses."

The priest waved a hand. "Never mind. That was three years ago. Tell me what happened since."

Emilia took a deep breath. On looking down, she saw she was wringing her hands. "A little over a month ago he..." She choked and then cleared her throat. "He raped me, Padre."

"Raped you! Tell me how that happened! You were with him, I suppose."

"No! He grabbed me from behind..."

Emilia told Refugio how Jedediah punched her in the mouth, threw her on the ground, held her down with a foot on her chest, how she had tried to kick him. The priest, leaning forward with avid interest, questioned her closely and forced her to reveal all the sordid details. "No one came to help me, Padre. God abandoned me."

"God never abandons any of us, my daughter. I am truly sorry you had to suffer such a brutal attack. Are you with child?"

"No, Padre. Mother and I came here today to pray and to thank Our Lady for interceding on my behalf. To thank her that I will not have to bear that monster's child."

"Do you wish to confess anything else?"

"No, Padre. The rape, that I was abandoned by everyone, even God, is what has brought me to you."

"But now you know that despite everything, God has shown you mercy. Therefore He exists and has cared for you."

"But He didn't stop the rape in the first place."

"We all must go through trials in this life, my child."

This exchange was going nowhere. She would end it. "Oh, I suppose so, Padre."

"Very well. Say your act of contrition, Emilia."

She obeyed, and Padre Refugio then told her what her penance would be. "I'll not prescribe a penance in direct connection with the rape, my child. However, even unknowingly, you surely did something to entice that man. All women are guilty, as daughters of Eve, of luring men astray. Keep that in mind and be more aware of your actions, young lady. Now, go home and say a full Rosary, and read the Book of Job. It teaches that no matter what hardships are inflicted upon you in this world, you must never give up trusting and loving God." He intoned the final prayer; Emilia responded mechanically, and when he stood up to go, she knew she was dismissed.

She stalked down the aisle, angry and frustrated. The priest's mind had been made up even before she told her story. His words, "You were with him, I suppose," echoed in her mind. No matter how horrendous the attack had been, according to this priest, she, not her attacker, was the guilty one, as a "daughter of Eve."

Dámaso Jiménez had been depressed for weeks. He missed the easy, breezy friendship he'd always had with Emilia, and couldn't imagine what was wrong. He'd been wounded, too, when she rejected his oblique proposal of marriage. No other girl had ever suited him so well. They'd known each other since childhood, and could almost finish each other's sentences. Besides that, she'd grown to be the most beautiful girl in Béxar.

He'd been avoiding her, working extra hours at the ranch and when he saw her in town, turning down another street. Once, he came into the Mercantile Store and saw her already there, moving toward him in the same aisle. He desperately wanted to talk to her, but no, she must be the one to say everything was fine, or at least to smile at him. When they reached each other, they turned their faces aside. His stomach clenched.

"Hello, Emilia."

A serious face. No smile. "Hello, Dámaso. How are you?"

"Fine."

Silence.

"Well then, please excuse me." Emilia brushed past him. "I'll be getting along home now."

He decided to seek priestly counsel in his pain and confusion. Padre Refugio was not an old man like Father Zambrano—he surely could understand far better than that ancient priest used to.

"Bless me, Padre, for I have sinned. My last confession was back in September."

"In what way have you sinned, my son?"

"I'm possessed by thoughts of a woman, Padre, and forget all my duties. I can think of nothing else."

"Continue, my son."

Dámaso poured out his heart to the priest, describing his feelings, his desire to marry this woman, her refusal, and her strange behavior afterwards.

"And who might this woman be, Dámaso?"

"I hadn't thought to reveal that, Padre, but since you ask, I don't see the harm in telling you. Her name is Emilia Altamirano."

Padre Refugio jerked back from the grille and blurted, "I would counsel you not to get too involved with that woman."

"Why, Padre?"

Silence from the other side of the grille. Father Refugio had backed himself into a corner by his spontaneous outburst. He cleared his throat as if to let Dámaso know he was still there. At last, he stammered, "She's... she's compromised."

"How? In what way?"

"I've said all I can on the subject. Now, say your act of contrition...."

Dámaso left the confessional convinced that Emilia had deceived him and had relations with another man. He spent a miserable night, his sense of injustice evolving into anger. The next afternoon, he saw her entering Potrero Street, on her way home from the serving the *Ayuntamiento*. Instead of avoiding her, he marched straight toward her, clenching his fists and glaring at her. She paused, expecting him to speak to her. He remained silent but stopped for a second to watch her reaction. Emilia gasped, her face twisted in surprise and hurt. He sneered and hurried away, leaving her standing, stunned.

Serves her right, he thought.

Emilia walked on, her brow puckered in worry. *What on earth is wrong with Dámaso? I only told him I couldn't accept a ring yet, not that I would never consider him at all.*

She entered the *jacal*, but not finding her mother there, she crossed to the kitchen. María was fully occupied in dinner preparations. Without a word, Emilia set to work helping her. They still hadn't exchanged a word as they served the meal to Andrés and Carmen, but Emilia caught her mother glancing at her with raised eyebrows.

Back in the kitchen, María placed her fists on her hips. "All right, *m'hija*, what's troubling you?"

Emilia looked at the floor, twisting her hands together. "It's Dámaso. He passed me just as I was leaving the *Casas reales*. He looked daggers at me. Clenched his fists. Didn't say a word, just sneered and walked on. I think he hates me. He's been avoiding me

116

lately, but that's because neither of us knows how to talk about our situation. Somehow confusion has turned to hatred."

María looked thoughtful, not answering right away. She stoked the fire and hung a kettle to heat water for washing the dishes. "You're sure you didn't misinterpret what you saw?"

"Oh, no. He only paused long enough to let his scorn sink in."

"It sounds as though someone has slandered you."

"But who could that be? No one knows about the rape except us and Padre Refugio—and Jedediah Crow."

"Then there must be some other reason."

"But what have I done?"

María took the kettle off its hook, poured steaming water into the tile sink and cooled it with water from the reservoir. She took up the dishrag and coated it liberally with the homemade soap. "There are some who envy you, you know. You've been too successful."

She washed the dishes, Emilia dried them and put them away. She was sure her mother was right.

Emilia carried on with the daily routine. On the third day, as she crossed Market Plaza carrying the usual covered plate of the day's sweets for the *regidores*, she saw Dámaso sitting on the church garden wall. Next to him sat Chipita. As Emilia approached, Chipita's arm snaked around his waist. She leaned in and kissed his cheek. Dámaso scooted closer and embraced her shoulders.

Emilia remembered how boldly Chipita had invited Dámaso to dance with her at the fandango. *She's been after him ever since then. Perhaps the slander comes from her? I need to talk to Dámaso—but how to approach him?* She walked past the couple. As she drew even with them, she turned and smiled. "Good morning, you two." Since there was no immediate reply, she walked on and mounted the steps of the *Casas reales*. By the time she arrived in the kitchen, she had already decided what to do.

Early each morning, Dámaso exercised horses for the soldiers and officers billeted at the Alamo. Today, Emilia thought, he had probably met Chipita as he came through town afterwards. She would rise at dawn tomorrow morning and meet Dámaso at the old mission. She'd offer to exercise one of the horses along with him. With luck, that would provide a good opportunity for a talk.

Emilia lay sleepless all night, worrying and planning what she would do in the morning. At first light, she rose and began to dress.

María opened her eyes and yawned. *"¿Qué haces, m'hija?"* What's going on?"

"I couldn't sleep, Mamá. I'm going for a walk before breakfast. You go back to sleep."

Sighing, her mother closed her eyes, turned on her side, pulled up the blanket and was still. Emilia watched for a few seconds, then silently left the *jacal*, in passing, snatching from a peg the britches she'd always used when she and Dámaso used to ride together. They hadn't done that for months. Once outside, she slipped on the britches under her smock, then set out for the Alamo.

The sun was not yet up when she arrived. She moved silently past the barracks and on to the corral. The horses, hearing her footsteps, congregated on her side of the fence. One of them gave a low nicker. Then she heard boots striking the ground behind her. Dámaso came up beside her before she had time to turn around. He heaved the tack for one horse on top the corral fence.

"What are you doing here?" His tone was frosty.

"I had to talk to you. It seemed the only way we could meet face to face."

"Up so early? Did you and your lover have a quarrel?"

"Lover? I have no lover, and never had one. You of all people should know that."

"That's not what I hear."

"Who's slandering me? Chipita?"

"No. It's someone whose word I believe without question."

"Who?"

He turned away. "Look. I have to exercise four horses this morning. I'm wasting my time on you."

Her words tumbled out. "We have to talk. It's urgent, before this goes any further. *Please!* You have to hear what I have to say. Tell me where the tack room is. I'll exercise two horses along with you."

Dámaso's body was stiff, his face wooden. "I guess I owe you a hearing. We were friends for a long time, after all. "

"Thank you! The tack room?"

"Over there." He pointed. "Take the saddle on the rack nearest the door. The blanket and bridle are with it." He moved away to the corral gate, opened it a few inches and slipped inside. He held a halter in his left hand as he moved among the horses. He slipped the halter over the nose of a tall bay gelding.

By the time she'd hauled the tack out to the corral, he had saddled and bridled the bay and tied him to the nearby hitching rack. "No need to go into the corral," he called to her, "I'll get Negrito for you."

That sounded friendlier. Dámaso led out a fine-looking black horse and tied him to the rack. She was already there with the tack, and he took the blanket, settled it on Negrito's back, then saddled and bridled him. "Follow me." He didn't offer to help her mount.

She didn't bother with the left stirrup, but jumped and pulled herself up by the saddle horn and cantle. Then she tucked her skirts under her legs and body, and touched Negrito with her heels. He responded at once, eager to keep up with his companion.

They circled the space inside the mission's walls once, then Dámaso led the way through an open gate and out the back, into the scrub brush of the nearby countryside. A path led straight toward a copse of live oaks a few hundred yards away. He touched his heels to the bay, broke into a trot, and Emilia on Negrito followed.

Dámaso rode directly into the knot of trees, stopping when they reached a small, grazed-over clearing. They couldn't see the Alamo, and no one could see them.

"All right. What is so urgent that you had to come all the way out here to tell me?"

"Be patient with me, Dámaso. This whole thing is terribly hard for me to talk about. Just let me tell you as best I can without you interrupting me. Please."

"All right. All right! Get on with it, then!" His voice told her that, in spite of his irritation, he was nonetheless intrigued, anxious to hear her story.

"About two months ago by now, I got hurt very badly. You came to visit me. You gave me that beautiful wolf carving."

He nodded.

"Well, I lied to you. I lied to everyone. I felt I had to. I didn't fall off that corral fence. I was grabbed from behind while I was up on that fence looking at a new horse. The attacker struck me in the face with a fist, slapped me, threw me on the ground and... and..."

Dámaso had stopped breathing and leaned forward, mouth open.

Emilia's voice broke and tears began sliding down her cheeks despite her effort to stop them. She dashed them away and gave him an accurate account of the rape.

Dámaso spoke between clenched teeth. "Who was it?"

Emilia's voice was tremulous. "His name is Jedediah Crow. He ruined me. I'm not fit to marry you, Dámaso. Not fit to marry anyone. At least I'm not pregnant with that brute's child." She wiped her eyes on the hem of her skirt.

Dámaso was less surprised than he'd anticipated. He'd been aware of Jedediah's behavior ever since the disturbance the man had caused three years ago at the fandango. He knew about several more unpleasant confrontations with the citizens of Béxar. The man openly despised and insulted the original settlers of the town.

And yet, he had not even purchased the land he occupied—he was a squatter. And now, a predator upon Mexican women.

"Whom did you tell?"

"After a month, when I knew I wasn't pregnant, I confessed to Padre Refugio. He's the only one who knows besides me, mamá, the rapist himself, and now you."

"I see...." Dámaso straightened, tilted his head back and stared over the treetops. "I went to confess to Padre Refugio, too. I told him I was obsessed with you, loved you, but you had just refused my... my almost-proposal of marriage."

"And what did he say?"

"That I should avoid you... that you were, uh... 'compromised' was the word he used. I took that to mean you'd been with another man."

"And he told me that I was at fault for having 'enticed' my rapist. All women do that, he said, because we're all daughters of Eve."

"Did you?"

"Entice him? Heavens no. I had barely noticed him in the mercantile store shortly before I went to look at the new horse."

Dámaso's voice sank to a steely monotone. His teeth were clenched. "I'll have to settle things with Jedediah Crow."

Emilia paused. "And what about Chipita?"

"She knows I'm not serious. She is, though, and I'll have to settle things with her, too." Dámaso remained silent for a while. "We'd better exercise the other two horses. We'll canter back and ride twice around the ring inside the mission wall." He nudged the bay, and they moved out of the grove and began to canter. Both horses were more than anxious to run, so they flew back to the mission, where they completed two circuits. Dámaso caught and saddled two more horses.

Around mid-morning, once all four had been walked, cooled, groomed, and fed along with all the other horses, Dámaso and Emilia left the Alamo. He took her hand. "You've had a terrible time of it. I'm sorry I made it that much worse. But we need to talk about what to do next. About us, you and me. I already know what to do about that *cabrón*, Jedediah."

"For God's sake, Dámaso, don't do anything rash! I want you safe!"

He smiled, his head tilted to one side. "Nothing and nobody is safe in this world, Emilia. You're the living proof of that."

"Papá, I'm going hunting."

"Why, Dámaso? We have enough venison on hand."

"It's not for our family, it's for someone else."

"Oh? Another girlfriend?"

No, Papá, not another. It's the same girl I've always loved."

Dámaso shouldered the M1819 Hall breech-loading rifle he'd traded his best horse for on the last trip to Goliad, the new name for La Bahía. He left the house without another word on either side. He hadn't lied to his father. Jedediah Crow was no better than an animal and deserved nothing better than to be hunted down like one. Dámaso had sacrificed his favorite horse for a gun he knew was worthy of the task. The very thought that such an evil low-life as Jedediah should have touched—even touched—Emilia stoked his fury.

He caught his second-best horse, Oropel, a handsome buckskin with black mane, tail, and stockings, and rode eastward to find Jedediah Crow.

He rode straight for the cabin. Dámaso knew he had a wife, but beyond that, nothing personal. his duty was to confront the criminal, now that he knew the truth about his assault on the woman he loved.

An early September morning mist covered the landscape. Shrubs, bushes and trees wavered and moved like nightmare beasts, but Dámaso trusted Oropel to alert him to any real danger. The horse extended his trot, moving without hesitation as if he sensed his master's urgency. It took only an hour to cover the distance. The sun rose above the horizon as they came to the trail that led to Jedediah's place.

The cabin looked deserted in the early morning light as Dámaso crouched to observe it. A wisp of smoke, almost a vapor, rose from the chimney. Apparently, the family was still sleeping. He didn't want to challenge Jedediah in his nightshirt, but decently dressed, so he could confront him man to man. Perhaps a few more minutes before calling him out. He watched the rising sun move the shadow of a prickly pear two inches, from one pebble to another. That must be about ten minutes. He stood and faced the door.

"Jedediah! Come out, you worthless dog!"

Only silence answered him from the cabin.

"Jedediah! I'm here to avenge your rape of Emilia Altamirano."

More silence.

"Jedediah! Don't make me come in after you!"

The door opened, and the man appeared, dressed in britches with suspenders, no shirt, a rifle in his hands. "Who the hell are you?" Jedediah moved a few steps away from the house.

"I'm Dámaso Jiménez. ¡*Pinche cabrón!* You raped my woman."

"Go to Hell, Greaser!" Jedediah raised his musket and took aim.

Dámaso was quicker. Both fired, the reports nearly simultaneous. Dámaso sensed the bullet that whizzed over his head, and Jedediah fell, bright red blossoming just below his left shoulder. Dámaso lunged forward as a woman, heavy with child, ran awkwardly from the cabin. They knelt on either side of the fallen man. Dámaso grabbed Jedediah's wrist and felt for a pulse while the woman embraced his body, supporting his head, heedless of the blood that soaked her gray shift.

"Jed! Oh, Jed! Stay! Don't go! Don't leave me!" She received no response—breath and movement were gone. Her first sob tore itself from her throat like the cry of a wounded animal.

Dámaso could feel no pulse. Her outcry startled him and he leaped to his feet, gazing down, struggling with a jumble of feelings: satisfaction that he'd avenged Emilia's rape, horror that he'd killed a fellow man, and pity for the pregnant child-woman on her knees, her hands and breast red with her husband's blood.

She rocked Jedediah's upper body to and fro, then looked up with hatred. She screamed. "You've killed my man! *Murderer*!"

He understood a few of her words, but felt a compulsion to help her. What would happen to this little woman and her unborn child? A child's cries came to them from the cabin. They both turned their heads.

The woman struggled to her feet. "That's my Bonnie! My little girl!" She took a step toward the cabin, then a step back, torn between love for her child and devotion to her dead husband. Dámaso took a step toward the cabin then another, then ran ahead of her to the door. Hardly knowing what he was doing or why, he pulled it open, scanned the interior, and yanked the blanket off the unmade bed.

He ran back to the corpse, straightened Jedediah's limbs and covered him with the blanket. He shouted at her, "*Vuelvo con ayuda*. I'll be back with help."

He'd have to leave her for now to care for the little girl. Someone in town would take her in—*must* take in—the pregnant wife and her daughter. He urged his mount into a run, then slowed to a trot, not wanting to kill his horse as well. *What will I say to Papá? I didn't think of that man's wife—and the child—children, if she lives through childbirth. I have to get help for her.* Still mulling over what he had just done, what must be done, what he might now have to face, he reined in his sweating horse before the *Casas reales*.

The *Ayuntamiento* was in session, and *Alcalde* José Miguel de Arciniega interrupted his argument as Dámaso strode into the room and stopped at the foot of the long conference table. The room fell silent.

"I just killed Jedediah Crow. I need someone to go out immediately to care for his widow and little girl—and to bury the body."

His appearance and words froze everyone in the room in a tableau; each man halted in mid-gesture: some writing, one raising his hand for recognition, several shaking their heads, one making a thumbs-down. Then everyone began moving and speaking at once. Erasmo Seguín, the senior diplomat and politician, tapped his water glass, and the loud clinking cut through the babble of voices. "Quiet! One person at a time! Whom did you say you killed, young man?"

Dámaso moistened dry lips and began to speak, but his voice came out as a croak. The nearest *regidor* passed him his full glass of water. Dámaso drank it all, cleared his throat, and spoke. "I just killed Jedediah Crow. He had a pregnant wife and little girl. The wife is a mere child, herself. I need... we need to help her and bury the dead man. She needs help right away... now."

The room remained silent until Erasmo asked, "Why did you kill him?"

Dámaso choked. "He raped and dishonored the woman I wanted... I-I want... to marry."

Emilia had been in the kitchen, preparing hot chocolate. Its fragrance followed her into the room as she appeared at the hall door. She had heard Dámaso's last words, his confession of guilt and his reason for committing murder. Without pausing to think of the consequences, she stepped forward and spoke, hoping her words would help the man she loved.

"I didn't fall, those weeks ago. Jedediah Crow raped and dishonored me. No one answered my cries for help."

José Miguel demanded, "But why did you keep the truth from everyone and pretend it was a fall?"

"I am a woman, Señor, and my honor had been stolen from me in the most brutal way. I had to wait to know if I was with child from that violation. I kept the truth from everyone including Dámaso, but when he found out what really had happened, he took revenge. He did it for me, to avenge my stolen honor."

The *alguacil*, Sheriff Gaspar Flores, a member of the *Ayuntamiento ex oficio*, stood. "Young man, we understand why you did what you did. Your action was like a duel, but fought with rifles instead of swords or pistols. However, I'll have to take you into custody for murder. You've killed an Anglo immigrant. I wish I could consult with Señor Austin about what legal procedure to follow that won't cause an uprising among the Anglo settlers. Right now, I'm escorting you to the Béxar city jail. Does anyone here know where the Crow homestead is?"

Andrés and four others replied, "*Sí*. About seven miles east of here."

Flores turned to his fellow *regidores*. "As soon as I return from the jail, we'll get over there to find out what needs to be done for the murdered man's widow and child. Those of you who know where to go, get ready. I'll join you. Does she speak Spanish?"

Dámaso replied. "No, but she seemed to understand something of what I said to her."

"Then we must do the best we can. We'll try to pick up tracks and any other signs that'll confirm or refute whatever Señor Jiménez's full statement will be. Now, come with me, Dámaso. Walk ahead of me, please."

Head down, Dámaso preceded him to the jail in the presidio.

Three men, Andrés Altamirano, Francisco Salinas and Rafael Menchaca, volunteered to fetch the widow and bury Jedediah.

Alguacil Gaspar Flores, who had been *alcalde* the year before, would make four. All of them were currently or had been members of the Béxar militia.

When they came near the cabin, they halted their horses and walked the rest of the way, carefully searching for traces of recent activity. They saw where Dámaso had dismounted and followed his footprints to a mesquite bush on the border of the clearing around the cabin. They checked Jedediah's rifle, and saw that it had recently been fired. Jedediah had fired at Dámaso, but missed. It was important to establish that Dámaso had not killed Jedediah in cold blood.

The three men approached the body, still lying under a blanket and guarded by a rangy brown and white spotted hound. The dog stood and growled, but Gaspar squatted beside him and talked to him, telling him he had to examine his master. The dog seemed to understand and allowed the men to examine the body. They verified that Jedediah had been shot in the chest from a considerable distance. That confirmed what they imagined the scene to have been: Dámaso had challenged Jedediah, they fired at each other, and only Dámaso had hit his mark.

Meanwhile, two of the searchers tended to the widow. They knocked, and not receiving an answer, entered the cabin. Slumped in a chair by the fireplace, she held her little girl in her lap, crooning to her in a soft voice. She stopped singing with a gasp and stood to confront them, drawing herself up to stand as erect as possible, her chin thrust out. Her face was swollen, eyes red from weeping. The toddler squirmed in her arms, turned away and began to whimper.

"I'm Kathleen Crow. This here child is Bonnie. She's two years old. I want you to know my husband was murdered in cold blood."

Gaspar Flores understood enough to interpret what she said to his companion. "Your husband's killer is in custody. He gave himself up. He's in jail. We need to bury your husband now, Señora, so the coyotes don't get to him."

Kathleen appeared to have caught the drift of Gaspar's words. She nodded and followed them out of the cabin.

"Where do you want your husband buried, Señora?" Gaspar accompanied his question with gestures.

She pointed, wordlessly, at a nearby tree. They dug a grave near the single gnarled live oak in the yard. Kathleen understood the words *"Padre nuestro,"* and said the Lord's Prayer in English while the men recited it in Spanish. She stared as if puzzled when they crossed themselves. After they had filled in the grave, the family dog, whose name, Kathleen told them, was Ben, lay down on the freshly-turned earth with a whine, head resting on his paws.

Gaspar scouted the little farm. He turned the two horses and the mule out to pasture and looked at the milk cow. He called to the others. "One of you bring this cow back to my place. She looks to be a good milker, and if she's not tended to, she'll either die of milk fever or go dry. See if she'll lead. If not, you'll have to drive her in. Besides, that little girl needs her milk."

They caught their horses and prepared to mount. They called to Ben, who raised his head, then laid it again on his paws, ears down, eyes mournful. Gaspar shook his head. "He'll follow us if he feels like it. We've got to get back to make our report." He mounted; Andrés lifted Kathleen to sit behind Gaspar, who took Bonnie in his arms. They started off at a walk, and when they began to trot, Kathleen passed one arm around Gaspar's waist and with the other supported her belly, trying to lessen the shocks to the fetus.

Along the way, the riders conferred with one another from horseback. Gaspar would take the widow and baby home with him for his wife to care for; then he would join the other members of the *Ayuntamiento* to report what they had seen. It was well after dark when they arrived at the *Casas reales*, but the windows were bright with oil lamps. Their colleagues had waited for them.

Marta, Gaspar Flores' wife, helped lift Kathleen off the horse. Kathleen groaned in relief—the ride had stressed her endurance to the limit. She prayed aloud, thanking the Lord for sparing the life of her unborn baby, and Marta understood both her prayer and her discomfort. She helped her into the house and the bedroom, where she gestured for the widow to lie down.

"I'll bring you some hot chocolate, directly. You just rest."

Kathleen spoke three Spanish words in a weak voice. "*¡Ah! ¡Chocolate! Comprendo.*"

Gaspar came in with the two-year-old girl, also at the end of her endurance. Kathleen took the toddler in her arms and asked, "Do you have any milk, *leche*? Bonnie needs nourishment."

Marta understood the gesture and the word *leche*, and nodded. Yes, there was milk to make the chocolate and to nourish the child.

Gaspar embraced his wife. "Rafael Menchaca's bringing in Jedediah's cow. Nice cow, her milk will give the little girl something she's used to. When they get here with her, settle her with some hay. If she'll let you, milk her as well. She really needs it. Well, I'd better get back to the others. We all must tell what we saw out there—it'll mean a lot in our decision what to do with Dámaso Jiménez. Just get some food into Señora Crow and the girl, and let them sleep."

Marta gave him a squeeze. "Of course, I'll take care of them. They probably need rest more than anything."

The *regidores* were assembled once again, by lamplight. *Alcalde* Arciniega heard statements from all four men, reporting just what they had observed and deduced from what they had seen.

"So, your unanimous conclusion is that Dámaso challenged Jedediah, who must have been armed when the two confronted each other, then they fired, and only Dámaso's bullet struck home. He then rode back here hell-for-leather and gave himself up to us. Is that a fair summary of your findings?"

A chorus: "Yes."

"Then, bring the prisoner in here for questioning, por favor, *Señor Alguacil*."

Gaspar nodded and complied. The men waited in silence, listening to faint noises of keys jangling, a long silence, then a double pair of approaching footsteps. When the *alguacil* and Dámaso entered, Arciniega gestured at the end of the table opposite him. "Take Francisco's chair, Dámaso. Sit where we can all see you. We have questions to ask."

Francisco Ruíz vacated the chair and moved to one side of the table. Dámaso sat, his body stiff, jaw muscles working as he clenched his teeth. He waited, silent. The seven assembled men, also wordless, leaned toward him, giving him their full attention.

Alcalde Arciniega, also acting as *juez*, judge, began the interrogation. "Tell us, Dámaso Jiménez, why you killed Jedediah Crow. Start from the beginning."

Dámaso's voice was hoarse, but strong. "The beginning? That was years ago when I came to know and admire, and then to love a girl named Emilia Altamirano. We've been close friends, but honorable, not lovers. I'd been planning to propose marriage for a while—two, three years, maybe, but could never get up the courage. I knew she liked me, and I had a good chance. I finally went to visit her, about six weeks ago, to propose. She'd been injured—looked like someone beat her up. Bruised everywhere, arms, especially her face, lips cut. Her hip was sprained. Told me she'd fallen off the corral fence out there." He gestured behind him toward Military Plaza. "Hard to believe. When I told her I was saving to buy a gold ring, she told me no, that maybe she'd never marry."

Gaspar interrupted. "Get to the point. When and why did you decide to kill Crow?" Andrés had been listing with the most intense interest, and now hitched his chair closer.

Dámaso nodded. "I was hurt, depressed. I became angry. I avoided Emilia. Thought she had deceived me, had a secret lover. She finally—weeks later—cornered me and told me the truth. She hadn't fallen, she'd been assaulted, beaten, and raped."

"Did she tell you who'd done it?"

"I had to ask her. Yes, she said it was that trouble-maker, Jedediah Crow."

"So, what was your reaction?"

"I saw white flames. Couldn't sleep. Traded a good horse for a new rifle, told Papá I was going hunting. I went out to the Crow place. It was early morning, and they were still asleep. I called Jedediah out of the cabin. I wasn't polite. He came out armed, called me a name and raised his rifle. We fired at the same time, but only he fell. That's all. Oh, yes, I came back here and told you, since I couldn't leave his wife and little girl out there to die too."

Arciniega looked around the table. "Any of you have any questions?"

Andrés and several other *regidores* shook their heads; one rounded his lips in a "no," and one made a downward movement with his hand.

"No? Well then, Gaspar, take him back to his cell. He'll be spending the night there." He looked at Dámaso. "I expect you're tired enough that the hard bunk in there will feel like a feather bed." He nodded to Gaspar, who ushered the prisoner out.

There was silence around the table for a moment or two, then, Arciniega spoke. "Andrés, would you please escort Emilia home?"

"*Sí, Señor Alcalde.*" Andrés offered his arm to his daughter, and the two left the room.

Francisco Ruíz stood and paced, hands locked behind his back. When he sat again, he surveyed the room. "*Bueno*, you saw the evidence and heard the guilty man speak his piece. What do you think we should do? We all know he's guilty of killing a man—with premeditation—but Crow was given an even chance."

Francisco Salinas raised a hand. "I don't think Crow had an even chance. He'd been asleep, probably was only half awake. I don't think I could shoot straight under those circumstances."

Menchaca spoke up. "Yes, but if I heard someone outside my cabin calling me names, and in Spanish, I think I'd be scared wide awake. He knew how miserably he'd treated us Tejanos."

Andrés Nava chimed in. "Dámaso was protecting his honor—his and Emilia's. My God, here she was, working for us all those weeks, and we never suspected a thing! In his place I would have taken vengeance, too. I vote that we let him go with some small penalty."

Erasmo Seguín, on a week's leave from the Legislature in Saltillo, broke in. "We know what we would do, if it were left up to us; we would uphold law and order as always. Ten years ago—even five—I'd have agreed that Crow was killed in a fair fight. However, Dámaso shot an Anglo-American."

Nava interrupted. "So? What difference does that make?"

Seguín raised a hand. "A lot. We have a few new Anglo settlers living among us, right here in Béxar, like that prominent merchant, George H. Bobbs, or the saddle-maker, Leroy Jenkins. And Thomas Portman has just set up a new mercantile store to compete with Veramendi and Navarro. These are prominent citizens who respect us and our ways. We don't want to alienate them." He stopped to wipe his forehead with his handkerchief. "More Anglos are coming to Texas every day. You all know that Señor James Bowie is courting Martín Veramendi's eldest daughter Ursula. Not only that, Martín and Bowie are planning together to build a cotton mill in Saltillo."

Francisco Ruíz growled, "So, what are you getting at?"

Erasmo raised a hand. "We Tejanos are in a delicate position, ever since 1824, when the central government combined Texas with Coahuila. Right now, I'd guess we have around five thousand new Anglo-American settlers—they and their 'indentured servants'— mainly in east Texas. They already outnumber our entire Hispanic population."

Ruíz dealt the table an impatient slap. "What on earth does all that have to do with Dámaso?"

"Everything, I fear. We don't want to do anything—even symbolically—that would show the opposing faction in Saltillo that we're not one hundred percent behind our efforts to increase our Anglo population. We also can't rile the local Anglos against us by causing them to think the *Ayuntamiento* is unjust and prejudiced against them. That kind of news spreads fast. In my opinion, we'll have to bind Dámaso over to the State Supreme Court in Saltillo. They'll have to determine his punishment for killing an Anglo. The matter is already out of our hands."

Heated discussion continued for another hour, after which the *Ayuntamiento* agreed that Dámaso would be sent to Saltillo under guard, to undergo a trial by strangers.

Their bodies tense, faces strained, Emilia and María sat across the table from each other in the *jacal*, seeking a way to cope with the situation.

María broke the silence. "I have something to tell you, *m'hija*. I borrowed Andrés's carbine and his work clothes and went to shoot Jedediah, myself."

Open-mouthed, Emilia stared at her mother. "*¡Mamá! ¡Dios mío!* I had no idea! But you didn't kill him, though. Why?"

"It was the day after the assault. I was burning with rage and lust for vengeance. You were in bed, dozing and reading. I left you with the impression I was going to talk to Pilar Chávez and let you rest. You accepted that."

"Yes, but you didn't kill Jedediah. So...?"

"I rode out to his cabin. He was plowing a garden plot, and his wife came out to bring him a canteen of water. She had a toddler—a baby girl—on her hip. She couldn't be more than fifteen, but she was a good seven months pregnant. I'd already drawn a bead on Jedediah, but when I saw those pathetic creatures, I couldn't kill him. All three, mother, child and unborn baby would've died of starvation. I rode home, and you were reading—didn't suspect a thing."

"Mamá! I always knew you had a will of iron and the courage of a tiger. To think you'd go that far! Thank you! And thank God you didn't kill him—you'd have murder on your conscience. But now, what are we going to do about Dámaso?"

"Do you know what their final decision was?"

"No, Andrés escorted me out before they began their deliberations. Hardly spoke on the way home and hurried back for the discussion. We can't plan anything before we know what they decided."

María, elbows on the table, cupped her chin in her hands. "Hmmm. Gaspar Flores is *alguacil* for this term. Why don't you go over and talk to his wife? If they came to a decision, she'll surely know what it was."

Emilia stood, her voice urgent. "Must be about ten. I don't think it's too late for me to go there—they're probably still discussing the whole thing. They know I'm 'an interested party,' so they won't be surprised when I show up. When I get back, we'll make a plan."

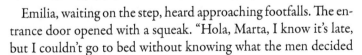

Emilia, waiting on the step, heard approaching footfalls. The entrance door opened with a squeak. "Hola, Marta, I know it's late, but I couldn't go to bed without knowing what the men decided about Dámaso."

Marta Flores stood framed in the doorway, silhouetted by the lamplight behind her. "Gaspar and I couldn't go to sleep yet anyway. He's out at the barn seeing if the new cow is eating. It was Jedediah's milk cow. She refused food at first. He'll be back in a minute."

"Where's your dog, Ferino? He usually greets me when I visit."

Marta shook her head and drew a long face. "He got snake bit and died about a week ago. Gaspar is even sadder about that than I am. Ferino followed him everywhere."

"Oh! I'm so sorry to hear that. I wish Mamá and I could keep a dog. But Juan Andrés won't hear of it."

"Don't just stand there. Come in, sit down."

As Emilia entered, her elbow brushed Gaspar's formal coat hanging on a peg to her left. Something shiny just beyond it drew her eye. On another peg nearby hung a large ring with several keys. She walked on, chose the nearest chair, an armchair, and sat. Marta faced her on the sofa. A child's whimper came from a neighboring room and Emilia started. "Whose child is that?"

"It's Señora Crow's toddler, Bonnie. Oh, of course you don't know. Gaspar brought Jedediah Crow's wife and child back here to stay with us."

After a moment's pause, Emilia exclaimed, "*Bueno!* At least the child will get the milk she's used to. I suppose you'll soon be a mid-wife to Crow's second child."

Marta squirmed a little. "Yes. That child-woman will need an understanding, helpful foster home for a time. But I expect she must be tougher than she looks, poor little thing."

"I expect she must be, to put up with that man. But I came to find out if Gaspar told you what will happen to Dámaso."

"Yes, he did. Dámaso will be escorted to Saltillo tomorrow morning and bound over to the court down there."

"Why didn't they reach a verdict on their own?"

"They did. Gaspar said Erasmo Seguín was most persuasive that we, up here, who used to run our own affairs and those of the rest of Texas, too, must not rile the Anglos. They're now in the majority and could save us from the Comanche as well as bring prosperity."

"So now we must run to Coahuila with our legal problems? I find that cowardly."

Marta clasped and unclasped her hands in her lap. "It's expedient, my dear."

"And my fiancé is to be the victim of this expediency. Well, thank you for telling me, Marta. I do think you and Gaspar are doing the right thing in taking care of the widow—a work of Christian charity. But now I must be getting back home. Please bid Gaspar *buenas noches* for me."

On her way out, Emilia again noticed what she'd seen on the way in: the keys to the *Casas reales*, the presidio and the jail cell. Emilia had seen the latter two keys often enough when she was admitted to Antonio's cell every morning for her reading lessons while he served his sentence for smuggling. She recognized them now.

María waited impatiently, and was pacing the *jacal* floor when Emilia returned. Her daughter blurted the news. "They're taking him down to Saltillo to turn him over to the courts down there and they're leaving in the morning."

"Well, then, there's not much time. How—"

Emilia interrupted. "The only way is to steal the keys to the jail and get Dámaso out tonight."

"So—where are the keys?"

"Hanging next to the front door in the casa Flores. I'll return there in an hour or so, wait until all is quiet, then simply open the front door, take the keys, release Dámaso, and return the keys. At least, they don't have a dog. He died about a week ago of snakebite."

A locked house door would be unthinkable. No one in Béxar locked their house doors at night. She shook her head. "I've got to do all that before dawn. That's next to impossible."

María grinned. "Not so. Sorry about Ferino, but that makes our task so much easier! Follow me." She picked up the oil lamp and the two crossed from the *jacal* to the kitchen. She went to the sink and took the bar of homemade soap. "Use this on the door hinges before you open it. There's plenty of fat in the soap. What kind of floor do they have?"

"Tile."

"Good. No problem there." She reached into the cupboard and fetched a rag from the shelf. "Here. Before you take the keys off the peg, wrap them in this. Be careful."

Emilia left immediately. The half-moon gave enough light to show her way without difficulty. Shadows of the one-story adobe houses on either side, however, were blacker than she'd ever seen. She stumbled once and caught herself on her extended hands. A dog in the house almost at her elbow began to bark. A moonlit patch lay straight ahead, and she hurried on. No harm done; the owner didn't come to the door or window, as far as she could tell. The casa Flores was dark when she got there, but she waited in the shadows across the street until she was sure all were in bed. Then she followed her mother's directions.

The soap was soft enough to make no noise when she applied it to the hinges. She massaged it into the crevices in the metal as best she could, then, slowly, she lifted the latch. The door swung open, silent this time. She took two steps inside. She heard a murmur from somewhere not far away—the bedroom, no doubt, and stood holding her breath until she was sure there was no further noise. The keys made a faint tinkle as she wrapped them and she again paused, but there was no reaction.

Heaving a sigh of relief, she stepped out and closed the door. She walked to the corner. From there, she ran. The moon lit most of the way in silvery light, but the huge shadow of the church, inky black, swallowed her. Her skin crawled at the thought of unknown danger hidden behind the garden wall. But nothing attacked her, and she continued to run across Main Plaza, to Military Plaza, and to the presidio.

She quickly picked out the right key and heard the lock click, but the door wouldn't budge. Alarmed, she pressed her shoulder against it and pushed with all her weight. The door popped open, banged against the wall, and she fell, bruising her knees on the threshold. *I hope to God no one is near enough to hear that!* She waited for a second or two, hearing only a scuffling noise from the direction of the jail cell, then scrambled to her feet.

"Dámaso?"

Muffled, from within: "Emilia? Thank God! But how—?"

In a whisper, "Shhhh! We must hurry!" She unerringly chose the cell key and this time, the door opened without resistance. "We'd better lock the doors behind us. I don't want anyone to suspect there's anything wrong until they come for you. Let's go!"

Once out in the moonlight, Dámaso embraced Emilia and kissed her fiercely. "You've probably saved my life! I'll love you forever!" He held her at arm's length. "I think I'll go to—"

"Don't tell me, Dámaso! The less I know the better. They'll try hard to get information out of me, I'm sure. Now run, take two horses so you can go twice as far—and fast. The men of the militia will be after you as soon as they know you're gone."

"You're right. I need to get away. *¡Hasta pronto, mi amor!* Wait for me!"

"*Ve con Dios, mi tesoro.* Of course I'll wait!" He ran. In the moonlight, his shadow rippled over the rutted ground as he raced across Military Plaza. Perspiration began to dry on her face. In her damp smock, she shook all over, her body reacting to the high tension of the past minutes. She must not stop now—the keys must be returned before they could be missed. She ran all the way to Gaspar

Flores' house, replaced the keys as she had found them, closed the front door, wiped the hinges with the rag, and then ran home. She burst into the *jacal* to find María waiting beside the lamp.

"Well? It's probably after three."

Emilia panted. "It worked! He must be... on his way by now. I only hope..." she swallowed, "nothing happens, no accidents... and that the militia won't capture him."

Oropel gave Dámaso his all for the first ten minutes of the flight southward from Béxar. It must be around four o'clock, and he needed to be well away from the town by sunrise. The moonlit landscape flashing by him consisted mainly of low shrubs and an occasional cactus, unidentifiable at this speed and in the faint light.

When he could sense that his mount and the mare he was leading, Pepa, were tiring, Dámaso dropped his speed to a deliberate trot and let both horses take a breather. After all, he needed their stamina to last all day, and by his reckoning, sundown was some eighteen hours away. The mare behind him, like Oropel, was a sturdy *mesteño*, what the new Anglo settlers were mispronouncing as "mustang." They were both wild horses he had caught and trained. Both, he knew, were devoted to him.

Dámaso had chosen the lesser-known of two trails, the one toward Monclova. Most traffic took the Camino Real south-by-southwest toward Saltillo. He knew exactly where he was heading. A wrangler, Chino Gutiérrez, whom he'd met in New Orleans two years ago, worked on the Fuentes y Culebra Ranch, west of Monclova. It was owned by a wealthy landowner from Mexico City who came north only occasionally to check whether his cattle-raising venture was still profitable and well run. The head wrangler had told Dámaso he had a chronic need of skilled cowhands. Dámaso knew he was skilled—one of the best.

After an hour at a working trot, he loped his two horses for a while and then slowed to a walk. It must be around six in the morning by now; light from the east had already transformed the scrub brush around him from black blobs to recognizable bushes. He began to detect the aromas of sage and creosote bush as the morning dew dried on leaves and branches.

At noon, he would switch and ride Pepa, and then, at sundown, find a place where he could hobble them, a place with water and grazing, where he could rest without fear of discovery. The day dragged on forever, hot, dry, and without food. He couldn't last long unless he could find water to refill his canteen, shoot a rabbit, a wild turkey—he fantasized about the game he might find. A deer would be too much, a waste.

The sun was well down its western slide when he spotted a clump of trees—just the upper branches; they looked more like bushes from this distance. They were well off the trail, but Dámaso urged his tired horses into a trot and came upon a rocky ridge. Below, a spring bubbled out of the limestone, creating a small pond and a stream that disappeared in the sandy soil not far away. Around the pond, shaded by cypress trees, grew lush grass, and on the pond swam a pair of wild ducks. He couldn't believe his luck. Slowly drawing his rifle, he aimed and fired at the larger of the two, the male by its coloring. Its mate flew with a loud whir of wings and disappeared directly into the sunset. Dámaso picked his way down the escarpment, leading his horses, found a fallen tree branch and fished the duck out of the pond. First, he tended to the horses, already thirstily sucking water into parched throats. He followed their example, knelt and scooped up the cool water.

He plucked and gutted the bird, and hung it by a branch over the coals to roast. He turned it from time to time until it looked and smelled right, then devoured it, without salt. It would certainly tide him over for the next day. He said a prayer and lay down to sleep, the saddle blanket under him and the saddle for a pillow.

On the fourth day, starving, dirty and exhausted, he rode onto the Fuentes y Culebra spread west of Monclova. He found the foreman, Emanuel, "Manu" for short, and introduced himself as Daniel Martínez. He told of meeting Chino, the head wrangler, in New Orleans.

"He'll be glad you're here, Daniel. I see from your outfit you've had ranching experience."

"Yes, Chino complained that he was short of cowhands. I'd like to sign on."

"Sounds good. It's about time to eat, so join us." Manu turned toward a building that advertised its purpose by the smoke from its chimney along with delicious aromas. "Cocí! We have another mouth to feed!"

A cowboy in a once-white canvas apron stood in the doorway, watching them. "OK, Manu. We've got plenty."

"If you see Chino first, tell him maybe he's got a new cowpoke." He jerked a thumb toward 'Daniel.' "Says he met Chino in Orleans." He turned back to Daniel. "We call our cook 'Cocí'—short for 'cocinero,' cook."

Cocí gave Daniel the once-over. "Looks all right to me. Starving, though."

"Damn right I am." 'Daniel' grinned.

'Daniel' was chewing his last mouthful of *estofado*, Cocí's tasty and aromatic stew, when he felt a hand on his shoulder. Chino stood looking down at him. "You look like you've been drug for miles through a mesquite patch."

"*St. Exacto*. Any room for a new wrangler in this outfit?"

"*Claro que sí*—if you're good enough, that is. What'd you say your name is?"

Dámaso crossed his fingers under the table. "Daniel Martínez at your service."

Chino slanted his head to one side with narrowed eyes. "Hmmm. That sounds a little off, but then, I'm probably misrememberin'. You come in from Béxar?"

"In four days. I'm pretty worn out, and my horses sure need a little rest."

"I guess you rode 'em half to death. Well, take it easy the rest of today, and tomorrow you'll ride with us."

"Great. Thanks, Chino."

Chino made an about face. "Manu, show this man where to bunk and if you haven't done it already, take care of his horses."

The next day, he rode out to prove to the wranglers that he ranked among the best.

Francisco Salinas crossed behind the presidio the morning after Dámaso's hearing. When he came near the rear of the jail, he called up to the barred window, "Dámaso, I hope you're ready for a long trip today."

No answer.

He called again. "Dámaso!"

Silence.

He jumped, grabbed the bars and drew himself up to the window. His eyes swept the interior. Empty. Were his senses deceiving him? "Dámaso!" he shouted again, but only a hollow echo answered him. His first thought was, *who has keys to the jail cell?*

As far as he knew, only the *alguacil*, and this term that was Gaspar Flores. Yes, it had seemed to him that Flores was a bit too sympathetic to the prisoner. He'd better confront Gaspar before the *Ayuntamiento* convened. Maybe he could catch him and Dámaso before they got away. He ran all the way to the Flores house and arrived dripping in sweat.

Marta answered his knock. "Francisco, how good to see you.... Oh! You must have come in a hurry. What—"

"The prisoner, Dámaso Jiménez, is gone. Where's your husband?"

"Why, he's eating his breakfast. Come in, come in! He'll want to know pronto!"

Salinas brushed past her and strode into the kitchen. Gaspar's hand, holding a tortilla loaded with *frijoles y huevo*, froze in midair. "Francisco, what's all this?"

"Dámaso Jiménez is gone. And you're the only one of us I know of who has the keys."

"What?" Flores leapt to his feet, almost upsetting the table. "Just a minute." He rushed into the salon and found the key ring hanging just as he had left it the night before. He quickly checked all the keys. "All here. Let's get over there." He grabbed his coat, and the two men rushed back to the presidio. Sure enough, the entrance door was locked, and so was the cell door.

As they stood in the echoing, empty jail cell, Flores mused, his hand stroking his chin. "Whoever did this had to have a duplicate set of keys. Andrés Nava, now... I thought he was a bit too sympathetic to the prisoner last night. We need to alert all the members and get them over here pronto. We have to be on that boy's trail as soon as possible."

From the middle of Main Plaza, as she approached the *Casas reales*, Emilia could hear the voices of men arguing. She continued to the door, carrying the usual platter of pan-dulces for the day. The angriest voices quieted a bit as she entered. She set down the platter. "What's happening, Señores?" She surveyed them all, her mouth open in puzzlement.

Arciniega cleared his throat. "Dámaso Jiménez has escaped. And someone here must have used duplicate keys. Everyone denies that, of course."

Emilia's mouth became a round "O" and her eyes opened wide. "Escaped? That's impossible!" Her expression changed to one of satisfaction. "But if it's true, I must say, I'm not sorry. He did it for me, to defend my honor, after all.... But you'd better get after him if you intend to catch him. I hope you don't, though." She turned and disappeared into the kitchen, pausing to hear what commentary would follow her performance.

Erasmo spoke first. "That was Emilia, through and through. She never tries to hide her feelings."

There were grunts of agreement. Then Arciniega delegated to Flores the task of organizing the men who would track Dámaso down. Gaspar summoned all twelve men of the Béxar militia. They were to split up in teams of four to search in the directions of Saltillo, Monclova, and Goliad. They set out shortly before noon.

A day passed with no news. On the second day, at siesta time, a man came to the door of the Altamirano kitchen and knocked on the frame. María, almost done with the dishes after *comida*, answered.

"Ah! Señor Jiménez! It's Miguel, isn't it?"

"Yes, it's Miguel, María. I... ah... I've come to ask about my son Dámaso. Maybe a week ago, he told me he was going hunting. I haven't seen him since. I had business out at the ranch, so I left right after he did. He wasn't home when I got back this morning, and now I hear gossip that he's killed a man. What do you know about this, María?"

María glanced around to check if either Andrés or Carmen was nearby. The less they knew the better. "Why come to me?"

"Because of what my son said as he left the house that morning. I asked him why he was hunting when we had enough venison. He answered that it was not for us. He said 'It's for the girl I've always loved.' That would be Emilia, your daughter. Did he bring you a deer or a pair of rabbits or a turkey that day?"

"No, Miguel. If you haven't heard this already, you soon will. You may remember that a couple of months ago, my daughter was hurt pretty badly—bruises, loose teeth, bloody nose, sprained hip and knee. We told everyone she'd fallen off the corral fence at Military Plaza. The truth was this: a man dragged her off that corral fence, beat her, and raped her."

Jiménez' mouth and eyes were wide open. "*¡Dios mío!* Who was the monster who did that?"

"A squatter named Jedediah Crow—the same man who caused a disturbance at the fandango three years ago. After Dámaso learned about the rape, he went out to avenge her honor."

Miguel covered his face with his hands. "Oh, God of mercy! No! That means he's now a fugitive from the law. He's killed an Anglo, and those people will soon be our masters. They're flooding into Texas and will soon take over..."

María patted his hand. "Miguel, "It's not *that* bad, not yet. You're right, though. The *Ayuntamiento* decided to bind Dámaso over to the Supreme Court of Coahuila y Texas in Saltillo. They were afraid to anger the few Anglo settlers already here. Somehow, during the night before he was to be escorted to Saltillo, someone opened the jail cell and allowed him to escape. All the *regidores* deny doing such a thing, but they all suspect each other.... Anyway, Dámaso escaped and has not been found."

Miguel nodded with a thoughtful look on his face. "I know my son. He'll find a way out of this mess. We simply have to wait. Sooner or later, he will come back to us."

The following day, the members of the militia that had searched for Dámaso toward Goliad and Nacogdoches returned, reporting to the *Ayuntamiento* that they had found no trace of him. The third party, the one searching south toward Saltillo and Monclova, was still out. Ten days had passed when they came in, also empty-handed. Young Juan Seguín, Erasmo's son and their best tracker, had led them. He reported to the assembled council.

"*Señor* Arciniega, *Señores regidores*, Dámaso must have figured we'd think he was headed for Saltillo, but I knew better. Who but a fool would take the most obvious escape route? He took the least traveled road to Monclova and left the most recent trail of hoofprints. He had two horses, riding one, leading the other. He spent the first night at a spring not far off the road. Shot a duck and ate it that night—didn't bury the feathers and bones. We followed him until his trail joined the road from Saltillo. There had been heavy traffic on that road, so we couldn't track him any farther."

"So you think he's in Monclova?"

"Could be, but I doubt it. He's no city boy. There are several ranches west of the city—he might have gone to one of them."

"We'd better search each one of them till we find him, then."

Weeks passed, and as far as Emilia knew, there had been no further search for Dámaso. Political struggles with the opposing Coahuila faction in the state legislature in Saltillo had occupied the *regidores'* attention entirely. Emilia fretted and walked the floor, praying that

Dámaso had found a safe refuge, hoping in vain for word from him.

María consoled her, saying she'd had the same agony of waiting to know the fate of her lover, Juan Andrés Altamirano. Unlike Emilia, she'd been pregnant with his love child—Emilia herself—and *General* Arredondo's hostile occupation forces in Béxar had been executing more victims every day.

Emilia sat with her mother in the evenings, questioning her about those violent times while she, Emilia, had enjoyed the relative safety of her mother's womb. María described how the women of Béxar—newly widowed, most of them—had been forced to work as slaves, also sexually, for the conquering Royalist forces. María had been spared much of that because of her pregnancy. She became cook and cleaning woman for the troops that occupied her "master's"—and lover's—house, where she still remained.

María sat back, her eyes distant. "Those who were wealthy enough had fled to New Orleans before the Royalist Army entered Béxar. A few came back before New Spain declared its independence. Carmen was one. Those refugees set a pattern, I suspect. Any time we, here in Béxar, are threatened again, those who can will flee in the same direction, although some will use their ranches as a temporary refuge. That's why the Veramendis, the Navarros, the Ruíz family and the Seguíns, among others, have built such luxurious ranches miles out of town. They're more elegant and better equipped than their homes here in Béxar, all because of their ghastly experience with Arredondo."

María's lips formed a bitter smile. "Interesting, isn't it, how that massacre back then has determined the whole history of Texas from then on—including mine and yours, Emilia."

José Miguel Arciniega reported a public nuisance to his *alguacil*, Gaspar Flores. "Have you seen that starving brown and white hound that's been wandering around our city? I can count his ribs, even from a distance. His belly's about to get stuck to his spine. Anyone would think he's ready to fall dead any moment."

"No, hadn't noticed. Why? D'you think he's rabid or something?"

"No, abandoned. But we ought to get rid of him, unless he's the ghost of an already dead and dried up hound." Arciniega chuckled.

"So what makes him a public nuisance?"

"He bothers people. Underfoot everywhere. He circles Main Plaza, sniffs around the church garden wall and inspects the vegetable booths and the fondas. Now and then someone gives him scraps of meat or a bone. He accepts their offerings politely enough, swallows the meat in one gulp and delicately takes the bones and retreats to a quiet corner to gnaw off any trace of flesh, but he won't stay in any one place."

Flores scratched his jaw. "So you want me to shoot him or something?"

"Either that or find someone to adopt him."

That evening, as the *Ayuntamiento* closed the session, Gaspar Flores with several other *regidores* descended the steps, and the hound stood waiting at the bottom as if he knew he'd been the subject of a recent conversation. He gave a *woof,* and approached Flores, emitting whistling whines through his nose and wagging his tail. Gaspar recognized him at once. "My God, it's Ben!" He squatted and stroked the dog's head. "I've been worried about you. How did you survive?"

The hound didn't answer, but pressed his forehead against Gaspar's chest. The *alguacil* looked up at José Miguel Arciniega. "This is Jedediah Crow's dog. He's been guarding his master's grave for weeks. I wonder how long he's been in town."

Arciniega cocked his head and took a better look at the dog. "He's been around here for at least a week. Always looking for someone, it seems."

Gaspar's voice had the ring of certainty. "He's looking for Señora Crow. She and her little daughter Bonnie are staying with Marta and me. He must smell them on me." He stood and took a few steps. Ben followed close at his heels. Gaspar said, over his shoulder, "Well, Señores, I'm on my way home, and I'm anticipating a joyful reunion."

His fellow *regidores* laughed and scattered to their own homes, while Gaspar, with a spring in his step, walked down Potrero Street, pausing now and then to stoop and pat Ben and scratch behind his ears. He'd been feeling guilty about abandoning the dog—he knew the horses and mule would survive—but he hadn't had time to ride out to see about Ben. He'd lost his own dog, Ferino, to snakebite and hadn't replaced him. Maybe Ben could fill the vacancy.

As they neared the house, Ben's tail began to wag. As they rounded the side of the house, he began to whine and bark. He ran ahead and burst into the back garden, where Marta had just gathered eggs and was carrying them to the house in a basket. Ben bounded to her, stood on his hind legs and, placing his paws on her shoulders, licked her face. She tipped over backward, spilling the eggs and breaking a few.

She sat up, pushing the dog away and holding him at arm's length. "Good heavens! What's all this? Whose hound is this, anyway?"

Gaspar, already at her side, lifted her to her feet. "Marta! Are you hurt?"

"No, but I did sit down harder than usual."

"It's Señora Crow's dog, come in from guarding Jedediah's grave. You must have been holding Bonnie recently—he smelled her on me, too—and came home with me."

For the moment, Ben was occupied licking up the broken eggs until only clean shells were left. Meanwhile, Marta replaced the whole eggs in the bottom of the basket, the cracked ones on top. "Looks like we'll have Spanish tortilla for our *cena* tonight."

A very pregnant Kathleen Crow appeared at the back door, looking as though the baby would come at any moment. Ben immediately gave a yip and made a dash for her. "Ben!" She held out her arm, palm outward. "Halt! Sit!" The dog immediately obeyed, smiling in delight, his tongue dripping out the side of his mouth. Kathleen knelt in front of him and put her arms around his neck, kissing his forehead. "Oh, Ben, I've been so worried about you! You came and found us!" Tears of joy flowed down her cheeks. Ben placed a front paw on her shoulder and licked them off.

After a few moments, she started to rise and looked around for help. Gaspar immediately gave her a hand. Once on her feet, she asked, "Can we have Ben inside the house, please?" She accompanied her request with gestures.

Marta understood. "*Sí, si puedes dominarlo*, Yes, if you can control him."

Kathleen cocked her head to one side. "*Dominar*... that means 'control,' doesn't it?" She nodded and answered in Spanish. "*Sí, puedo*, Yes I can."

Chapter Twelve
1830–1832

Dámaso worried constantly about his inability to communicate with Emilia. In the beginning, he thought it best not to try, for fear of revealing his whereabouts. One man at the ranch, the cook, knew how to read and write. He kept the books on profits and losses, on numbers of head of cattle and other animals, and of supplies. Dámaso felt tempted to approach him to write a letter, but kept his distance, in case the Béxar militia came looking for him. Cocí was a gossip, always telling yarns and revealing details about one wrangler or another that they'd rather not have told—usually to general laughter over supper at the ranch or around the campfire.

A few weeks after Dámaso had settled in at the ranch, members of the Béxar militia did come looking. *Desayuno* had just finished, and he'd begun to saddle Oropel, preparing to ride out for a day's work, when three riders arrived. They must have camped out for many nights, since they looked dusty, unshaven and unwashed. He knew them: Francisco Salinas, Andrés Nava and Juan Seguín. They were among the best trackers in the Béxar militia. In a way, he was surprised they hadn't found him sooner.

They walked up to the cookhouse and were welcomed by Cocí, who pointed out how they could wash up before he fed them.

Dámaso waited until they were inside, then mounted Oropel and headed for the herd, where the rest of the wranglers were working that day. He could only pray that Cocí wouldn't immediately single him out.

At noon, as usual, the two-wheeled food cart appeared on the horizon, only this time, it had a three-rider escort. Cocí found a level spot, parked the cart, and hopped down to get everything ready to dole the main meal of the day to the hungry cowpokes.

Dámaso, unsurprised, observed from a distance. *I guess I'll go without food for a spell.* He turned Oropel and rode into the nearby hills. He knew a good place to wait until sundown, a pocket valley with a lone oak tree on one side. The grass had recently been grazed by the herd, but the new growth would be high enough for Oropel to feed, and there was shade for him. After hobbling the horse and unsaddling him, Dámaso gave him a friendly slap on the haunch and let him go.

He walked for a while, making a circuit of the lush little valley, keeping an eye out for cow piles, and daydreamed about Emilia. A plan for their life together at the family ranch on Calaveras Creek began to form itself. He would build a couple of extra rooms on the cabin, since they would surely have children, at least three. He could see himself teaching them how to ride, how to handle and tame a horse, how to herd cattle. Often, Emilia would be riding at his side. He paused, picturing her grace and dexterity. He conjured up her dimpled smile. He smiled too, but tears blurred his vision. Would he ever get home? Ever see her again?

By mid-afternoon, he spread his saddle blanket under the oak, using his saddle as a pillow, and took a siesta. It was sundown when his hunger woke him. He rose, got ready and rode back to the ranch. He could see no strange horses, so he approached the cookhouse. No visitors. He could safely go in for supper.

Chino spotted him first. "*Caramba*, Daniel, *dónde diablos*, where the devil have you been?"

Dámaso had a half-believable story ready. "I spotted a yearling calf up one of the draws out there, followed it. Couldn't catch him. Finally did when I was almost all the way to the Aguas Frias Ranch. Damned if it wasn't a stray from the Aguas Frias herd. Had their brand on him. Wasted the whole afternoon. I'm plenty hungry."

Cocí strolled over, plunked a steaming plate on the nearest table and gave him a push toward it. "There was three cowboys come out here looking for someone named Dámaso Jiménez. Seems he killed a man back at Béxar and gave them the slip before they could get him to trial over in Saltillo. You know the guy?"

At the mention of the name, Chino raised his head and gave sharp looks at Dámaso and then at Cocí. Perhaps he remembered "Daniel's" real name from meeting him in New Orleans.

Dámaso didn't change expression and kept his voice conversational. "Yeah. I know him. Pretty nice chap. I'm surprised he'd kill anybody. Did they describe him to you?"

"Said he was tall, dark haired, brown-eyed, slim, a *mestizo*."

"Sounds like it could be any one of us cow hands in here—except for Güero over there." He gestured toward a skinny, freckle-faced wrangler with red hair. "Sorry I missed the fun. It would've been good to talk to those fellows; I bet I know them, too." He turned and began shoveling beans and tortilla into his mouth.

Chino had gone back to eating, Cocí disappeared in the kitchen, and nothing more was said about the day's visitors.

A year passed, and Dámaso had more than proven his expertise as a wrangler as well as his knowledge and love of animals, especially his love of horses. He taught the cow pokes at the Fuente y Culebra Ranch how to capture and tame wild horses, *mesteños*, without brutalizing them. Even the roughneck hold-outs were convinced when they saw how the formerly wild horses now ate out of Dámaso's hands.

1831

A number of stray cattle had drifted far from the main herd, south and west of the ranch. They found water and good grazing in a rough tract of land, its low hills cut by steep, narrow and winding canyons. The western border of the hills lay about two miles from one of the well-traveled roads from Monclova to Saltillo with a branch to Monterey. A team of eight wranglers, including "Daniel," worked to round up the cattle and move them to join the main herd.

Once the strays were gathered, they would spend the next few days branding the yearlings to lessen the probability of theft. Another disagreeable task was castrating the bull calves—all but two or three chosen ones that would be allowed to mature into intact bulls. The only redeeming aspect of the task, at least in the opinion of the wranglers, was the evening feast on the testicles, *los cojones*, "prairie oysters."

Dámaso had ridden to the top of a ridge to overlook the steep little draws that crisscrossed the hills with a narrow valley beyond. The landscape around him was rugged but green, providing both ideal grazing and snug hiding places for the cattle. Below him, he could see two cows and a calf in the left-hand draw and a small knot of cattle in the more distant valley. There must be water there. He turned his horse's head to descend the steep slope into the draw, but as he turned, the glare of the afternoon sun caused him to raise a hand to shade his eyes.

A cloud of dust on the horizon interspersed by occasional brilliant flashes of reflected light drew his attention. It moved slowly but steadily, gradually drawing nearer. He waited. Details began to emerge. Colors: flags on staffs waved in the distance, individual horses ridden by men wearing clothing that twinkled with stabs of light that shone and then disappeared. Probably medals, epaulettes, brass buttons and such on fancy uniforms. Cannon on wagons drawn by teams of oxen lumbered behind the horses. A horde of men marched on foot in ragged clothing, alongside and behind the cannons. There must be a thousand of them. Bringing up the rear, a motley crowd of women, some driving goats, pigs or a milk cow, some riding donkeys, some with wagons drawn by skeletal mules. The Mexican army and its camp followers!

He'd heard horror tales of the army, how men from teenage to sixty were seized and summarily pressed into service. A cold shiver traveled down his spine. He turned his horse to get out of sight, but before he could ride off the hill, he caught a more intense flash of light. An officer was close enough to use a spy glass—trained on him. Before he could react, the man's arm rose, pointing in his direction. Two riders broke from the pack and ran straight toward him. He scanned the tract of land the wranglers had been combing for strays. There! In the right-hand draw! He dug heels into Oropel's sides, running along the ridge until he came within shouting distance. "Juanito! Get out of here! The army's after us! Run! Tell the others!"

He descended into the gray sagebrush at the bottom of another narrow, twisting canyon. Ahead, another pair of his friends. "Francisco! Manuel! The army! Run! Tell the others—tell Manu, Chino! Run!"

Dámaso rode off at a right angle in a side draw, hoping to lead his pursuers away from his fellow wranglers. A horse whinnied on the ridge above him and he looked up, hoping it was one of his friends. It looked like the officer who had spotted him with the spy glass. Dámaso on Oropel ran for his life, but the draw ended in a vertical stone wall. He wheeled and galloped back the way he'd come. The two riders waited at the opening of the draw and blocked him. He looked up. On the ridge, the officer had his rifle trained on him. Trapped!

They made short work of him. One dropped a noose around his upper body, pinning his arms and securing the knot. Another took his rifle from its scabbard. A third grabbed him, ready to pull him off Oropel, but the lieutenant, who had joined them, barked a command.

"Let him ride back to the troops. It'll save time. You can confiscate his horse later. Fine horse, that. Fit for an officer."

A duet replied. *"Sí, Capitán Gálvez."*

Dámaso twisted his neck until he could see the captain. "Why are you treating me like a criminal?"

Scornful laughter. "Because you *are* one. You just tried to evade service in your nation's army, didn't you? That's crime enough." He turned to the mounted men. "Move! Get him back, pronto!"

Filthy Gachupín! To his horror, he'd said those words aloud, under his breath, instead of merely thinking them.

Capitán Gálvez reacted. *"Gachupín*, eh? I'll teach you what a *gachupín* can do to a *mestizo*!" He gouged his horse's flanks with cruel spurs. The animal launched itself into a dead run, and the four riders galloped back to the army. Once there, the captain gave a brutal yank on the reins, and his horse squealed and reared in protest. "Get him off that horse and strip him!"

His captors obeyed immediately, yanking him off by the rope around his body and with rough hands. They grabbed his sombrero, released the rope, stripped off his vest, his chaps and his boots, leaving him his socks, shirt, and homespun trousers tied at the waist with a drawstring.

Gálvez called, *"¡Teniente Moreno! ¡Aquí tienes tu nuevo caballo!* Here's your new horse."

A short, square-built officer dismounted from a raw-boned nag. *"Mil gracias, Señor Capitán."* He tossed the nag's reins to a sergeant and strode to Oropel. After looking him over, feeling his legs and checking his hooves, he sprang into the saddle, digging his spurs into the horse's side. Oropel, who had never been harshly used, gave a squeal and lunged forward. Lieutenant Moreno cut him over the haunches with his whip and ran full speed in a tight circle, yanking him to a skidding stop next to the captain.

"Fine horse, this. Thanks again, mi *Capitán*. I'll see that it gets used to my style of riding, pronto."

Gálvez chuckled. "I'm sure you will, *Teniente*."

Oropel, breathing hard, eyes wide in fear, looked to his master, who stood denuded of his outer clothing, hands now tied behind his back. Dámaso shook his head and lifted his shoulders in apology. He hoped his faithful mount would understand his helplessness. *God protect you, Oropel. You've done nothing to deserve this.*

The captain turned to one of the men guarding Dámaso. "Now you, Mateo, show this new *soldado raso*, this buck private, where his place will be."

"*Sí, Señor Capitán.*" Mateo produced a knife and pressed the blade against Dámaso's neck. "*Por aquí.* This way."

Dámaso, his neck angled at full stretch, stumbled in the direction Mateo pushed him. The army had not paused in its march for the little drama of recruiting a new soldier. Half of the ragged, mostly barefoot troops had already passed by, when Mateo halted.

"Here's your place, among the recent recruits to our glorious army. Serve us well, kill when you're ordered to, or you'll be shot." Mateo cut the rope that bound him and shoved him into one of the ranks of miserable-looking men, but not before allowing his knife to graze the skin of Dámaso's neck. The sting meant he'd been lightly cut, as did the blood that ran down and brightened his shirt collar.

He fell in step with the man next to him. "Do they treat all new recruits this way?"

His fellow solder gave him only a quick glance. "Mostly. Unless you volunteer. We are the ones who tried to get away."

Dámaso's socks were already working their way off his feet. He hopped on one leg and pulled one sock up, then the other. "Where are we headed?"

"Monclova. I think we're ordered to make a show of force there. Someone high up is worried about a movement to separate Coahuila and Texas—something like that. We're to frighten the ringleaders."

Dámaso kept pace with the man next to him, although he soon began limping, and every time he stepped on a sharp stone, his feet hurt him more. "You appear to know more about politics than I'd expect from a common soldier. How's that?"

"Because I, like you perhaps, am a Federalist. I was a lawyer in Zacatecas. I was 'persuaded' to serve in the army just as you were. I'm Pablo Ochoa. Pleased to meet you even in these extremely unpleasant circumstances." The soldier glanced at him, then back at the road in time to avoid a fallen branch of mesquite.

Dámaso jumped, barely missing it. He nodded, thrusting out his hand. "I'm Daniel Martínez from Béxar in Texas. Pleased to meet you, too." He had only partially grasped the political implications of the man's statement. They ceased talking and shambled on as miles slowly passed. Dámaso's attention was increasingly drawn to his feet. By now, his socks were in tatters and he began to leave bloody footprints. He gritted his teeth against the pain and kept on walking.

They made camp just outside the city. The troops lined up to pass by the cook wagons to receive a foul-smelling, lukewarm slop made of boiled oats or barley.

"Damn!" a solder ahead of him cursed, "This is what we had last night, only by now it's spoiled."

The lawyer replied. "Yes, but eat it all the same. It's all the food we'll get. If we can keep it down, we might get a little good from it." He turned to Dámaso. "Sit over there on that boulder. I'll get some help for those feet. If we stay here near Monclova for a few days, you'll have a chance to get better."

Dámaso collapsed on the boulder, brushed bloody mud off the soles of his feet and tried to assess the damage. Hard to tell in the coming night, with only a small, nearby fire to see by. Exhausted, he slumped into a stupor, his pain receding into the distance.

A gentle hand on his shoulder roused him. A dark-skinned woman, unwashed for days from the smell of her, bent over him.

"What...? Who...?"

"Shush. I'm Rosa, a camp follower. I know a lot about curing hurt feet. Lots of practice." She knelt and took hold of one ankle then the other, examining his lacerated and bruised soles. "I'll get some water from a cook wagon and wash them first and then I'll doctor them. Be still and wait here."

She rose and hurried away in a rustle of skirts. He lapsed again into oblivion. Much later, she returned with a pail of water and a rag. She tore it in thirds and with the first she washed away the dirt, pulled out thorns and embedded pebbles. With the second, she dipped into the pan, now with much less water and white powder in the bottom, which quickly dissolved. The liquid stung, but not for long.

He was fascinated. "What's that?"

"It's nothing but salt water. It will keep the wounds from festering." From around her waist, she unwound a length of white cloth and moistened it in liquid from a bottle she had carried in the cloth, sling-like. When she removed the cork, he recognized the smell of vinegar. "I'll dip your feet in vinegar and wrap them in these cloths. That will keep anything harmful from getting to your skin during the night." She wrapped one foot, tearing the cloth to make a strip and tying a firm knot, then repeated the process with the other foot. "Your cuts will seep through these bandages by tomorrow night. Then I'll need to tend you again. Walk as little as possible until morning." She picked up the pan and vinegar bottle and stood. "I'll get more vinegar in Monclova. We have to have a good supply on hand. There's always someone with cuts and even wounds to tend."

"My feet feel so much better! How can I repay you?"

She rose to her feet with a groan and patted Dámaso on the shoulder. "Don't thank me until you're all healed. I'll try to find you a pair of huaraches in the city." She disappeared into the darkness.

Dámaso looked for his fellow soldier to thank him for bringing help, but not finding him, he crept close to a pair of cook wagon mules to share their warmth, curled up in the dust just inside one of the wagon wheels, and slept.

He awoke to the sound of a bugle. He crawled out from under the wagon, brushed himself off and stood, stiff and footsore, looking around him, confused in the dim light of dawn. On one side, the city spread below him, mostly low adobe buildings graduating to taller, official-looking stone structures, with the cathedral and its single tower marking its center. On the other side, rugged mountains, the eastern extension of the Sierra Madre Oriental. Fellow soldiers were already leading teams of mules and oxen to the river to water them for the day ahead. He was thirsty, too, but had no idea if he could get to the river without being shot.

He itched all over and began scratching. Of course! He'd picked up fleas and probably lice as he slept in the dust last night. Damn! They'd be his constant companions from now on.

A familiar voice behind him made him jump. "Hola Daniel! I see Rosa did her magic on your feet. Without her, you'd not be standing today. Let's go get a drink; you must be as parched as I am."

"Hola, Pablo. You startled me. D'you mean we're free to move around that much?"

"Yes, but," he pointed, "only inside this area surrounded by sentry patrols. They'll shoot anyone crossing their line."

"So, at least we're free to get a drink and wash up. I was wishing I were a horse or a mule; *they're* getting plenty of water! Do we get any food?"

"Yes, we usually get a couple of tortillas and beans. Best meal of the day. Soon after that, we'll line up in rows to be counted. Then we'll likely parade through the city to frighten the magistrates into abandoning the idea of federalism."

This must have to do with the idea that Texas separate itself from Coahuila, something like that. We've always got ourselves in trouble over the idea of independence of one sort or another. Dámaso tightened his parched lips and hobbled alongside Pablo to the river. They chose a spot upstream from the animals and drank as much as they could hold of the river water. As he washed, Dámaso wondered if he'd ever again have a chance to shave. Probably not for weeks. A sudden thought made him straighten abruptly.

"Pablo! My girl back home needs to know where I am. I never learned to read and write—except for my name—but it's been months now that she hasn't heard. I pray to God she hasn't married someone else."

"Was she the fickle type?"

"No, steady as a rock."

"Well, in that case, she's probably sick with worry but still holding onto hope."

"Can you put what I want to say on paper?"

"No problem. The problem is getting it out of the encampment and on its way. Where did you say you're from?"

"Béxar, in Texas."

"You'd better keep that quiet. The supreme commander of the army, behind the scenes, mind you, considers Béxar a major trouble spot. One of the primary reasons we're here is that the Tejano representatives from Béxar are moving here to Monclova, trying to make this the capital of Coahuila y Texas. The powers that be don't like that move, so we're here to intimidate them."

Just as I thought. Dámaso, silent, sat contemplating that bit of news. He could picture the faces of the very men most likely leading the movement: Erasmo Seguín, Juan Martín Veramendi, and José Antonio Navarro. Their images transfixed him with a sharp pang of longing.

He burst out, "If any of the Béxar representatives are here, maybe you could get my letter into their hands. I know they would deliver it. Especially if you could give it to José Antonio Navarro. He knows my girl well."

Pablo watched the river currents for several minutes. "I'll give this a try, Daniel. The hard part will be getting it into the right hands. We'll write it tonight by candle or firelight."

The clanging of a bell called them to the cook wagon where Dámaso had been served "supper" the night before, and where he had slept. He devoured his tortilla and beans and wished for more, but more was not forthcoming. Barely had he licked his fingers when the bugle sounded. Dámaso limped into the line and stood at attention beside Pablo.

Teniente Moreno inspected the ranks. When he came to Dámaso, he stared at his feet and poked him with the end of his crop. "You. Get yourself to the cook wagons and find out where you can be of service. You'd make a sorry impression if you were to march through the city. Now, fall out!"

Dámaso spent the day performing any task that didn't entail much walking. The troops returned from the day's parading through Monclova just past five o'clock by the cathedral bell. Pablo found him making tortillas—the cook, Manolo, had taught him how. They would be used to wrap shredded meat from a cow donated to his wagon by one of the camp followers. The cow had died the day before of some unknown illness, so Manolo saw that the meat was well cooked. It would be tough—even though the cook and he had spent the afternoon shredding the well boiled meat—but it would be a welcome change from beans.

Pablo appeared and eyed the interior of the cook wagon. "*¡Dios mío!* It smells divine! Well, Daniel, did you make yourself useful today?"

"Hope so. My feet are plenty sore, so I hope the cook will keep me on for a few days. I've done my best to learn what he wants and follow his orders. Also to figure out what's needed even if he doesn't give orders."

"You'll be helping him serve, then. We'll get together after that, so stay close to this wagon." Pablo turned and strode away.

Later, by firelight, after Rosa had doctored and rebound Dámaso's feet, Pablo produced a piece of paper and a pencil. They made sure no one was near, and then Dámaso began. "First of all, Pablo, you need to know I was running from the law, so the legislators from Béxar might not want to accept my message. I was to be turned over to the court in Saltillo, but escaped and worked on a ranch near where I was dragooned yesterday."

"So I'm associating with a criminal? I guess you *do* need a lawyer!"

Dámaso marveled at Pablo's light tone. Perhaps he'd been a criminal lawyer. Pablo soon interrupted his thoughts. "Well, let's get on with this letter."

During the day, as he did menial tasks for Manolo, Dámaso had worked out what he would say. He began at once:

> Dearest Emilia, I found a kind friend who can read and write. I spent months on a ranch where no one but the cook could write, and I didn't trust him. Yesterday, I was forcibly conscripted into the army. God knows when I'll get free to come to you. I think of you every day, loving you. Please wait for me, my treasure. D.

Rosa, who enjoyed unhindered and unsupervised access to the city, bought supplies along with a bottle of vinegar and then consulted a clerk in the shop nearest the courthouse—a florist—about whom to contact to get information on the legislators meeting in the building across the street.

The florist was happy to tell her. "Ricardo, the janitor in 'his courthouse', as he considers it, knows just about everything that goes on over there. He prides himself on his vast knowledge of court and legislative procedure, but I think he's mostly just a busybody."

Rosa nodded and smiled. "Thank you! A busybody will probably be willing to tell me what I need to know."

She entered the building and, after asking a guard stationed at the foot of the staircase leading to the court and conference rooms, located the janitor in the basement.

Startled to see a strange and somewhat disreputable woman in his domain, he challenged her. "Who are you and what do you want? Not a handout, I hope."

"No. My name is Rosa and I follow the army that has been parading through these streets. I bear an urgent message from one of our heroic soldiers to a legislator from Béxar in Texas."

"I hope this is not a political matter."

"No, it's a sentimental matter. A love letter. Do you know any of the legislators from Béxar?"

"There's one you can't miss. He's taller than most others, walks with a cane and limps badly. His name, I've been told, is José Antonio Navarro. Their session usually ends around five-thirty or six. I'll have to ask you to wait outside the courthouse, though." He finished his words with his nose in the air.

"Thank you kindly, Señor. I'll wait at the head of the entrance stairs."

The janitor, visibly pleased at her use of Señor, nodded and waved her away.

Late that afternoon, a group of men in formal dress exited the main door. Among the last to emerge was the tall man with a limp. He slowly descended the steps and turned to follow a street opposite, away from her, walking with surprising speed. She hurried to follow, not wanting him to slip out of sight. He rounded a corner, and when she got there, he was nowhere to be seen. She scanned the doorways as she hurried down the street. One had a barred gate instead of a doorway. Señor Navarro was at the end of the entrance hall, about to enter a large interior garden.

She dared to raise her voice. "Señor Navarro! I have news!"

He hesitated but did not turn. She shouted louder. "*Señor*! This matter is urgent!" Her voice trembled in her anxiety, and that more than her words seemed to stop him. He turned, shaded his eyes, and she knew he could see only a silhouette at the opening of the corridor. He began to come back. Now, he took his time, limping down the long hall to the gate.

"What is this urgent matter?"

"It's a message, Señor, from one of your Béxareños to another. You know them both, I'm told. But one of them is in danger right now." She shoved the folded paper between the bars.

He unfolded it and read. He spoke, mainly to himself. "This should have been sealed, but I'm glad it wasn't. Now the mystery of Dámaso's disappearance is solved. Emilia should be overjoyed. But the army... that may take months to undo." He looked up from the note. "Thank you.... What's your name?"

"Rosa. I follow the army and do a bit of nursing."

He slanted his head to one side, looking her over with a faint smile. "Thank you again, Rosa, for delivering this message. You found the right man. I'll be sure to get it to the proper person." He fished in his pocket and gave her two *reales*—a fortune in her eyes.

"Oh, thank you Señor!" She turned the coins over in her fingers as if she couldn't believe her good fortune. "That little soldier must be someone very important."

Navarro smiled. "In many eyes, he is indeed."

Chapter Thirteen
1832–1835

After a cool, humid and overcast day, late afternoon shadows gathered over Béxar. Emilia, home from the cabildo for an hour, heard a loud knock on the frame of the jacal door.

"Emilia! María! I have news!"

Emilia knew the voice as well as her own: José Antonio Navarro! She beat her mother to the door by a yard. "Yes, Tío, what news? It must be important for you to come to us."

"I finally got a free moment to bring it. Here, Emilia, read it for yourself." He handed the folded slip of paper to her.

She took the paper, her heart beating wildly, and hurried to the lamp on the central table. "Come in, Tío. We have no secrets from you."

María said, "Please, sit at the table where there's more light."

He sat, while Emilia stooped closer to the lamp, read the terse note, then kissed it and pressed it to her bosom. Without a word, she handed it to her mother. María also leaned toward the light and read, then passed the note back. Her tone, dry and practical, brought Emilia down from a cloud of romantic fantasy.

"If you continue to wait for this boy, *m'hija*, you'll be a spinster for another few months—maybe years. Ever since *Señor* Bowie married Ursula Veramendi last year, everyone seems to be thinking of unorthodox weddings, and young hopefuls have been buzzing around you. It seems you're not considered *déclassée* once you've made yourself indispensable at the *Ayuntamiento*."

Antonio raised his head. "Most of them think marrying Emilia would be the quickest way to get a political foothold in Béxar. Come to think of it, they're probably right."

Emilia shook her head. "I don't believe that, and anyway, they're out of luck, Tío. I love Dámaso. Always have. Of course I'll wait for him!"

Navarro's eyes narrowed. "It just occurs to me, Emilia, that *you* might be the culprit who freed Dámaso that night. Hmmm. You'd just have to steal the keys from Gaspar Flores's house—or else you had a set of duplicates all along. I happen to know you visited Marta Flores that night."

Emilia hesitated, tempted to 'reveal all' to Antonio, but decided against it. "Ye-e-s, I do know the culprit, Tío, but my lips are sealed as to who that is and how it was done."

June 1834

Emilia walked home slowly after a long day with the *regidores*. Instead of well-earned satisfaction after providing them with a merienda of tasty pastries that María had baked last night, she felt a hollow in her stomach. Goliad and lately, Gonzales, had been stricken by a severe outbreak of cholera.

She rounded the Altamirano house and entered the kitchen, expecting to see the lamp lit and María starting dinner. But the kitchen was dark. She hurried across to the *jacal*, pulling open the cowhide flap. Emptiness and darkness greeted her. Where was her mother?

Manuela Salinas, her childhood playmate, hurried up just as Emilia re-entered the *jacal*. "Emilia, The messenger, the man who brought the news from Goliad, is very ill. Your mamá is caring for him at our house. She's been there all afternoon."

A cold quiver shot through Emilia's body and she hugged herself. "Ill? In what way?"

"He's throwing up and—pardon me for saying, Emilia—but he's pooping every few minutes, groaning, and stinking something awful."

Emilia could barely move her lips. "That's how they describe cholera. Where is this messenger by now?"

"Still at my house, as far as I know."

"I'll be over in just a minute. I must tell the family here." Emilia gestured toward the house, "They'll be expecting supper. You'd better tell everyone you meet, all your friends and their parents, their children, their servants—everybody!"

"You're right. I'll start now." Manuela hurried away.

Emilia entered the house. Andrés and Carmen were seated at the dining table, the lamplight revealing impatient faces.

"Why isn't supper ready? Where is your mother?" Carmen's tone was sharp.

"She was called to tend a sick person sometime this afternoon."

Andrés looked perturbed, not cross. "A sick person? Who? It must be serious."

Emilia twisted her hands together. "Very serious. It's the messenger from Goliad. I'm sure you heard about him coming in—he was warning us that cholera is devastating Goliad. I just got here from the *Ayuntamiento* and one of the Salinas girls met me and told me."

"His symptoms?" Andrés stood.

"Vomiting and evacuating his bowels every few minutes."

Juan shoved his chair back and strode toward the door. "I must inform all the *regidores* so they can warn the citizens. Padre Refugio should ring the church bells so our *alcalde* can make the announcement. I'm afraid cholera has come to Béxar, and instead of warning us against it, this man has brought it to us."

Emilia followed him out but turned away to run toward Dolorosa Street and the Salinas house. Despite the cool air, she arrived panting and wet with perspiration. By now, it was full dark, and so was the house, its curtains drawn across the windows. She knocked. No answer. As she raised her fist to knock again, the door opened. Señora Salinas stood silhouetted against the lamplight.

"Ah, Emilia!"

"Is my mother here?"

"No, she left some time ago. The poor man died, and she left after washing him and wrapping him in a sheet, and then cleaning the room. She was a great help. Padre Refugio is here now."

"Thank you, Señora." Emilia turned and ran back toward the Altamirano house. She almost collided with a huddled, dark figure, a woman, hurrying along, muttering to herself. Emilia gasped when she recognized her mother. "Mamá!" She reached out and found her mother's clothing sopping wet.

María's voice came, hoarse and slow. "Don't touch me, *m'hija*. Only God knows if I'm contagious."

"I went to the Salinas house. You weren't there. I was frightened, Mamá... for *you*!"

"I prepared that poor man—Rubén was his name—for burial, then left the house. I felt filthy, crawling with the disease. I hurried to the river and waded in, clothes and all. I scrubbed—I took a piece of lye soap from the Salinas's—kept soaping for nearly half an hour, and let the fresh river water wash over me. The water was cold, and I felt numb. I thought maybe I'd faint and drown, so I crawled out and started home."

"Let's get you there so you can warm up. It's not far, now."

María's teeth chattered in answer.

Emilia's voice shook with fear. "Oh, Mamá, is it cholera?

"Yes, Preciosa, I've seen it in Saltillo."

Once in the *jacal*, Emilia tried to help her exhausted mother strip off the soaked shift, petticoat and underwear, but María would not let her touch the clothes. She accepted the wool blanket that Emilia wrapped around her, then lay down with her daughter's help, and snuggled into still more blankets. Emilia chafed her mother's hands, cold despite the warm June weather.

María pulled her hands free for a moment and pointed to the heap of wet clothes on the floor. "*M'hija*, before you do anything else, get a stick and carry those things outside without touching them. Burn them. They were splattered with vomit and feces, and I'm sure you could still catch cholera by handling them. Let them dry a little, then burn them."

"So why did they call you, of all people in Béxar, to nurse the messenger with cholera?"

"I'm not sure, but I think it's because they know I'm an Indian, and all of us Indians are supposed to know things about medicine that the whites don't know."

"But you were brought up as a Spanish lady!"

"I told them that, but they still urged me to come. No one else would help them—so I went. There was nothing I could do for poor Rubén except urge him to drink water and watch him die."

"I suppose all cholera epidemics must start with one person. I pray that he not be the one."

"I've been told the time from exposure to coming down with the disease varies from a few hours to four or five days. Rubén came down with it after four days, most of that time on the road from Goliad. I've been thoroughly exposed, so I suppose I'll be next. You must keep your distance."

"Oh, Mamá! Don't even think such thoughts! I couldn't live without you!"

The church bells began to ring the alarm pattern. María laid her hand on Emilia's arm, but jerked it away as if fearing her touch would spread cholera to her daughter. "Go see what the *regidores* will recommend."

Emilia got to her feet. "Yes, we must know. I'll be back soon, very soon." She darted out.

A crowd had already gathered in Main Plaza, with more coming by the second. Manuela and Andrés had been efficient in spreading the news.

The latest *alcalde*, Juan Seguín, stood on the *cabildo* steps and made a short announcement. "Today, a messenger came from Goliad to deliver a message to the *Ayuntamiento*, warning us that his town has had an outbreak of cholera. Not long afterwards, he came down with it himself, and..."

Exclamations and cries of fear from the crowd drowned him out. He held up his hands, and the people quieted.

Seguín continued, "...and the unfortunate man died only an hour or two ago. We must take countermeasures. For now, we must stay in our homes and avoid places where many people congregate— like now. There will be no regular work until we know whether anyone else has come down with the disease. Padre Refugio will ring the bells when further announcements are to be made."

A voice rang out near the front of the crowd. "Who nursed this messenger? Where did he die?"

"He was nursed by María, Juan Andrés Altamirano's servant. Manuel Yturri Salinas took him home to give him a meal after he delivered his message. He died there."

A buzz of consternation ran through the crowd, then Seguín continued. "That's all we know at present. If any of you falls ill, the *Ayuntamiento* has commandeered the Veramendi Palace to serve as a clinic. Go there if you need help and otherwise go home and keep to yourselves."

The next morning, both mother and daughter slept until broad daylight. When Emilia finally rose and hurried to prepare *desayuno* for Carmen and Andrés, they didn't complain about the late service. No one came to see the women until noon, when Marta Flores knocked on the *jacal* door.

"*¡Hola, María, Emilia! ¿Estáis allí?* Are you there?"

"Yes, we're here. What is it?"

"Two more people have taken ill. Señor Salinas, who welcomed the messenger into his home and a young woman about your age, Jacinta Jiménez, who was the first person the messenger met when he arrived in Béxar."

Emilia' hands went to her mouth. "*¡O Dios mío!* Jacinta was also my playmate when I was little. I must go help her."

Marta, María and Emilia entered the Veramendi house to find that the Salinas' housemaid and one of her children had been added to the list of sufferers. Before she took over the task of nursing from Señora Salinas, María warned her daughter: "Whatever you do, don't touch your face. Keep your face averted when you work with anything that can splash you. If it gets inside your body through the eyes, nose and mouth, you'll surely get sick. It's only logical."

Emilia wondered how her mother knew this, but accepted the sensible advice. She set to work at once nursing Jacinta, washing her, carrying out her slops and dumping them in the Veramendi outhouse. She returned and washed her hands with lye soap before trying to get Jacinta to drink water.

"You need to drink water—lots of it, Jacinta! You're losing all the fluids in your body. Please drink this!"

Her friend took the glass with shaking hands, sipped twice, then set it aside. "I'll just throw it up anyway, Emilia." And, abruptly, she vomited into the bucket Emilia held for her—only now the liquid was black.

An hour after Emilia and her mother had arrived, Jacinta went limp. Emilia began to tremble. "Mamá! Is there nothing more we can do for her?" Her choked voice sounded strange to her own ears.

María came close to Jacinta's bed and stared at the pale form, then she beckoned to Padre Refugio, hovering in the background. "No, Preciosa. Only Extreme Unction. She'll be leaving us soon. Pray for her immortal soul." She made a move as if to embrace her daughter, but instead glanced at Emilia's face, beaded with perspiration. She pointed to a pile of clean rags on a shelf. "Wipe your face with one of those and see that it touches nothing else. Remember, don't let your bare hands touch your face!"

An hour later, Jacinta's breathing stopped. Emilia stared at her friend, eyes open but sunken and expressionless, black liquid still pooled in the open mouth. *This body is not Jacinta. Whatever made it my lively, loving friend is gone, like a puff of smoke.*

For a time, she could not cry. And then, while she bathed her friend's body, her tears began to drop into the pan of soapy liquid.

A practical but useless thought came to her: *If I only had some kind of gloves. Mamá and I would last longer if we didn't have to use bare hands.*

She and María wrapped Jacinta in a clean sheet. Two servants of the Salinas household laid the body in the entrance chamber next to the messenger, waiting for Padre Refugio's decision about how and where to bury them.

After nursing all day and mostly in vain, the two women repeated what María had done the previous night: they went to the river that ran close behind the house and waded in. They both did a thorough job of washing themselves, clothes, bodies and faces, with bars of lye soap. They returned home, exhausted, teeth chattering in the cool night wind.

They felt warmer upon entering the *jacal* where there was no breeze. Emilia spoke for the first time since they had left the river. "There's no sense in burning all our clothes, Mamá. We'll be going back tomorrow, so we'd better let them dry and wear them again, day after day, until we both drop dead."

They spread their clothes on bushes outside, and the next morning donned them, damp as they still were.

Three more days passed in a blur. On the fourth day, Emilia tried repeatedly and in vain to convince Jacinta's father—still sick but still alive—to drink water.

"My beautiful daughter is dead. She was my treasure. Why should I continue to live?" He pushed her hand away.

A warm hand on Emilia's shoulder gave her a start, and a male voice spoke next to her ear. "I brought a supply of straws to help with that. Most patients are too weak to hold a glass and drink normally."

She felt a surge of pleasure. A familiar voice! She turned to see a tall Anglo, dressed in black, his hand extended toward hers, offering four or five straight lengths of golden hay stems. They were hollow, approximately eight inches long.

Emilia stared at the newcomer. *His name... something very Anglo... I must speak to him.* "I remember you! You're... you're..."

"Charles McCray. It's now Dr. Charles McCray. I heard cholera was moving up-country from deeper in Mexico, that it had struck Goliad and Gonzales... and I feared it might have come to Béxar. I see I was right."

She remembered him as not much taller than she, with a shock of blond hair that shone like golden threads in the sunlight, and clear blue eyes. Now, he was at least a head taller. His hair and eyes were the same, although his expression was more serious, more mature.

"I'm so glad to see you Dr. McCray. We've been in desperate need of expert help to cope with these poor patients."

He nodded. "I fear no one is an expert when it comes to cholera. It's still Charles, not Dr. McCray, to you, Emilia. You see, I do remember your name. I've thought a lot about you over the years since we met on that bridge."

Back then, she'd given him two large, fresh-dug potatoes to go with the fish he'd caught. "Did you and your father enjoy your dinner at the campfire that night?"

Charles' smile broadened and his eyes lost their sharp focus, as if he were remembering that long-ago, happy time. "The fish... the potatoes were delicious. But here, try one of these drinking straws and see if your patient will drink that water you're holding."

Señor Jiménez drank the whole glass and another as well.

Charles handed her another straw. "Replace that one, Emilia. It's beginning to wilt. And give him as much water as he'll drink. It may save him." He turned to help María nurse another patient.

At the end of the day, he showed Emilia and her mother how to use hot water and that same lye soap to clean themselves adequately instead of bathing in the cold river water. "I'll stay here and watch over these patients until you return. Now go and get some rest."

Back in the *jacal*, Emilia fell immediately into a deep sleep, woke once in the dead of night and heard Maria tossing and turning. She woke again when it was barely light and saw her mother fully dressed, moving toward the door.

"Mamá! Where are you going? It's so early!"

"I couldn't sleep. I'll be at the Veramendi Palace, *m'hija*. You go back to sleep. You need it."

Emilia's eyes closed, still exhausted despite her sense that duty called her to go with her mother. She rose at the usual time, built the fire in the kitchen stove, and while it was warming, made tortillas. She cracked eggs onto the parrilla, added salt, chopped a couple of slices of onion and chile peppers, scrambled the mixture, scooped the food onto plates and made hot chocolate. She then carried the loaded tray into the dining room.

"*Buenos días, Señora Carmen, Señor Juan Andrés, ¿cómo amanecieron?* How are you this morning?"

Andrés looked haggard and allowed Carmen to speak first. "I couldn't sleep last night—neither of us slept. We're going to leave Béxar and go to friends in Victoria. We can't stay here; we're too frightened we'll catch this disease. If you catch it, you die, I know."

Emilia answered obliquely. "We're doing our best to save as many as we can. Dr. Charles McCray from *Señor* Austin's colony arrived yesterday to help."

"Well, *is* he helping?" Andrés looked skeptical.

"Señor Jiménez was still alive when mother and I left last night. Dr. McCray thinks he might get well."

Emilia waited impatiently in the adjoining room until the couple had finished their meal, then collected the dirty dishes, stacked them unwashed in the kitchen and hurried to the Veramendi Palace. She felt a creeping anxiety. Something was not right. She burst through the door of the clinic and looked around for María. She was not among the nurses bending over patients in various stages of the disease. Then she saw her. A haggard white face with hectic red spots on her cheeks. Charles McCray set a bucket on the floor next to the bed.

"¡Mamá! ¡Mamá!" The cry tore itself from her throat as she ran to María's side. She reached out to embrace and kiss her mother, but Charles threw his arms around her and forced her back. She broke into desperate sobs.

"No, Emilia, you mustn't touch her. I'm so sorry!"

María spoke in a hoarse voice. "*M'hija*, Preciosa, I knew I'd caught it that first day... all that time splattered with feces and vomit... before I could take that cold bath in the river. Too little, too late."

"But Charles will make you well! Please, Mamá, do everything he says."

María's mouth widened in a brief smile. "Padre Refugio gave me Extreme Unction. I'm ready."

Charles handed Emilia a glass of water and a straw. Like Jacinta, María drank only a little, then pushed it away. "I need the bucket."

Charles barely lifted it in time, and she threw up black liquid. Within an hour, she lapsed into unconsciousness. By now, Emilia knew the various stages of the disease. Some people lasted for days, like Señor Jimenez. They might recover. But most died within a few hours, like Jacinta. Like her mother.

She stood, stiff and unmoving, watching her mother's chest rise and fall, rise... and fall.... Then no more movement. Like Jacinta, María underwent an indefinable change. The spirit was no longer there; she had become a thing. Emilia couldn't cry; the loss was too enormous. She felt Charles' hand on her shoulder, his voice soft in her ear.

"I'm so sorry, Emilia. We did all we could. Nothing more I could do."

She spoke, not answering, but revealing the depth of her grief. "I am nothing without her, Charles. She was my guide. Wisdom. Strength. Protection. She taught me how to be human."

Charles signaled Padre Refugio, who came immediately to the bedside. Wordless, he placed the stole he held in his hands over his shoulders and began the ritual for the dead. He was pale, hollow-eyed, his shoulders bowed, not in reverence but in exhaustion. He'd been repeating this ritual all day, and would soon lead the graveside service over a mass grave.

Emilia watched him, almost vacantly. *Strange. I no longer feel resentment for his having bungled my confession and broken his vow when he spoke to Dámaso. He's only human like the rest of us, makes mistakes. Has limited vision and understanding.* She forgave him, using the ritual words he was muttering over María's dead body. "*Te absolvo in nomine Patris et Filii et Spiritus Sancti. I absolve you in the name of the Father and of the Son and of the Holy Ghost.*"

That night, Emilia, alone in the silent *jacal,* wrung her hands and broke into painful, deep sobs that wrenched her entire body until she nearly suffocated. At last, drained and exhausted, she fell on the bed and slept.

Emilia rose the morning after María's death, prepared *desayuno* and carried the tray into the dining room. She braced herself,

trying to think of a way to tell the dreadful news to the Altamiranos. As she entered, Andrés sat staring at his plate with a worried
frown, but Carmen examined her face. "*¡Dios mío Emilia! ¿Qué te
pasa?* Good God, Emilia! What's wrong?"

Emilia felt a tiny surge of gratitude. Carmen had relieved her of
having to invent a way to tell them.

"Mamá died yesterday. She's gone."

There was nothing more to say. She gently set down the tray and
fled the room.

Voices murmured behind her and a chair scraped. She hurried
through the kitchen and was seated at her own table when Andrés
pushed aside the door-flap and came in.

"May I sit with you?"

"Of course, Señor Andrés."

"Emilia, I am your father. You surely know that."

"Yes. The priest, Zambrano, told me when I was seven."

"And you kept my secret all these years."

"Yes. For Carmen's sake."

"Yes, and Carmen just ordered me, 'Go, console your daughter.
I've known for years.' I've been a fool, a fool!" He pounded the
little table with his fist. "I... I've forfeited years... the chance to love
my only child. Instead, I called her 'slave.'" His voice broke. "And
I loved your mother, too. Just didn't know how to handle it all....
And now that it's too late, too late, María's gone and I feel it like
losing a vital part of me, an arm, a leg." He reached toward Emilia's
hand, then drew back. "Forgive me! I've sinned against you both."

She nodded and took his hand. "I forgave you years ago, but
Antonio took your place. He loved me as a daughter and I loved
him back, my dear 'Tío Antonio.'"

"And now, what can we do, the few who're left?" Andrés sounded like a lost child.

"Be kinder to each other from now on, papá." She paused.
"'Papá.' That feels strange in my mouth. The secret of my birth is

ours, now, not just yours. But for everybody else, we'll go on as we've done all my life. I wouldn't know how to behave otherwise. We'll just be kinder, that's all."

Tears had spilled down his cheeks, and he withdrew his hand to grope for his handkerchief and mop his face. "Will you sit with us at our table?"

She had to smile. "Perhaps just for a moment now and then. We'll go slowly. But now, you must take Carmen and get out of Béxar. Today. Now. I want you safe." She stood. "And I must go back to the Veramendi Palace. They need my help with the nursing."

"But you'll be in danger!"

"I'll be careful. Now come, wrap your arms around me. That's a start on being a good papá. Then I'll help the two of you to pack and leave Béxar immediately."

She gave a final wave to the retreating buggy on its way to Victoria. Like the Altamiranos, most of Béxar's population had fled to their ranches or their nearest safe town. Many of those who had remained were now buried in trenches in the San Fernando graveyard. Emilia made a quick visit to the *Ayuntamiento* that seemed to be in perpetual crisis. Not only because of cholera but also due to the political situation in Monclova and in Mexico City. There, the new president, someone named Bustamante, seemed bent on destroying Texas's hopes for freedom to run its own business.

Her main occupation, however, remained the sick ward at the Veramendi palace, caring for the victims of the waning epidemic. Now that her family had gone, she had no regular duties at home. None of the other external things moved or interested her. She performed her duties like an automaton, feeling nothing, barely responding to those who expressed compassion and sympathy for her loss. Her own life seemed trivial, its essence dead and buried. She wondered why she hadn't caught the disease and gone to join María.

A week passed and then another, and the epidemic dwindled to one or two patients left in the Veramendi clinic. Charles took her hand as they left the building one evening.

"I'll be leaving tomorrow morning for Nacogdoches, Emilia. Cholera is mowing down the people there, too."

She answered almost automatically. "Must you go so soon, Charles? You need to rest, sometime."

His smile was tender, head canted to one side. "I'm a doctor, my dear. That's what I trained for."

Her voice sounded dry, like husking year-old corn. "But if you can't stop it, don't know what causes it, what good can you do?"

He took her other hand. "Relieve their suffering. That's something, after all."

"I suppose so. I'll miss you."

"And I you." He bent slightly as if he would kiss her, except for the danger.

He squeezed her hands once more and pulled free. Expressionless, she watched him stride away toward Señora Herrera's boarding house.

May, 1835

Dámaso, alone now that his fellow soldiers had retired, gazed into the campfire. He dropped his gaze to his sturdy new boots, dyed a warm orange by the flickering fire. He'd snatched them from a cobbler's display during the sack of Zacatecas. And they fit, the first comfortable shoes he'd worn since his forced entry into the Mexican army three years ago. Civil war had broken out between Federalists and Centralists, and Zacatecas was an important Federalist stronghold. The army, as usual, fought on the Centralist side.

The atrocities, killings, burning and looting in the aftermath of the Battle of Zacatecas had sickened him, but he'd taken advantage of the chaos nonetheless. He felt in his pocket and drew forth a wedding band that glinted in the firelight. As his squad had passed a jeweler's shop, he'd spotted it in the broken display window, the only thing left after looting. He'd snatched it up. At a glance it seemed about the right size for Emilia. Now, he tried it on. It passed only the first joint of the little finger of his left hand. He turned his hand back and forth to catch the light, picturing Emilia proudly wearing the ring. He wriggled his toes, enjoying comfort of wearing proper footwear at last, and his guilt lessened.

His lot had improved, once he was transferred to *General* Urrea's army. *Sargento* Padilla, commander of Dámaso's squad, praised his skill with any firearm—be it rifle, pistol or musket—his cleverness at tracking, his unerring sense of direction. He was an asset to the army and to the men around him, earning Padilla an occasional commendation. At separate times, the sergeant had given him a sheet of duck cloth, woven of linen and hemp, as a shelter, and passed on to him a nearly new shirt, a decent pair of trousers, and a leather belt. No more rags—until he wore these clothes out, too.

He appreciated the friendly relationship with his sergeant, suspecting him of being a secret Federalist, but he missed his friend, Pablo Ochoa, who had simply disappeared during the campaign against Zacatecas. Pablo had saved Dámaso's life back when his army ordeal had begun—by saving his feet. Rosa, the camp-follower, had somehow found a pair of huaraches that fit, more or less, and he'd marched in them for hundreds of miles. Over the past two years, a little short of three, he'd moved with the army alongside Pablo in any direction unrest or rebellion had threatened.

Pablo had taught him many survival techniques that had served him well. One of those, to seize any opportunity that presented itself, prompted Pablo to escape into a narrow side street in his home town. Dámaso wished him well and hoped for the same chance, especially if they were to march northward to Texas.

When he'd been captured and tied like a yearling calf, dragooned into forced service in the army, all his prized possessions had been confiscated: boots, hat, vest and chaps, his tack, his rifle, ammunition, and his horse Oropel. However, he'd been able to save his horse from possible early death due to the new master's brutal treatment. Dámaso began a whispering campaign, telling Pablo and Rosa that the horse had belonged to the Barón de Bastrop, given to his father for a favor he'd done the baron. The horse, he said, had been trained by one of Mexico's most illustrious horse-handlers (himself), and was far too fine for such a cruel, ham-handed upstart and ignorant ruffian as *Teniente* Moreno.

Less than a week later, Dámaso, who knew where Oropel was picketed, saw a young, fair-haired, aristocratic-looking *capitán* walking around the horse, feeling his legs, inspecting his hooves, and shaking his head as his fingertips brushed the fresh and half-healed spur wounds on Oropel's ribs and flanks. That evening, Oropel was no longer picketed with the junior officers' animals. A week later, Dámaso saw his horse on parade, groomed and gleaming, his rider splendid in a dress uniform. Oropel pranced with his neck arched, tail curved high, safe and proud for the moment, at least.

General José de Urrea had commanded Dámaso's army until recently. Presidente and *General* Antonio López de Santa Anna had then taken command of the army to attack Zacatecas. Dámaso considered him a heartless opportunist. He had usurped the presidency from Anastasio Bustamante by pretending to be a Federalist, only to reveal his real essence as a Centralist dictator. Dámaso had seen more than enough of what he could do to those who opposed him.

He jumped as a figure materialized out of the darkness and directly approached him. A private halted before him, peering doubtfully at him in the half light. "You are Private Daniel Martínez?

"Yes, you've found him."

The private looked furtively in all directions. "I have a message from *Sargento* Padilla. He says to meet him at the stable tomorrow morning before reveille."

Dámaso scratched his head. "Odd. Well, thank you, Private."

Without another word, the private vanished into the darkness.

Chapter Fourteen
1835

Dámaso spent a sleepless night, wondering why the sergeant would summon him in such a mysterious way. It had to be important, and had to be something Padilla wanted to keep secret. With the first faint light of dawn, he rose, dressed, and stood in a shadowy spot near the stable, restraining himself with difficulty from pacing or otherwise fidgeting. An hour crawled past, while Dámaso watched the light changing on the makeshift tents and stretches of bare, trampled earth around him, listened to the stamping and occasional snort of the horses inside the stable, and smelled the mingled odors of horseflesh, manure, and the gusts of clean morning air from nearby Bufa Mountain.

He heard Padilla's boot-falls before he rounded the stable corner. As he passed Dámaso, he jerked his chin toward the stable door. They entered together.

"Over here, Private Martínez, is *Teniente* Castañeda's favorite horse. Lead him out and watch."

Dámaso opened the stall door, attached a lead rope to the halter the horse wore, and led him out. "That's a bad limp. Let me look at it." He moved his hand down the gelding's right front leg and lifted the hoof. "As I feared, a crack from the bottom of the toe well into the corona, the quick. The shoe he's wearing isn't holding the crack together, so there's no chance of healing." He straightened and faced Padilla. "What do you want me to do?"

"The *teniente* has been told the horse is useless. He'll have him shot tomorrow morning unless you can convince him otherwise."

"Surely, he's had the best vet look at him?"

"The army vet, yes."

"And he told the *teniente* what?"

"That it would take months to heal under the best of conditions."

Dámaso turned and ran his fingers through the horse's wavy mane. The horse's head hung low, his weight on the other three feet. "That's true. But this is a magnificent beast, surely worth the effort to save."

Padilla placed a hand on Dámaso's shoulder. "That's what you need to tell the *teniente*. Demonstrate that to the *teniente*!" he ended forcefully.

"Why me?"

The sergeant's voice became more urgent. "Simple. This is the *teniente's* favorite horse. If you save him, you'll be his favorite, too. He's been ordered to take a hundred troops to reinforce *Colonel* Ugartechea in Béxar. You want to be one of those hundred."

"Ugartechea in Béxar? Why?"

"Santa Anna fears an insurrection in Texas. Béxar is the hotbed of Federalist fervor for independence. Ugartechea is now the military governor."

Dámaso pounded his right fist into his left palm. "*¡Maldito sea!* Sounds like a repeat of Arredondo's occupation after the War of Independence! I need to get up there."

"I thought so. The *teniente's* away until tomorrow. I'm relieving you from all your duties today. Get busy and work on that horse's hoof."

"A day's not much time, but I'll do my best."

Dámaso flew into a whirlwind of activity. As he entered the stall, he noticed a small card tacked to the doorpost. He slowly sounded out the letters printed on it, cursing himself for never learning to read. A-U-D-A-Z. That's Ah-oo-dáhss. Audaz, the bold one! Must be the horse's name. He turned to the horse. "Steady now, Audaz, I'm going to lift that right foot." He made precise measurements of the horse's ailing hoof and sought out the camp farrier. The man was holding a mule's front leg between his knees.

Dámaso tapped him on the shoulder. "Can you make me a bar horseshoe? Here are the measurements."

The farrier dropped the mule's leg and stood, fists on hips. "What? Which horse? On whose orders? Who the hell are you anyway?" He turned as if to stoop again.

Dámaso sized him up. The man was pushing forty, short and wide, not fat but all muscle. He looked like a man who would understand. "*Teniente* Francisco de Castañeda will have his horse, Audaz, shot tomorrow if we don't stabilize the crack in his hoof."

The farrier paused and straightened, shaking his head. "Audaz, eh? Damn my eyes! About to be shot? I know that horse. Fine animal. Not gun shy, even after being wounded in battle. When do you need the shoe?"

"Yesterday." Damaso laughed. "Surely, you have shoes almost the right size that you can alter? And add a bar?"

"For that horse, I'll make an exception. I'll do that next and put off the other jobs, claiming orders from the *teniente*."

"*¡Mil gracias!* Meanwhile I'll prepare glue for the hoof." Dámaso gathered hoof parings that lay around the farrier's quarters, borrowed a pot from a cook, added water to the parings and brought the smelly mess to a boil. He waited until it thickened, then carried the pot and contents to the farrier, who had meanwhile re-forged a shoe and added a bar.

The farrier held out the shoe, still too hot to handle, with a pair of tongs. "How does that look?"

Dámaso squinted at it. "That should fit him fine."

The two entered the stable. The farrier removed the old shoe, cleaned the hoof and applied the glue, using a thin knife blade to introduce it as far up toward the corona as possible. Last, he fastened on the new shoe.

When all was done, they led Audaz out of the stable for a brief walk. After a few tentative steps, he began to put his weight on the injured hoof.

Dámaso shook the farrier's hand. "*Dios mío,* how can I thank you? Without you and the proper tools, we could never have finished on time."

The *teniente* returned the following morning and found his horse standing on all four feet, relaxed, out of pain, head high, with a fancy new shoe on his right front hoof. He nickered when his master approached the stall.

Teniente Castañeda turned to his orderly. "Who did this? Go ask the farrier!"

Within a few minutes, Dámaso stood before him at attention, saluted and said, "*Daniel Martínez a sus órdenes, Señor Teniente.*"

"You did this?"

"*Sí, Señor,* with the help of the farrier, *claro.*"

"On whose orders?"

"Señor, I heard that this fine animal would be shot today. I know horses well, and could see that he could be saved, even though it will take months for him to be ready for normal duty. I took it upon myself, *Señor Teniente.*"

"Who is your sergeant, Private Martínez?"

"It is *Sargento* Padilla, Señor."

The lieutenant again summoned Private Martínez a short time later. "I understand that you would like to supervise the healing of my horse, Audaz. Is that correct?"

"*Sí, Señor,* certainly."

"Then you must be transferred to my detail. I am leaving for Béxar, in Texas, tomorrow morning. I am informing you of the transfer."

"*A la orden, Señor Teniente.*" He saluted. "Your valiant horse, Audaz, very important to me, Sir."

After Dámaso had packed his meager belongings on a supply wagon, he sought out *Sargento* Padilla. "Señor, I cannot thank you enough for what you've done for me. I'll be able to see my family and my sweetheart again."

"Private Martínez, I've owed you a favor for months in return for all the good turns you've done me. My recent commendation was thanks to you. For your future, I wish you a successful career in the army and steady promotion. You deserve to become an officer."

Dámaso cocked his head with a pensive expression. "But perhaps I'm better off among the enlisted men, mi *Sargento.*"

The sergeant's eyebrows shot up, but nonetheless, the two men embraced and clapped each other on the back.

July, 1835

The trip to Béxar took over a month, since the distance was nearly six hundred miles, and Castañeda's company included a cannon hauled on a wagon by a double team of oxen. Dámaso's feelings were mixed: he was so anxious to reunite with Emilia that he wept sometimes at night from the pain of the delay. On the other hand, he knew that the slow pace was best for Audaz, whose hoof he kept clean at all times, especially after they had slogged through heavy summer downpours. By the beginning of July, the crack had grown out below the corona, and with any luck, would be completely gone in six more months.

When they had come within a few miles of Béxar, Dámaso went to his commander. "Señor, I respectfully request a day or two of leave when we arrive in the town. My family lives there, and I've been unable to contact my intended future wife for years."

Teniente Castañeda pursed his lips. "Private Martínez, your service so far has earned you at least two days' leave. Your family, or what is left of it, might still be in town, but what makes you think your fiancée has waited for you for years?"

Dámaso shrugged with a faint smile. "I know her, Señor. When she says she'll do something, she does it."

"She made you a promise?"

"An informal one, but I'm optimistic, Señor."

Castañeda gave a barely visible head-shake. "I grant you two days' leave—no matter what you'll find when you get there."

Dámaso raised his head and sniffed. The aromas reaching him from the town ahead were familiar: the scent of live oak trees slightly damp from the recent rains, the marshy smell from the river, the perfume of cooking fires. His stomach clenched with conflicting emotions, anxiety and joy. He was home. He had already given instructions to the private who had been his aide throughout the trip, and now he hurried to inform the lieutenant that he was beginning his leave.

Castañeda waved him away. "*Vete, Daniel, vete. Y suerte.* Go, and good luck."

When the company was about to cross the San Pedro Creek bridge and enter Military Plaza, Dámaso ran ahead to Rosita's Fonda, now owned by her daughter, Gabi. The Plaza was crowded with native Tejanos, but also with a few strangers, Anglos, whom he judged to be settlers. He raised his eyes to the low building next to San Fernando Church and saw, over the door to the fonda, a new sign, "Rosita's Fonda," in bright red letters outlined in black against a white background. Gabi needed to advertise her business to the settlers, but she still kept Rosita's name, honoring her mother.

The interior was dark as usual, the only light coming from the doors. Four tables with six customers each were wedged into the small space between the counter and the wall, and all seats but one of the stools at the counter were occupied. He scanned the faces. Many were familiar, but no names came to him as yet. They glanced back, a few eyes lingering and narrowing as if trying to remember who he was. All were Tejanos. Dámaso quickly seated himself on the last stool. He was closest to the parrilla and to Gabi.

When she turned to place tortillas and beans on a waiting plate, she faced him, halted and stared, nearly dropping the tortillas. "¡Dios mío! ¡Dámaso Jiménez! ¿Levantaste del sepulcro? Are you risen from the grave?"

All eyes in the place immediately focused upon him. He blanched, then felt the blood rushing back—heat rising up his neck, cheeks, and forehead. "No, Gabi. I went to Monclova all those years ago and was snatched up by the army. You don't easily get away from the army. I'm here with reinforcements for *Colonel* Ugartechea. I need to know about Emilia Altamirano. About my family." He glanced nervously around, wishing he didn't have such an eager audience.

"Hmph." Gabi first took the plates to the customers, then returned to face him. "Emilia's probably across the plaza with the *ayuntamiento*. Your papá's still alive and so is your little brother. Your uncle Tomás was very sick. He lived, but his daughter, your cousin Jacinta, died."

"How?"

"Cholera. It struck earlier this year."

"My papá lived, and... my sister Luisa?" His question was breathless.

"They're fine. No problem. They stayed out at the ranch until the epidemic was over. Oh, yes. Emilia's mother, María died too."

Dámaso felt a knife twist in his gut. María dead? How could Emilia live without her? And Jacinta, his little cousin, once his playmate and Emilia's? How could this be?

Now it was his turn to cry out. "*¡Dios Mio!* Emilia! I've got to find her!"

He stood, knocking over the stool but catching it before it hit the floor. He was outside in an instant and ran, weaving through the crowd toward the *cabildo*. As he approached, the heavy, paneled door opened and Emilia stepped out, her expression intent, as if she were on an errand. Dámaso came to a halt, watching her, paying no attention to the rider swearing at him, whose horse had barely missed running him over. Both plazas were filled with soldiers like himself, and he knew it wasn't likely she would pick him out among the throng. Now careful to sidestep more foot and animal traffic, he stared. Still beautiful. Had she grown taller in three years? She seemed a mature woman, dignified, with none of the sunny lightness he knew. She wore her hair tied back in a French roll that would look severe except for a few escaped wavy tendrils around her face.

He continued working his way through the crowd to cut her off before she slipped away on her errand. "Emilia! Emilia! Wait!"

His call froze her where she stood, and she frantically looked in all directions until she saw him coming toward her. "Dámaso! Dámaso!" She fought her way to him, and threw her arms around him. "I'd know your voice anywhere. Can it be true? At last!"

"*¡Mi Tesoro! Sí, soy yo.* Yes, my treasure, it's me." He bent his head and they kissed passionately, ignoring stares of passers-by, a few low murmurs, and scandalized glances from older women.

"Let me look at you." She placed her hands on his shoulders and pushed him back. "You look tired." His face had matured: a three-day beard, cheekbones wider and firmer but with hollows beneath.

The strong cleft chin she remembered and those voluptuous lips. She admired his broad shoulders, deep chest, tapering waist and narrow hips. "You're a grown man now."

"We're both grownups. These years have been hard for us both."

Her head drooped. "Yes, they have. Especially since mamá..."

"I know. Gabi told me. I'm so sorry..."

She placed a hand over his lips. "Yes. The pain's too deep for words." Her voice ended in a croak and she paused, looking away. "Have you eaten?"

"No. Maybe Gabi's?"

Recovered, she smiled. "Might as well. That way, everyone will know everything much quicker." Some of the old mischief danced in her eyes.

The fonda had half emptied by the time they arrived. They sat at a table. Midway through their meal, Dámaso burst out, "Next, I'll have to confront the *regidores* to see if they still want to put me on trial. Then I must find my papá."

"Your papá will be overjoyed to see his favorite son back from the dead. I expect the *ayuntamiento* will be happy to pardon you, but they're in recess right now. I just left our Political Chief sitting at the conference table, all alone. We must see him before we go to your papá."

They walked back to the *cabildo*, hand in hand. "José Ángel Navarro is our *Jefe Político*, doing his best to keep *Colonel* Ugartechea from arresting everyone sympathetic with the Federalist cause. Tío Antonio has been gone most of the time since 1831, when Governor Viesca appointed him Land Commissioner for Green DeWitt's land grant. He's busy creating the ideal colony down there and even set up an *ayuntamiento* in Gonzales. I just don't see him anymore."

Dámaso caught the wistful note in her voice. He squeezed her hand. "He was gone when you most needed him."

"Yes," Emilia nodded. "But at least he was spared the threat of cholera. It was at its worst in the city centers."

They climbed the steps and entered the silent *cabildo*. Ángel sat alone at the head of the long conference table, a pile of papers at his elbow. Chin propped on his left palm, he stared down, brows furrowed, as if deep in thought. He jumped as they entered the room.

"Ah! You startled me, Emilia."

He rose, moving to the side of the table so the two young people were no longer silhouetted against the bright light of the window. "Dámaso! You're back! And you're in uniform."

"Yes, Señor José Ángel, I fled to Monclova the night I escaped, worked on a ranch for a while, and then the army captured me like an animal and forced me to serve. I've been fighting battles for the Centralists ever since."

Ángel's lips widened in a bitter smile. "Then you're not in danger from Ugartechea. I just received his orders. All Federalist members of the *ayuntamiento* are to be arrested, in particular my brother José Antonio and cousin Francisco Ruíz." His voice took on a sarcastic inflection. "I'm the exception, because of my glorious history, having fought alongside *General* Arredondo during the Battle of Medina."

Dámaso asked, "Then where is everybody else? Have they been detained already?"

"Most of them have taken their families and gone to their ranches. Ugartechea doesn't want to spare the manpower to send troops in all directions to hunt them down. I would dearly love to be with my wife at our ranch on San Gerónimo Creek, but I'm stuck here trying to keep the peace, as far as that's possible." He resumed his seat and ran a weary hand through his hair.

Dámaso pulled out a chair for Emilia and they both sat, unbidden. "What caused the *colonel* to issue that order. I wonder?"

José glanced out the window. "Mainly the hostility of the Anglo settlers. Even under the best of circumstances, they disregard our laws and customs, speak only English and despise our religion. But now, under military restrictions, they spit and curse: 'God damn Ugartechea! The Devil take Santa Anna!' The *colonel* hears that, and he's furious—and afraid they'll start a real uprising."

Emilia stood. "We'd better go find your papá before Ugartechea calls you up for duty, Dámaso."

He rose also, but paused to ask, "What about my case? I did kill someone, you remember."

Ángel raised both hands and shrugged. "I say, you can go your way, Dámaso. The army is like prison for privates anyway—you're serving your term. I don't think any one of us wants to bother with a cold case. Too much else to worry about. A crisis is coming and we'll be lucky to come out of it in one piece."

They rode to the Jiménez ranch on two of the Altamiranos' horses.

Dámaso swept his eyes over the cypress trees, the roomy log cabin, the barn, corrals, and the hill beyond Calaveras Creek. He shook his head. "Something feels wrong about the place."

"Why? What?"

"It's too still. There are no horses grazing on the hill and only a cow or two. Nothing in the corrals. I see no activity around the house, even though it's mid-afternoon and warm. No cooking smells. No dog. He should be barking to alert papá or Inés and Alonso, our caretakers, or at least be lying in the shade somewhere in plain view."

As they approached the cabin, Dámaso called, "Papá! It's me, I'm home!"

A tall teenage girl stepped out the door. Emilia saw at once her resemblance to Dámaso. Glossy black hair to her shoulders, fine arched eyebrows over large, black-lashed brown eyes, the same full lips, and the shadow of a cleft in her chin. The girl stared at Dámaso and he at her.

"*¡Dios mío! ¿Eres Luisa?* Good Lord! Is it Luisa?"

"*Sí, idiota. Y tú eres Dámaso. Por lo menos* yo *te conozco a* ti. Yes, idiot, and you're Dámaso. At least *I* know *you.*"

Both laughed. Dámaso exclaimed, "Luisa, you were still a little girl when I left. Now look at you!"

The door opened again, and Miguel Jiménez stepped out. Dámaso leapt off his horse and the two reached each other in two strides and embraced.

"Papá, I get the feeling things are not going well out here. What's wrong?"

"The Comanche, son. Six weeks ago. They killed Inés and Alonso in the most gruesome way. Then they slaughtered all the cattle they could find and stole all the horses. They even killed our dog, Paquín."

Dámaso panicked, fearing for his brother. "Where's Pedro?"

"He's in Goliad, selling three *mesteños* we've trained since the raid. He's fine. All three of us were in Béxar when they came. I still can't imagine why they didn't burn down the cabin. But I thank God they didn't."

Emilia had remained standing next to her horse, watching the drama of the family reunion. Dámaso turned to her. "Papá, I don't know if you ever actually met my girl, Emilia Altamirano. Emilia, this is Miguel Jiménez, my father."

Emilia shook his hand. When he embraced her, she reciprocated, her arms around him. He kissed her lightly on the cheek. "I saw you in church from the time you were little, Emilia. I knew Dámaso loved you already when he was twelve. Who else was he carving wolf figurines for? Somehow, we never officially met."

Dámaso broke in. "Papá, where are Inés and Alonso buried?"

"In San Fernando graveyard. But I put up two memorial crosses over there beneath that lone oak. They were butchered near there."

Dámaso blinked back tears. "They were second parents to me. Emilia, would you go with me and say a prayer for them?"

Emilia nodded and followed him. As they crossed through a patch of high grass, she noticed a clump of Indian blanket flowers in bloom. She plucked six and caught up with Dámaso. "We'll put three at each cross."

He knelt near the first cross while she placed her flowers at the second and then came and stood next to him. They bowed their heads for a moment of silent prayer. Dámaso began the Lord's Prayer, choking back tears. He felt Emilia's sympathetic presence as her voice also cracked. Then they recited, "Grant them eternal rest, O Lord, and let eternal light shine upon them. May they rest in peace. Amen."

They returned slowly hand in hand to Miguel and Luisa. She had already prepared the noon meal, with plenty to include the two visitors.

Seated at the table, Dámaso gave Luisa a grave look. "*¡Gracias a Dios!* Thank God you were not here when the Comanches came. And Pedro: he's... what... nineteen now? *¡Caramba!*"

He turned to his father. "And what happened to my sweet horse, Romero?"

"They stole him, son. I'm so sorry."

"And Oropel was taken from me when they forced me into the army. I've lost three of the smartest, best tempered horses I've ever known. My best horse I traded for the rifle I used to take vengeance on the man who dishonored you, my love." He reached for Emilia's hand and kissed it.

Luisa blushed and looked at her hands, but Miguel seemed not to notice. "You'll find other good horses, Dámaso. They're out there."

They continued to talk of the ranch and what they'd done to restore its former prosperity. Pedro had caught and trained half a dozen *mesteños*, three of which he was selling at that very moment. Miguel had rounded up a number of unclaimed "wild" cattle and brought them home. The herd now amounted to thirty-five head.

He turned to Emilia. "I think I owe my son's escape from Béxar jail to you, too, don't I? María told me about it."

She laughed. "Yes, you do. Just a matter of stealing the right key. Simple."

Dámaso laid his hand on top of hers and gave it a squeeze. "Nothing simple about it. I saw how you were sweating, Emilia. Every move you made must have been at a dead run."

She nodded. "Yes, I had to act fast."

Dámaso spent the day outside with Miguel, helping with mundane chores like mucking out the stables, but also sizing up the three *mesteños* penned in the corral. All three were fine looking horses and one, a sorrel with a blaze, who snorted and reared when Dámaso dropped inside the corral fence, impressed him as a possible replacement for Oropel. Emilia helped with household chores and with preparation of the evening meal.

As afternoon shadows began to lengthen, Dámaso and Miguel washed up at the pump, then came in to sit at the table. Dámaso explained, "I have to report for duty tomorrow morning. I'd love to spend the night here, in my home, and ride back early tomorrow. That would mean getting up before dawn and leaving."

Emilia broke in. "Then I'll come with you."

Miguel rapped on the table. "Luisa, you get up tomorrow morning and make them *desayuno*. I have fresh coffee beans. Use them. Dámaso, you can sleep in Pedro's bed. Luisa, you and Emilia can work out sleeping arrangements between yourselves. Any objections, Emilia? Dámaso?"

The two chorused, "No objections, Miguel/Papá."

"And Emilia, you can call me 'papá,' too."

Emilia nodded. "Thank you, Mi—, uh, Papá." She paused for

a moment. "Luisa, I'd better be getting ready for bed if we're to get up so early." She rose and began clearing the dishes.

Dámaso turned to Miguel. "When do you expect Pedro to get back?"

"He has a girl in Goliad. He might stay a week. If you're not gone on some Centralist military goose chase by then, I'll send him into town on an errand, and he can find you."

"Come to think of it, since I was on the run three years ago, I gave my name to the ranch foreman where I worked as Daniel Martínez. When the army seized me, I gave that name. I'm still Daniel Martínez to the army. Pedro might have a problem finding 'Dámaso Jiménez.'"

"I'll keep that in mind. That might come in handy if you should ever think of leaving the army without notice..."

"Yes, papá, the thought did occur to me." He yawned. "I'm off to bed, too."

Emilia showed her efficiency as she helped clear the table and wash the dishes. Luisa hung up the dishtowel. "That's done, then. Come upstairs and I'll show you where you'll sleep." Over Emilia's objections, she gave up her bed, sleeping instead on a cot in the spare room.

A few short hours later, Luisa knocked on the door when the world was still sunk in darkness. Her lamp, held aloft, sent a beam of light through a crack. "May I come in?"

Hearing Emilia's sleepy reply, Luisa entered and lit the lamp on the night table. "Breakfast is ready and Dámaso's already at the table. Hurry; it feels like rain, and you've a long way to go."

September 1835

Dámaso's thoughts accompanied his stride on his way to the *jacal*, where he and Emilia, now acting as secretary to José Ángel Navarro, had arranged that they meet while both were in Béxar. He rapped twice on the sapling door-frame and heard the immediate invitation.

"*¡Pasa, pasa, Amor mío!*"

They embraced, kissed, and sat at the table where Emilia and María had talked and planned for so many years. They joined all four hands.

"I've just been appointed orderly, so I hear more gossip among the officers at headquarters. It seems that *General* Martín Perfecto de Cos landed in Copano Bay day before yesterday with five hundred men. With him, Santa Anna begins his campaign to wipe out those in Texas still loyal to the Federalist Constitution of 1824."

Emilia gripped his hands tighter. "This is crazy, Dámaso. We're repeating history. My father joined the Royal Army of New Spain, believing he was doing the honorable thing, following in his father's footsteps, fighting for the King of Spain. Then when the fight for independence began, my father and Ángel Navarro were caught on the wrong side. The same thing is happening to you. When they call you up to aid *General* Cos, what're you going to do?"

"I'll have to obey orders."

"So did my papá, and so did Ángel. Both of them have tried to counteract their service with Arredondo with service to the community. But there's always a shadow, whispering behind backs. And now—the irony of it!—because Ángel was in your position, he's been named *Jefe Político*. The *regidores* think, with his 'shady' reputation, he can deal with the Centralists and be believed. Now, they turn to him for protection."

"I don't know what else I can do."

"Neither did my papá. You see? Life can set traps that can ruin a person forever."

"I haven't been called up yet. So far, this is idle speculation. Look! I brought a bottle of Rioja wine. The best, from the *colonel's* stash. Let's drink it, and then..." He glanced toward the straw mattress.

Emilia raised her eyebrows. "I've been thinking, *Amor mío*. With Cos moving on Béxar, you'll be ordered into action, like as not. Time is short. It's barely dark outside. Why not go over to the priest's house and arrange for Padre Refugio to marry us. We need only two witnesses—we can check that with Padre Refugio—and enough money to pay the priest something. We can do that now, and drink the wine afterwards."

Dámaso was already on his feet. "Splendid idea. But you should have a big, glorious wedding!"

"Don't be absurd, mi Amor. I'm a poor girl with no dowry; a 'slave girl' even now, to many good Bexareños. A quiet, simple wedding is what I want."

The windows of the priest's house, a short walk away, were bright with lamplight. Dámaso knocked, and Father Refugio opened the door, a napkin tied around his neck. He looked from one to the other in surprise. "You've finally found your way to each other, I see!"

Dámaso replied, "Please excuse us for interrupting your *cena*. Yes, Father, it has been a long, difficult road, but we're here to ask you to marry us as soon as you can."

"You need two witnesses, you know."

Emilia stepped forward. "Yes, I'm confident we can find them by tomorrow."

"All right. Let's say about ten o'clock tomorrow morning."

Dámaso reached out to shake the priest's hand. "*Bueno, mil gracias*. We'll be here then."

They walked away hand in hand, glancing back to see Father Refugio still standing in the door, his head tilted to one side, hands on hips.

Emilia shook her head. "He still thinks of me as 'compromised,' it seems."

"But he'll marry us just the same."

They paused in the shadow of the church to kiss.

Chapter Fifteen

September 1835

The next morning at seven, *Teniente* Castañeda summoned Dámaso. "Private Martínez, bad news. Colonel Ugartechea sent a small delegation to Gonzales about ten days ago, asking that they return the six-pound bronze cannon that belongs to Ramón Músquiz. He lent it to them two or three years ago to help them fight off the Comanche. They haven't needed it, but the alcalde of Gonzales refused. Instead they took the delegation members prisoner and finally released them with the message that they will not, under any circumstances, give up the cannon. They say they need it for their own defense against Centralist forces and they'll fight for their rights guaranteed under the Constitution of 1824."

Dámaso, taken aback by the probable conflict with his plans to marry Emilia that morning, shook his head. "And what has *Colonel* Ugartechea decided to do about that?"

"He's sending a hundred cavalry this morning to take the cannon by force."

"Oh-oh! That could be the spark that starts an explosion." Dámaso clenched his fists.

The captain's eyebrows drew together. "I fear so, too. But I must obey my orders."

"*Sí Señor, desde luego.* Of course."

"And so do you. You'll be coming as one of my cavalry. I've seen how well you ride and manage a rifle from horseback, and I'll see that you're promoted to sergeant. By the way, will I be able to ride Audaz on this expedition?"

"Not yet, *Señor Teniente.* Another two or three months and he'll be ready. The cracked hoof has grown out two-thirds the way to the bottom. He's progressing nicely. Right on schedule."

"*¡Caramba!* I was hoping he'd heal faster than that. God knows what we'll be facing before long, and I'd prefer to ride my favorite mount."

"Just be glad he won't be shot or stabbed in the next few months, Señor. And many thanks for the promotion. Totally unexpected."

"It may take a week or so. Paperwork, you know."

Dámaso hurried to make preparations for the expedition. By nine o'clock, the cavalry had mustered in Military Plaza behind the church, and he had only a moment to ride by the *cabildo* to inform Ángel—and Emilia—that he'd been summarily promoted to sergeant of the cavalry, and would be riding out at once to put down a rebellion in Gonzales and to seize a cannon there.

Emilia met him at the door, where he told her his news. She squeezed her temples with both hands. "*¡Mala suerte! ¡Siempre mala!* Heaven itself seems determined to keep us from marrying. But you need to tell Jose Angel."

The *Jefe Político* made a wry face. "This looks like a competition for dominance. Ugartechea doesn't need that little cannon. He already has several at the Alamo mounted for battle and at least eighteen unmounted. He just wants to show who's boss, and his vanity will get all of us into a major conflict. *¡Caramba!* Why didn't he consult with me first?"

Emilia set her jaw. "He's endangering everybody with this nonsense."

Dámaso turned to go, and Emilia followed him out. "*Por favor, Amor Mío*, use all your experience to avoid getting shot by one of those settler-soldiers. And don't you shoot unless you have to."

He saluted with a laugh. "*¡A la orden, Señora!* I'll be very careful. Don't worry, I'll come back safe, and we'll be wed." They embraced, and he mounted to join the troop already assembled in Military Plaza.

She held on to his stirrup. "I'll tell Father Refugio to postpone the wedding."

"Pray to God we'll live to have one." He blew her a kiss and trotted out to join the regiment.

She'd hidden her fear from him, but now marched up and down in front of the *Casas reales*, her fists clenched and arms rigid, fighting tears. She prayed, "Dear God, don't take him away from me when we've waited so long, when we're about to be married. Please!"

The next few days were agony. Emilia managed to intercept the messengers who arrived at least every other day, take their dispatches, and then deliver them to Ángel. Once read, he mercifully let her know any news that concerned her. She learned that Centralist *General* Cos was making rapid headway toward Béxar. However, the next message reported that on 2 October, Captain Castañeda and the cavalry had surrendered to a band of settlers at Gonzales without retrieving the cannon, and had suffered a number of casualties. She paced the floor, praying that Dámaso was not among the wounded.

He and the cavalry arrived two days later. Several men still in the saddle wore bandages on legs, arms, chests and heads, and two men lay on a wagon severely wounded, perhaps dead already. Horses, too, had been wounded. Dámaso wore a bandage around his left bicep and guided his horse with the right hand. The sun had already set and lamps were lit when he finished the necessary formalities and reports. Among other things, he obtained a week's sick leave. Then, certain that Emilia was home, he walked to the *jacal*, entered without knocking and ran straight into her arms.

She immediately saw the bandage and the sleeve, black with dried blood. "My poor love! You're wounded! How badly?" She led him to a chair where he sat with a sigh.

"It's a puncture wound, a splinter off a tree trunk. The settlers—they call themselves Texians—fired the cannon we went to confiscate. Twice. We were only four hundred yards from their position. For a cannon, that's point-blank range. One shot struck a tree. Two men were hurt seriously. I fear they died on the way back here."

"How foolish of those settlers! This will mean all-out war against Texas." Her tone was calm, however, as she assessed the wound, realizing she must cut off the sleeve to see its extent.

He nodded. "War. Most likely. *Teniente* Castañeda was surprised that they decided to attack after the parley where he told them we were unwilling to fight and only wanted to recover the cannon. He even told them he supported the Constitution of 1824. But still they fired on us. Afterwards, he ordered the bugler to sound the call to retreat and we did, taking the wounded men and animals. We had to shoot two more horses on the way back. It took me a minute to realize I had a piece of wood sticking out of my arm. I jerked it out. It bled—you can see that on my sleeve—and I bound it tight."

Emilia took charge. "Come into the kitchen. That's where Mamá kept medicines and things." She carried the lamp and led the way. Inside one cabinet door were soap, a rolled-up strip of cotton bandages, a jar of ointment, and a pair of scissors. She turned to Dámaso, removed the bandage and cut off the sleeve, stiff with blood and sticking to the edges of the wound. She bathed the arm with soap, gently removing as much clotted blood as possible without restarting bleeding. Darting outside for a moment, she cut a spike of the aloe plant growing next to the garden, slit the spike lengthwise and applied the jelly liberally to the wound.

Dámaso, meanwhile, had remained stoic, his smile showing his appreciation and admiration of her skill.

Using a generous strip of the bandage, she wound it around his arm. "We'll leave it for a day and keep an eye on it. If it doesn't turn red and irritated, we can leave it longer. I suspect it will heal with no problem."

"You'd make a good nurse!"

"Yes, I learned a lot from my mother and from Dr. McCray during the cholera epidemic. I suppose, if you stay in the army, I might need these skills again."

"*¡Que Dios te libre!* God forbid!"

Emilia persuaded Dámaso to spend the night in the *jacal* so she could watch over him in case he showed signs of fever or infection. She left a candle burning and felt his forehead from time to time, holding the candle high to take a close look at the arm in case there were streaks of redness. Dámaso slept the sleep of exhaustion, and in the morning, awoke at daybreak sore but alert, feeling stronger.

Emilia, tired but happy, placed before him a plate of scrambled eggs, pickled jalapeños and tortillas.

"*Querido*, do you feel up to coming with me to set the time for the wedding?'

"Of course! For that, I'd rise from my death bed."

"Don't be so gloomy! But, really, how do you feel?"

"I won't be using my left arm for much, but otherwise I'm fine."

"Is tomorrow too soon to celebrate the wedding? What do you think?"

"I should be well enough by then. Yes! Let's do it!"

"Right now, I'll serve breakfast to Carmen and Andrés and then we'll walk over to the priest's house."

She served the breakfast, and as she poured weakened hot chocolate, the last they had, she asked, "Andrés, Dámaso and I are marrying tomorrow. Could you give me away? We also need two witnesses, and find out if Father Refugio is available. Carmen, could we count on you to be a witness, please?"

Andrés laid down his napkin, paused, staring at his plate as if thinking of all he hadn't done over the years for his long-unacknowledged daughter.

Carmen, watched him, tapping her toe under the table. Her tone was sharp. "Well, Andrés, I think that's most appropriate. And I'll of course be there as a witness, if women can count as such."

Andrés beamed at her. "Yes, Emilia, I'd be more than happy to do that for you and Dámaso. You realize, when you walk into the church on my arm, everyone will finally know for sure what I've been hiding for years."

"They surely know already. They tell me I resemble you in many ways."

Carmen laughed. "You certainly do. Same wave in your hair, same eyes.... That's why you're so beautiful. When would you need us?"

"I think, if possible, around ten tomorrow morning, if Father Refugio can manage it. Would that suit?"

Andrés nodded. "I think so. Just let us know as soon as you can."

"Of course."

Emilia bustled back into the kitchen. "Dámaso, Andrés agreed to give me away, and Carmen will be a witness. Let's go see Father Refugio. Along the way, we might find another."

Dámaso chuckled. "My ever-efficient wife-to-be!"

Father Refugio again came to the door with his napkin tied around his neck. "Emilia! Dámaso! Just finishing breakfast. My first mass was at six, you know. I got your message postponing the wedding.... Are you here to set a new date?"

Emilia asked, "Are you free at ten tomorrow morning?"

"Yes... I think so...." He paused, thinking. "Yes, after mass I have nothing before noon."

"*¡Maravilloso!* Then, if we can find one more witness, we'll be here tomorrow at ten. *¡Mil gracias, Padre!*

They walked in the direction of the *Casas reales*, and saw Gaspar Flores coming around the corner. Emilia called to him. "Gaspar! Could you be a witness at my wedding? Dámaso and I are to be married at ten tomorrow morning."

"Married! Hija mía, I'd be delighted! There are other *regidores* in the *cabildo* who'd like to witness the occasion, too. I'll go in and see."

"Then you'll meet us at the altar tomorrow?"

"I'll be there, with others, I'm sure."

The following day at ten, her left arm in his right, Andrés escorted Emilia into the dim nave of the church. He wore his formal suit; she her Sunday dress, a belted lavender smock with lace around the collar. María's white mantilla covered her glossy dark brown hair. When their eyes adjusted to the gloom, they saw six *regidores*, including Ángel, the Seguíns, father and son, Andrés Nava, Gaspar Flores, and Carmen. A low rumble and elbow nudging had greeted their entrance. The *regidores* thus greeted Andrés's symbolic declaration of his fatherhood—at last.

Father and daughter approached the altar, where Emilia gave Andrés's arm a squeeze, mounted the steps of the altar and took her place beside Dámaso, handsome in his dress uniform. Against custom, she turned to face the gathering. "Thank you so much for coming! I only wish Antonio could be here."

"He's here in spirit," Ángel assured her.

Father Refugio, vested in a white chasuble, took his place before the altar. He began by greeting the guests, then turned to the couple, asking them the traditional questions before the Consent and then received their vows. Next came the blessing and giving of the Ring. To Emilia's astonishment, Dámaso produced a gold band and placed it on her finger. Only slightly too large, it fit well enough not to fall off.

After the Prayer of the Faithful and The Lord's Prayer, Father Refugio's eyes shifted from the couple to Andrés. Carmen handed her husband a bundle consisting of two large, ornate rosaries of jet and silver, joined by one large silver crucifix: the *Lazo*. He stepped forward and looped one rosary around Dámaso's shoulders, then the other around Emilia's in a figure eight, the crucifix between them. The priest then blessed the *Lazo* as the symbol of their sacred union, and intoned the Nuptial Blessing:

> O God, who by your mighty power created all things out of nothing, and... formed man and woman in your own image, making the woman an inseparable helpmate to the man, that they might be no longer two, but one flesh, [you] taught that what you were pleased to make one must never be divided....
>
> Look now with favor on these your servants, joined together in Marriage, who ask to be strengthened by your blessing. Send down on them the grace of the Holy Ghost and pour your love into their hearts, that they may remain faithful in the Marriage covenant....
>
> And now, Lord, we implore you: may these your servants hold fast to the faith and keep your commandments; made one in the flesh, may they be blameless in all they do....
>
> Amen.

He then informed Dámaso, "You may kiss the bride."

Dámaso drew Emilia to him with one arm; she embraced him with both, and they demonstrated what "two becoming one" might look like. Smiling, Father Refugio blessed the congregation and concluded the service. Moved to tears by the words of the Nuptial Blessing, Emilia turned to Carmen and Andrés. "Oh, thank you for the *Lazo*! What a beautiful gesture! I'll never forget this moment! So sacred!" She lifted the rosaries off their shoulders and returned the *Lazo* with a fervent embrace. "You have hearts of gold!"

Ángel broke in. "Come! Back to the *cabildo*! Let's celebrate the happy couple!"

They left the shadowy church and trooped across the plaza to the *Casas reales* and filled the chairs around the conference table, the couple at the head, Erasmo Seguín at the foot. He and his son Juan disappeared into the kitchen and returned with a dark green magnum, Juan carrying a tray of nine glasses.

Erasmo held up the large bottle. "It's the finest *champán*, bought in New Orleans two years ago. It's still cool from the wine cellar." While he spoke, he unwound the wire around the cork and began prizing. The cork gave way with a pop and hit the ceiling, white foam pouring onto the table. Juan hurried to catch much of it with a wineglass, then filled the others and passed them around.

Erasmus raised his glass. "Here's to the Newlyweds! May they live in peace and prosperity despite the grim circumstances. So sorry we can't offer you a wedding cake or other refreshments."

Emilia waved a hand. "No need to explain. We understand all too well!" She raised her glass. Here's to Andrés, who chose a beautiful way and a meaningful moment to tell you all that he's my father." Cheers and a gabble of congratulations erupted, with audible words like "finally" and "at last."

Dámaso rapped on the table. "And here's to the members of the *Ayuntamiento*. They know how to honor Emilia, who has faithfully served them refreshments and as clerk for many years."

Glasses were raised again and refilled while lively conversations continued around the table.

The couple arranged to use the lovely Veramendi villa for their honeymoon, near the river and Misión San José, south of Béxar. The house where Jim Bowie and Ursula Veramendi had spent their honeymoon in 1831, it held a special attraction for the newlyweds, not only for that reason but also for the beauty of its setting. Graced by ancient live oaks, rose bushes still in bloom and mountain laurel surrounded it. A small stream, diverted from the nearby acequia, filled a decorative pool. The porch, shaded by confederate ivy, held a table painted white, with matching chairs.

Emilia stretched her arms wide. "Smell the air, Dámaso! It's so fresh out here. And listen to the birds! The trees are full of them."

"Yes, *Querida*, a Paradise for our love."

That night, Dámaso waited for Emilia to admit him into the master bedroom. "Are you ready, *Preciosa*?"

"*¡Sí! Pasa, Amor mío.*"

He entered and found her sitting against a bank of pillows, her long hair falling to her shoulders, her white nightgown highlighting the warm tones of her complexion. He hurried to the bed, knelt and kissed her, then crawled in beside her. He was surprised by a sudden stiffness in her responses. She began to tremble.

He drew back. "What is it, *Preciosa*?"

Emilia was silent for a moment and then spoke in a quiet, hesitant voice. "I'm frightened, *mi Amor*. That monster hurt me so badly. The pain and horror of his attack still haunts me, blinds me. I'm afraid I'm not right inside, and normal love will be agony for me. I'm afraid to confront all that again. I'm so sorry, *mi Tesoro*."

He kissed her hands. "I understand. He wounded you, body and soul. I could kill him all over again for what he did to you!" He gently embraced her, holding her close until her trembling lessened.

"How will we go on, *Querido?*" She brushed his naked body with one hand.

"What we'll do, *Preciosa*, is go slowly. We'll begin by exploring each other's bodies with our hands. You've already begun. Whatever happens after that will be gentle and loving—you needn't be afraid, *mi Alma*. Then we'll go to sleep in each other's arms."

"That sounds lovely." Her voice was uncertain, but both hands were already on him. "Such velvety skin!" Her voice sounded calmer, quieter.

They consummated their love that night, in joy and rapture, then settled down like two spoons, one behind the other, and fell asleep.

Chapter Sixteen
9-27 October

General Cos, who had learned of the defeat at Gonzales, made haste to advance to Béxar. He left twenty-seven men at La Bahía Presidio, a similar number at Lipantitlán, and a few at Goliad to guard supplies he could not carry with him. He arrived in Béxar on 9 October and spent two weeks fortifying Main and Military Plazas and the Alamo.

Messengers from Juan Seguín brought news that the Texians, after their victory in Gonzales, named Stephen F. Austin their commander and began a slow march toward Béxar, collecting more men as they went. These grew to 400, including Seguín and his company and James Bowie. After Bowie's scouts had reconnoitered the outskirts of Béxar, the Texians, on 27 October, occupied a grove of trees on the San Antonio River near the former Mission, *Nuestra Señora de la Purísima Concepción*.

Meanwhile, Dámaso reluctantly returned to the Mexican cavalry from his honeymoon idyll. On 29 October, sent by *General* Ugartechea to deliver a message to Ángel, he found the *cabildo* abandoned and the conference room deserted. In the kitchen,

Emilia drummed her fingers on a tabletop, awaiting the return of Ángel, the *Jefe Político*, who'd been summoned to a consultation with *General* Cos and *Colonel* Ugartechea. Dámaso, who had unknowingly crossed paths with Ángel, greeted Emilia with a kiss and sat opposite her at the table, near the back door in case Ángel should return that way.

Emilia spoke first. "I wish you were not out there every day in danger of being shot by our own Texian settlers! Were you in yesterday's battle? We could all hear the gunfire and the cannon. Then the soldados came streaming back like beaten dogs. What happened?"

"You probably knew that the Texian army arrived day before yesterday and camped down by the old Misión Concepción."

She nodded. "Yes, Ángel receives word of troop movements on either side."

"We were called up yesterday morning before dawn in that heavy fog. My cavalry were assigned to cut off their escape route."

"Fog! That must have been made fighting treacherous for both sides. Go on."

"We surrounded them, our infantry with artillery in front and on their flanks, cavalry behind them on the opposite bank of the river. When the fog lifted, we could see they had cleared the brush from the field of fire and had withdrawn behind the high banks of the river. My troop was where I could watch the whole battle. The Texians were amazing. I recognized James Bowie, commanding them. He had the men hide under the steep riverbank and dig niches in the earth where they could stand, take a shot across the cleared ground, then duck down again. Our troops—Cos's troops—fired the cannon twice. They were loaded with grapeshot. But all that did was tear the leaves off the pecan trees and shower the Texians with ripe pecans."

"Which they gathered?"

Dámaso chuckled. "What they could reach."

"How did it all end?"

"Cos's soldados were being mowed down and not hitting a single Anglo. The army retreated, and the Texians pursued them to the edges of Béxar, then turned back. More than fifty men killed on Cos's side, I think, and many more wounded."

"How many on the Texian side?"

"I have no idea. Maybe one or two."

"Incredible."

"They have better weapons—and in this case, better tactics. James Bowie is a remarkable man." Dámaso sat silent for a while, staring at the floor with a frown. He acutely felt split loyalties. He hated to see his friends in the Mexican army hurt or killed, yet his political beliefs, his loyalty to the constitution of 1824, allied him to the Texian side.

He balled his fists in frustration. "Damn it, Emilia, I can't stand the strain. My friends are getting killed by people whose politics I agree with. I've got to find a solution before I go crazy!"

Emilia covered his fists with her hands. "I know, *mi Amor*. But you never asked to be stuck in the Mexican army." She gently opened his fist, straightening his fingers one by one until his hand lay palm down, relaxed on the table. She repeated this with the other hand. ""We'll find a way through this, *amor mío*." She stroked his hands. "We'll just take things as they come."

For a month, there was a lull in combat with only a few minor skirmishes. The town, however, was under siege by the "Federalist Army of Texas." Meanwhile, the Mexican Army buried its dead, healed the wounded, and the remaining soldiers occupied themselves mainly in searching for food. The Bexareños had already supplied as much as could be taken without starving the population. *General* Cos finally sent Ugartechea south to Laredo to get supplies and fresh fighting men.

For ten days, the Texian siege of Béxar continued. Then, at three in the morning of 5 December, Dámaso, in the Alamo, awoke to the crackle of rifle shots and the roar of cannon fire. Béxar, the town itself, was under direct attack. He ran to the rear barracks window and could hear faint cries from people in the town. He ran back to his bunk, threw on a shirt and pants, pulled on his boots and grabbed his musket and cross-belt holding his cartridge box and bayonet sling.

Emilia! I've got to get her out of town. She could be killed any minute by a Texian's stray bullet. The ranch! I'll take her there. Need horses. Andrés and Carmen will need their two.

Chaos reigned in the dark open area in front of the barracks. Infantrymen ran in all directions, obeying shouted orders from junior officers. Dámaso simply ran for the stables. Relative quiet prevailed there, since cavalry would be of no use in street fighting. He saddled the nameless bay gelding assigned to him during the siege of Béxar, led him to the gate in the east wall, and found it undefended and unlocked. He crossed the acequia and headed south.

He led the horse for a bit, then mounted, feeling his way through *suertes*, vegetable gardens plowed and awaiting spring planting. *At least I'm not crushing people's tomatoes and squash at this time of year. I'll get on Villita Street and follow it to the ford, then cross the river and head west. It's roundabout, but I neither want to be seen nor shot.*

He had some difficulty persuading the bay to enter the cold water, but once in, the horse walked confidently to the other side. So far, they had seen no one. Most people had either left town or were lying low. He rode the bay on through Paso Street and dismounted once they reached Potrero Street. He crept to the corner and peered in all directions. The crackle of rifle fire still seemed blocks away to his left, concentrated around the plazas, so he scurried across leading the bay. Mounted again, he rode to the river bank and turned left, hoping the row of houses along Potrero would keep him from being seen or fired at. His luck held. He took a right where the river paralleled Soledad Street, and emerged behind the Altamirano house.

Lamps were glowing in the windows, and Dámaso knew that Andrés and Carmen were planning to leave for Victoria while it was still possible. He rounded the house to the kitchen and the *jacal*. Emilia was in the kitchen, packing a basket of leftover tortillas and beans, a few boiled eggs and apples for the Altamiranos to take with them. He called her from the doorway.

"Emilia! Tell them the basket is waiting for them. Then come with me immediately."

She took a sharp breath, then grinned at him. "*¡Gracias a Dios!* I was afraid you'd be out there fighting. You've got a horse. Good thinking!" She ran to the rear house door and shouted, "A basket of food is waiting in the kitchen. Come through here on the way to the stable. I'm leaving right now with Dámaso!"

They heard a muffled reply from the bedroom, then left the kitchen. "One moment. There's something I won't leave behind." Emilia darted into the *jacal* and came out at once, tying a handkerchief around two small objects. She attached the bundle to her waistband. "Now, let's go!"

Two small black silhouettes and one large, bulky one trotted through the deserted streets, returning the way Dámaso had come. They heard a boom, then a whistle, and then an adobe house fifty yards to their right seemed to explode into a plume of dust.

"The Texians are firing cannon. We'd better move east until we can get out of town." Another boom and whistle and the cannonball smashed into a house not far behind them. "*¡Dios mío!* They're shooting at *us*!" Dámaso caught a flash of white teeth and knew Emilia was making a grim joke. Rifle fire rattled again, behind and to the right.

They increased their pace to a run, the horse still keeping up at a trot. Cannon fire had ceased for a moment, and gunfire seemed concentrated southwest of the plazas. Dámaso halted the horse and boosted Emilia into the saddle. "I'll ride behind you, but I do need the stirrups. I'll hold you around the waist." He vaulted upon the bay. "If we keep this horse, we'll have to name him."

"Of course. The very thing uppermost in my mind."

"You're still making jokes!"

He took the reins in one hand and passed the other arm around her waist. "¡*Ai Diablos!* What the devil do you have tied to your waistband?"

"I'll show you when we get to the ranch. Just don't squeeze too hard. They're delicate."

They rode on in silence, listening to the sounds of battle as they faded with distance. Once on the road away from Béxar, they allowed the horse to walk while they marveled at the contrast. The countryside was at peace. The aromas of the earth, of the fallen leaves and yellowed grasses, wet from yesterday's rain, rose around them. Birds began to call in the broad-leafed oak trees overhead, and dawn was not far off. Their knotted muscles relaxed, and even the bay horse shook his head and snorted away his earlier fright and tension.

The ranch, seventeen miles from Bexar, was built beside Calaveras Creek, shaded by the tall cypress trees that marked the stream's course. When they arrived in the early afternoon, all seemed peaceful. The chickens foraged near the house, cows and horses were visible on the hill beyond the river, but there was no visible human activity. Emilia entered the house at once and found it deserted. Dámaso tended to the tired bay, cooled, brushed, and stabled him with a fork of hay. He then walked to the cabin, staggering here and there with exhaustion.

"They're not here! Where could they be?"

"We have relatives in Victoria. Perhaps they went there. Maybe we'll find a note or something. But right now we need to eat. We should have taken that basket of food you left for the Altamiranos."

"Never fear. I'll find something. I wasn't your guest here without learning where the food is." She opened a door on one side of the kitchen and entered a small storeroom hung with *carne seca,* jerky, and dried herbs "Here. Gnaw on this strip of jerky. That should keep you until I can get something hot for us."

She took down strips of carne seca and chopped them. She found flour in a bin. Then, with eggs from the hen-house and with hot chocolate, they were soon sitting at table with hot tortillas, carne scrambled with eggs, and the hot chocolate to wash it down.

"You're a miracle worker, Emilia. Now, tell me, what is in that bundle at your waist? It's still tied there."

She slowly undid the knots and gently opened the kerchief. Lying in her hands were two beautifully carved wolves. She held them up and tears came into his eyes.

"I couldn't leave them behind," she said. "They've meant so much to me over the years. The thought that anyone... *anyone* would take the time and trouble to carve such exquisite objects for me... for *me*... gave me the strength to go on after that assault, after you disappeared, even after Mamá's death. Do you see?"

"I see, but I'm amazed they mean that much to you. You say these poor little carvings of mine really helped you?"

"Dear love, they've saved me from despair at other times as well."

"Then I thank God you had my work to remember me by."

Emilia rose and hugged him, then went to the most centrally located shelf in the kitchen, cleared a space, and placed the two wolf carvings where they could be seen by everyone. She turned back to him. "I know we must discuss what you'll do next, whether rescuing me means you've deserted, and what that would mean. But we need sleep. Let's go to Pedro's room."

Dámaso smiled, allowing himself a huge yawn. "Yes, we need clear heads for planning."

Emilia rose early the next morning, but Dámaso's side of the bed was already empty, and he was not in the house. She began making *desayuno* and was sitting down to wait with a cup of coffee from the beans she'd just ground when he came striding in, holding a freshly killed rabbit.

"We'll have fresh meat for supper!" He stood a long-barreled rifle in the corner.

"Congratulations, O mighty hunter! Where did that gun come from?"

"It's papá's. It's like the guns the settlers use. Very accurate. I bagged the rabbit at fifty yards. Don't know why papá left it behind."

"I suppose the army confiscated your good rifle when they conscripted you."

"Yes, and gave me a musket. I'm so happy to have a decent gun again."

She reached for the rabbit, still clutched by its ears in his left hand. "Later, I'll scout around to see if anything edible is growing here in December. I found rice in the storeroom. We'll dine royally tonight."

Serious talk started right after breakfast. Emilia began with a question. "Do you intend to stay or go back to your regiment?"

Dámaso answered without hesitation. "All along, I'd planned to desert when the opportunity arose. The attack by the Texian army last night gave me the perfect way out. And it reunited me with you. Almost too good to be true! They'll be looking for Daniel Martínez whose physical description fits half the men in the regiment, so I don't foresee a squad coming out here to arrest me. Besides, the Texian attack will keep them plenty busy for a while. We're well out of Béxar. I just hope most of our fellow citizens can get away from the house-to-house fighting."

"I wish the Altamiranos well... and hope they're safely on their way to Victoria. But what about us? Will we simply hide out here until one side or the other wins? Which side are you really on, my love? I know you're not a Centralist, but are you a Federalist? Or just haven't decided?"

Dámaso made an exasperated noise in his throat. "Where else could I be except on your side? I'm a Federalist, of course! Look—I was a soldier in the battle of Zacatecas, on the wrong side, sad to say—and saw how merciless Santa Anna is. He thinks nothing of slaughtering troops, not just in battle but prisoners, too. He learned a lot from Arredondo, whose lieutenant he was as a young man."

Emilia went to the window. The sky was cloudless and the early afternoon sun warmed the sprouts of new grass, where the white chickens scratched for food. A paradise, she thought, except for us humans. We spoil everything. She turned back to her beloved husband. "Very well, then, what do you think we should do?"

He rose and in two strides stood beside her, looking out at the splendid morning. "First of all, I want you safe. But I must know what's happening in Béxar. Some of those cavalrymen are my friends. I need to know what's happening to them, even if I can't help. With Santa Anna's armies closing in on Béxar, doom is hanging over all of us and Béxar's the center. I feel I must ride there every other day or so to keep up with the news."

The following day, 7 December, Dámaso donned old work clothes left behind by his papá. By now he was worried about his father's and Luisa's whereabouts; it wasn't like them to walk off and leave the farm unattended. He feared something terrible might have happened to them. Still, the need to know the fate of Béxar drew him even more and he rode close to town, circling to be far enough from concentrated gunfire but close enough to make out what was going on. He questioned Tejanos living on the outskirts, who helped him piece events together.

Meanwhile, Emilia kept as busy as possible, watering and feeding the animals, mucking out the chicken coop and the cows' and horses' stalls. Having finished the chores, she walked out on the hill overlooking the creek and the ranch buildings, watching the muted colors—the brown blur of the cypress branches, naked for winter, and the dark green of live oak—the color fading toward black as the wintry sun went down behind a bank of dark grey clouds. Stormy weather, perhaps, tonight. *Oh, if only Dámaso would come home! And where are Miguel and Luisa?*

Back in the house, she cooked a full meal for more than the two of them, still hoping Dámaso and his family would arrive soon. He'd been gone since dawn. At last, well after dark, the horses in the barn whinnied and she heard an answering whinny from some distance away. Dámaso... or somebody! She waited at the door until she was sure, then fetched a lamp, holding it high to light his way to the house.

"*¡Dios mío, Querido!* I was afraid..." She set down the lamp and reached for him.

"*Todo bien, Querida, aquí estoy...* Everything's all right, Love, I'm here."

They hugged and stood in the warmth and safety of their embrace, then drew apart as they heard hoof beats—maybe two horses—coming closer. Emilia lifted the lamp high again. Once they had come close enough to be recognized, Emilia exclaimed, "Miguel and Luisa! We were so frightened! Where on earth were you?" Her words tripped over each other.

Dámaso's father dismounted and raised both hands as if in apology. "Our nearest neighbor, Raúl Osuna, came to us about a sick cow. He thinks I'm an expert with cattle. I couldn't leave Luisa here by herself, so we rode over. Didn't think we'd be gone long."

Dámaso asked, "When did you leave? We got here day before yesterday afternoon."

"That morning. We may have missed you by two or three hours."

"What kept you?"

Miguel shook his head. "Mysterious disease. First cow died after we got there, then another got sick. Buried them both, burned the hay they'd bedded down in, spread lime in the stalls, threw out the water in the trough they'd used and scoured it with lye soap. That took all this time."

"You must be exhausted. Come in. Supper's ready." Emilia lighted the way to the kitchen.

As they ate, Dámaso narrated what he'd seen that day in Béxar. "Worst of all, I think, was the death of one of the Texian generals, a man named Ben Milam. He was standing outside the Veramendi Palace when a Mexican sniper shot him."

Miguel and the two women shook their heads and murmured condolences.

"The main problem is that Cos has mounted two cannon in the San Fernando church tower. The shooters can see every movement for miles from up there."

Emilia smiled faintly. "How well I remember that view when you and I were up there as children. How clever of Cos to find the best location to defend a besieged city!"

"But the Texians found a way to frustrate even that. They dug through adobe walls from one house to another and when that proved impossible they simply darted from behind one wall to another. They fought through to Zambrano Row and forced their way into one of the houses overlooking Main Plaza. They took the Navarro House, and I think they had their eye on the priest's house, still occupied by Cos's men. If they win that, it would give them another strategic position on Main Plaza."

Miguel nodded. "Those Texians are tough."

Dámaso nodded. "And persistent. While I was there, I saw our cavalry ride out of the Alamo and head north. From the gunfire, I think they tried to destroy the Texian base camp. But they were driven back and came in with wounded men and horses." He looked down. "Some of them were friends of mine. From what I could see and was told, they'll live. Oh yes, and I heard that on the Texian side the important scout, Deaf Smith, was wounded, too."

Emilia asked, "Badly?"

"I have no way of knowing. But if they lose him, they lose one of their best and most experienced scouts."

Two days later, again over supper, Dámaso began with a seemingly grim announcement. "You won't believe it, but yesterday Ugartechea returned to Béxar with reinforcements."

Emilia sat open-mouthed. "Oh, no! Did he drive the Texians out of Béxar?"

"No. The Texian commander at the base camp, Burleson, sent a hundred fighters to join the battle, house to house. They mounted two cannon near Main Plaza and blasted the church tower. That ended sniper and cannon fire from up there. And then, you won't believe this either, all of Cos's fighters in the city retreated to the Alamo. Shortly afterward, the entire cavalry, all my former comrades, rode out of town, abandoned the fight, and deserted the army altogether. My count says that's around a hundred eighty-five men and horses. The Texians are in possession of Béxar!"

"So Ugartechea didn't help after all?"

"No. Those reinforcements were raw recruits, most of them. They didn't know how to fight. But that's not all. After the withdrawal, Cos was bottled up in the Alamo with over a thousand troops and all the camp followers to boot. They must have nearly smothered. Anyway, this morning, they displayed the white flag of surrender."

Miguel wagged his head with a grin. "They must have been damned hungry, too. And with no cavalry support, they had no safe line of retreat."

"Right." Dámaso took a last spoonful of flan and wiped his lips. "There will have to be an unconditional surrender. At least, with a mass defection by the cavalry, I won't have to worry about being hunted by anyone now. Too many of us to punish."

Two days later, on 11 December, Dámaso brought back joyous tidings. Cos had signed the surrender agreement, pledging to withdraw his troops across the Rio Grande and to support the Constitution of 1824.

Emilia raised her eyebrows. "Hah! How long do you expect him to keep that pledge? Isn't he Santa Anna's best friend or something? If he seriously became a Federalist, he'd be shot."

Dámaso nodded. "Probably true. By the way, I saw a number of families moving back into town. You and I should do the same—we're just too far away out here. The travel is too time consuming."

"Good idea. If the *jacal* hasn't been blown to bits, we can use it, at least for the time being."

They prepared to return the next day. Emilia would ride a *mesteño*, tamed by Dámaso's brother Pedro, and Dámaso the bay gelding who had saved them on the night the Battle of Béxar had begun. As he cleaned the horse's hooves that morning, Dámaso noticed the start of a crack in his left front hoof. "I'll bet he did that stumbling into a boulder when we forded the San Antonio River that night. Lucky we didn't get hit by a cannonball from that *falcón*, the small cannon the Texians were firing."

Emilia nodded. "Falcón! That's a good name for the horse. After all, he's a war-horse."

"Good idea. Hmmm. I wonder what's happened to *Teniente* Castañeda and his horse Audaz. That hoof must be healed by now. Castañeda may have ridden him out of Béxar with the rest of the cavalry. Guess I'll never know."

They rode toward Béxar at a leisurely pace, enjoying the warmth of an unusually bright day for mid-December, stopped under an evergreen oak where a fallen log made a convenient seat and ate the lunch Emilia had prepared.

Emilia sighed. "It's blessed moments of unexpected peace like this we'll remember for the rest of our lives."

Chapter Seventeen

December 1835–March 1836

Béxar was already a hive of activity, with Tejanos busy repairing their battle-damaged homes. The Texians had taken over the Alamo and were fortifying it, placing captured cannon in all imaginable defensive positions, including three raised above the front wall of the Alamo church. They shored up the walls where there were weak areas. Dámaso joined a crew repairing the San Fernando church tower, a badly needed vantage point for spying out any unusual movement—especially approaching troops—from any direction.

Three prominent members of the *Ayuntamiento* welcomed Emilia when she visited the *cabildo*. José Ángel Navarro was about to finish his term as *alcalde* and *jefe político*, and Nicolás Flores was preparing to replace him. Juan Seguín, who'd been *alcalde* in 1834, sat with the other two, all three with chins in hands, when Emilia entered the council chamber. The three men leapt to their feet to greet her.

"Emilia!" they chorused. Ángel continued, "No one had seen you for days. We feared the worst. Thank God you weren't injured or killed during the fighting!"

Emilia smiled and pointed at the chairs. "Please sit, gentlemen. Dámaso Jiménez, my husband, took me to his family ranch. We stayed there until Cos surrendered and marched out of here."

Juan Seguín gave her a sharp look. "A few people, like me, know that Dámaso wears the enemy uniform. They also said they'd heard him called by a different name."

"Yes, he was conscripted into the Mexican army shortly after he escaped three years ago. You just missed him when your search party arrived at the Fuentes y Culebra Ranch west of Monclova. He'd given his name to the foreman as Daniel Martínez."

Seguín slapped the table. "Damn! I had a feeling the foreman was hiding something when I questioned him about Dámaso. So what happened in the army?"

"When the army took him, he kept the false name. All along, he planned to desert when the opportunity arose. He served for three years, got the opportunity to come up here to reinforce Ugartechea, and found the moment to defect when the Texians began bombarding the city."

Nicolás Flores nodded. "Well, we welcome you back, Emilia. Sad to say, there's no sugar and damned little flour in the city to make pasteles. If we all get together, we'll let you know and you can at least make us hot chocolate."

"Chocolate is most likely gone as well, Señor," she replied.

The Christmas celebrations and the midnight mass were particularly lively and hopeful, although the Bexareños were woefully short of food and other goods. The Mexican troops as well as volunteers gone to help the Texians had beggared the city. Emilia knelt on the left side of the nave, admiring the blaze of candles on and around the altar, illuminating the crèche with a youthful Virgin Mary draped in a blue cloak, kneeling beside the manger where a cherubic baby Jesus lay, abundant brown curls making him look at least a year old. *I wonder when I'll start having babies... if I even can.*

Her thoughts were interrupted by Padre Refugio's homily. He thanked God and the Texian army for liberating Béxar of the horde of troops. He asked God to move *General* Cos's heart to honor his pledge to respect the Constitution of 1824. Emilia looked around the nave. She saw perhaps four Texians among the congregation. *These Texians are not loyal to any of the pledges they made on coming here, to respect and honor what we stand for—language, traditions and religion. I fear for our future once they take over. And they're about to do just that. They have the power, thanks to their sheer numbers.*

January came, and spies kept Béxar and the Texian army informed of Mexican army movements south of the Río Grande. In late January, Santa Anna conducted a Grand Review of six thousand troops he had gathered in Saltillo. They began their march northward to the Rio Grande.

Juan Seguín sent his cousin, Blas Herrera, to keep an eye on Santa Anna's movements. When his army crossed the Rio Grande on 18 February, Blas raced back to Béxar and reported to his cousin. Seguín then went to the Alamo, asking to speak to the commanders of the Texian army. William Travis and James Bowie granted him a joint audience.

"I have fresh news that Santa Anna's army has crossed the Rio Grande and is on its way here. They will arrive in a few days, Señores."

Travis, known to consider all Spanish speakers potential traitors, sneered. "Impossible. This sounds like a rumor intended to waste our efforts on premature preparations."

Bowie had known Seguín for years and trusted him implicitly. "*Mil gracias, Juan.* We'll begin preparations immediately." He glared at Travis.

Seguín shook Bowie's hand, gave a curt nod to Travis, turned on his heel and walked out. As he left, he heard the two men arguing, Bowie berating Travis for discourtesy and prejudice, Travis cursing Bowie for being a credulous fool.

The news of Santa Anna's approach spread in Béxar, from Seguín himself, from his cousin Blas, and from other Tejano scouts who had returned from the Rio Grande. Many citizens, especially those with a family, packed up to take refuge in an outlying rancho, or, if they had no such property, on a friend's or relative's ranch. A few got away only after Santa Anna's army was within sight or even entering the town itself. Carts laden with household goods clogged all the roads out of Béxar.

Dámaso had to decide what to do. "I'll go find Juan Seguín's militia. They're somewhere south of town right now. I'm pretty sure they'll soon join the Texians in the Alamo; meanwhile I can be of help to them. But I won't go if you'll be in danger."

"I'll keep out of sight. You're needed where your skills will be of most help. I'll stay in the *jacal* until they come to occupy it—if ever. There may be things I can do to help the people inside the Alamo. Don't worry; I know how to take care of myself."

At the Alamo, preparations for battle began, although slowly, until Texian scouts confirmed Seguin's message. Santa Anna entered Béxar on the afternoon of Tuesday, 23 February. He hoisted the *degüello*, the blood-red flag signifying "no quarter," atop the belfry of San Fernando church and made the Yturri House on the northwest corner of Main Plaza his headquarters. The siege began with an exchange of cannon fire and attempts by Bowie and Travis to talk terms with Santa Anna's adjutant, Juan Nepomuceno Almonte, known to be more diplomatic than his superior. The attempt to parley failed with the dictator's response by letter delivered by Santa Anna's aide-de-camp, *Colonel* Batres, that unless there be an unconditional surrender, there would indeed be no quarter.

~☙~

Emilia busied herself finding supplies for the women and children now marooned in the Alamo. If there was no active fighting, she thought she, a woman, might be able to deliver food and medicine—and news of the outside—to the people behind barricades. Mexican soldiers had not yet moved into the Altamirano house, so food was still available in the kitchen. She milked a neighbor's cow, since their own had gone dry, cut a large chunk of a chorizo sausage the Altamiranos had left behind in their flight to Victoria, dug potatoes and onions. She decanted the milk into a leathern flask and made tortillas, wrapping them in a clean cotton rag. She filled a small bag with beans, another with rice, adding salt and chiles. These riches she packed into a large wicker basket with a bail and lugged it to the entrance to the Alamo.

The main gate to the compound had been impressively fortified during *General* Cos's occupation by a semi-circular stone redoubt, its wall eight feet high and extending about fifteen feet south of the original gate. It had two small doors on the east and west sides. These could easily be blocked and defended from within. Emilia approached the imposing structure from the east side.

A Mexican sniper guarded the gate against any entrance or escape. Since Emilia took a direct approach, he stepped out of hiding. "*¡Alto o tiro!* Halt or I'll shoot!"

Emilia greeted him like a neighbor. "*Buenos días Señor. Traigo comida para las mujeres y los niños.* I'm bringing food for the women and children."

He scowled at her. "*Muéstrame*. Show me."

She set down the basket between them and lifted off the white dishtowel cover. "You see? Rice and beans and potatoes and sausage... and milk for the baby."

He squatted and ran his fingers among the food items, lifting a few out to look at them, then replacing them.

She asked him, "Where are you from?"

"Toluca."

"Do you have a family?"

He raised his eyes to stare out over the town. "Yes... a wife and three children, two boys and a girl. We lost the fourth child a few days after birth...." His voice trailed off and she could feel his grief.

She placed her hand lightly on his upper arm and drew it back. "I'm so sorry. I know how much that must hurt. I'm sure you'd like to be with them right now."

He looked down, his face puckering momentarily. "Yes, I truly miss them." He paused for a minute or two, still looking at the ground. "I'll let you go in. But don't take too long."

Emilia made four such trips, until all food was gone. On each trip she paused to speak with the guard. Besides bringing what food she could scrounge, she sometimes included medicine, but never anything suspicious. He trusted her, and under other circumstances, she would have liked him. But now, he could at least be a convenience. An assured and easy entry into the Alamo might come in handy, soon.

Emilia returned home by way of Main Plaza, noting that Béxar seemed almost a ghost town. Soldiers were everywhere else, leaving Main Plaza to the few citizens still in town. The usual crowd of birds had migrated to Military Plaza, where the cavalry mustered and droppings were abundant. No civilian dared to ride a horse in town these days for fear of having it shot or requisitioned. But to her surprise, Conchita Alvárez walked in her direction, one of the few young women who had stayed. Without taking time for polite greetings, she ran to Emilia, placing both hands on her shoulders. Her expression hinted that her news was not deadly serious. "Emilia! You'll never believe this!"

Eager to hear of something other than casualties and persecution, Emilia asked, "What? What?"

"*General* Santa Anna is marrying a girl from La Villita!"

"You can't be serious."

"Yes. One of the battalions was looking for ready-cut timbers, to build another bridge, or maybe for a battering ram. *General* Castrillón and *Colonel* Miñón were with the soldiers. They were tearing down vacant *jacal*es in La Villita when they came into one that was occupied. It belonged to the widow Oliveira and her daughter Dolores."

"You mean Captain Ramón Oliveira's widow and that beautiful daughter of theirs?"

"The same. Castrillón and Miñón asked why they were still in La Villita when the area was often under fire and therefore dangerous. Widow Oliveira told them she was not afraid, and anyway they had no place else to go. When Castrillón reported the matter to his general, Santa Anna ordered him to bring the girl to him—he was eager to see her, and if she was truly beautiful, he would ravish her."

Emilia's voice filled with loathing. "The nasty old goat!"

Conchita nodded. "Exactly. Others thought the same. *General* Castrillón bowed out of the whole thing, saying he wouldn't have anything to do with such disgusting behavior, but *Colonel* Miñón had no such scruples. He returned to the widow with the general's orders.

"Señora Oliveira defied him. She replied that Santa Anna was not her president, she was not afraid of him, and under no conditions would she release her daughter except for a legitimate proposal of marriage. She and her family had always been honorable, and she was in straitened circumstances due only to her husband's untimely death."

Emilia applauded. "Good for the widow. But obviously, there's more to this story."

"Yes. The *colonel* returned later with the General's proposal of marriage."

"Incredible! I've heard Santa Anna's already married and has several children."

"He is. But just wait. Miñón told the general he had a man in his outfit who knew enough to impersonate a priest—convincingly. They borrowed vestments from Father Refugio—under threat, I suppose—and held a false marriage. The impostor carried it off well enough to convince Señora Oliveira—and Dolores."

"I see. So poor Dolores is now snuggling in the arms of the Devil himself. There's no end to Santa Anna's evil, is there?"

News filtered to Emilia day after day, while the siege continued with minor clashes at irregular intervals. On 27 February, she heard that the acequia that supplied the Alamo had been cut about a mile upstream. She hoped the well they had dug would supply enough for their needs. Any food left in the town had already been devoured, although some, like her, had hidden enough to keep themselves alive. She watched cavalry escorting wagons headed for the Seguín and Francisco Flores ranches to confiscate corn, hogs and beef for the starving Mexican army. For her, this revealed another flaw in the general's planning, competence and character. *Apparently, Santa Anna didn't bring adequate supplies to feed his army. He's a disaster as a commander, only thinks of himself.*

She longed for news from Dámaso, but heard nothing. She prayed fervently and often that he remain safe and could soon come back to her.

Rumors abounded, for instance, on 28 February, she overheard that two hundred reinforcements for the Texians were on their way from Gonzales, and noticed with satisfaction that despite their overwhelming numbers, reports of reinforcements kept the Mexican forces on edge.

Emilia walked the floor at night, worrying over Dámaso. On 2 March, during her visit to the Alamo, she learned that on the previous night, thirty-two Texians, led by John Smith, had arrived to reinforce the little garrison. Meanwhile, more Mexican wagons left Béxar to take more corn from the Seguín and Flores ranches.

During that visit to the fort, an Anglo-American woman, Susanna Dickinson, had accosted her. Her attitude seemed combative, as if she were telling Emilia an unpleasant truth. "You must surely be aware that our commander, *Colonel* Travis, doesn't trust any of your people."

Emilia took a step backwards. "Why ever not?"

"He has good reason. A group of your Tejano fighters left the Alamo. They might even have gone over to the enemy. *Colonel* Travis cursed them and called them traitors."

"Ah. I know why they left. They went with permission, perhaps from *Colonel* Bowie. As part of Juan Seguín's militia, they're rounding up reinforcements for the defenders."

"I believe what the *colonel* told me, that they are deserters, and there are only three Tejanos left in the Alamo. He believes all other Tejanos, townsfolk like you included, are public enemies."

"Susanna, I'm really sorry to hear this. It's slander. It depresses me that the commander misunderstands and mistrusts my people so thoroughly. I hope there will be time and opportunity to change his mind."

Emilia moved away. *So many Texians think of us that way. If they understood more Spanish, they would know how wrong they are.*

That night, Emilia heard something scratching against the doorpost of the *jacal*. She had blown out the lamp hours earlier, but had been unable to sleep for worry over Dámaso. Frightened, she rose and approached the door on silent feet. Through the crack between the cowhide door-flap and the doorpost, she could tell that a man—a Tejano from his clothing—stood there.

"*¿Quién es?* Who is it?"

"*¿Señora Emilia?*"

"*Sí, soy yo.*"

"Dámaso sent me. He's been south of here on scout duty, tracking *General* Gaona's troop movements, but he'll be coming in later tonight or tomorrow night. He wanted you to know as soon as possible."

"*¡Gracias a Dios!* He shows us mercy, after all!"

The man faded into the darkness without telling her his name.

Emilia lit the lamp and waited until the blackness turned to gray in the east. Quiet steps sounded outside, then the door-flap moved aside and the lovers flew into each other's arms. They stood pressed together, kissing and murmuring endearments. At length, Emilia caught her breath enough to say, "We have six eggs and a potato from the garden. We'll have breakfast and you can tell me where you've been and then get some sleep. Right now, I'm the happiest woman alive."

Santa Anna held a council of war. The choice lay between immediate attack, beginning at midnight the following day or to wait until the seventh, when *General* Gaona with seven- hundred more men and two twelve-pound cannon were due to arrive and would surely open a breach in the already crumbling Alamo walls. Opinion was split: reason counseled the latter, but the general was eager, not reasonable. Many of his officers were aghast, but their entreaties were rejected. Santa Anna burned with fury over his good friend Cos's humiliation and he already had nearly three-thousand troops he could immediately deploy. That was enough. He wanted revenge. He wanted it in blood. He remembered Arredondo.

In the Altamirano *jacal* the next day, Emilia and Dámaso sat at the table, holding hands across the top. Dámaso gave Emilia's hands a squeeze. "I've decided what I must do. I'm joining the Texians in the Alamo."

Emilia gasped and gripped his hands hard. "Why? Just tell me why!"

"I'm a Federalist. I've always wanted my own independence, and I want Texas's independence under the Constitution of 1824. Santa Anna has robbed all of Mexico and turned independent states into servile departments. I won't tolerate that. I'm a patriot, a loyal citizen of the Mexico we had before that bastard rose to power. I'll fight to restore that."

Emilia's voice shook. "But, *Precioso*, that's not why those Texians are fighting! They want Texas for themselves. They're fighting for complete independence—severance from Mexico entirely."

Dámaso's tone was firm, decisive. "I know that and I don't agree with them, but I feel enough kinship that I'll join them in this fight. Anything to get rid of Santa Anna." He stood and picked up his father's long-barreled rifle.

"Wait, *mi Amor*, just wait a moment. There may be two hundred men up there in the Alamo, but Santa Anna has thousands, and he has decreed "no quarter." You don't stand a chance. You are throwing away your life and our future. Will anyone remember your sacrifice?"

"Surely General Fannin will arrive from Goliad with reinforcements. Any victory Santa Anna might win will cost him dearly, with or without Fannin's troops. If we can delay Santa Anna's march on East Texas, we can save hundreds, maybe thousands of our people. They'll have time to get away. I can fight for that, even die for that." Dámaso's jaw was locked, his face set, eyes flashing. "I'm going up there now."

Emilia knew there was no arguing with such resolve. "Then I'm coming with you. There are already wives and children behind those gates. If you're going to sacrifice your life, I want to die with you."

"My darling, I want you to live!" He laid the rifle on the table and embraced her. "We defenders still might survive the battle, but if not, someone must live to tell the story."

"There are some who will tell it, never fear. But you and I are one. Our wedding vows say so, and it's true. I must be with you to the end, however it comes."

He held her at arm's length and looked long and deep into her eyes. "You truly mean this. *Bueno*: it gives me great joy to have you with me—and courage, too, body to body, soul to soul." He picked up the rifle again. "Then let's go, my love, as one."

They avoided the plazas, where they could hear shouted orders and the tramp of many feet, the rattle of arms. "They're organizing for the assault," Dámaso said over his shoulder.

"God have mercy on us," Emilia replied.

They dodged a few soldiers as they approached the Alamo, but when they arrived before the gate fortification, they found no Mexican guard. This absence struck them as a sinister sign. Dámaso knocked on the eastern door with the butt of the rifle, thinking correctly that it would make enough noise to be heard. The door opened a crack. "Who goes there?"

Dámaso knew enough English to reply, "A volunteer."

The gate creaked open wider. "Good. We're undermanned. Come in."

A tall, wiry soldier with an unkempt, grizzled beard and in worn civilian clothes sized them up. "Hello, little missy. Funny how you Messkins bring your women in here. Just more mouths to feed."

Emilia used her small stock of English words. She pointed to herself. "Nurse. You need me."

He stood back, allowing them to pass into the large Alamo compound. "Report to *Colonel* Travis. He'll tell you where to go."

Dámaso looked puzzled, but Emilia understood. "Where *Colonel* Travis?"

He pointed to the left wall and to a barrack halfway down and held up two fingers. "Second door."

They moved in that direction, while the gatekeeper bolted the gate. A sentry stopped them before they could reach the second barracks door. "Who are you and what do you want?" He spoke Spanish.

"I'm a volunteer. I understand that you're undermanned. You need me. This woman is a nurse."

"Very well. Report to *Colonel* Travis." He pointed to the door.

Dámaso knocked, then entered. They stood before a small desk, where the lieutenant *colonel* was writing something, probably a letter. He looked up, eyebrows lifted, lips pulled down at the corners. "Yes? What is it?

Dámaso stood at attention and saluted smartly, Emilia at his shoulder, a step behind him. "Sergeant Dámaso Jiménez reporting for duty, Sir."

Travis had a wild look in his eye. Emilia thought he must be considering that one hundred eighty-odd men inside the old mission-fort had no chance. His tone conveyed the impatience of a man whose train of thought had been broken. "What do you want?" So far, he had spoken English, Dámaso Spanish.

Dámaso, apparently sensing that Travis might have a problem understanding, spoke slowly. "I was a sergeant in Santa Anna's army, but a Federalist. I want to fight with you to restore the United States of Mexico Constitution of 1824."

"So you're a turncoat." Travis' lip curled.

"I was a conscript, seized against my will. I waited for a moment to get away. I'm now here, offering my life to fight for a cause allied with mine."

Travis paused before answering. "What did you say was your rank?"

"Sergeant of the cavalry, Sir."

"Your marksmanship?"

"Excellent, Sir."

"Then you'll be rifleman from the emplacement in the northwest corner." He turned to Emilia. "You. Why are you here?"

"I am a nurse, Sir. I know how to stop bleeding, bind wounds, set bones."

"Then go find the women and children. When the battle begins, use your skills wherever you see they're needed. Now, dismissed. Go! Dismissed!" He waved his hands with increasing emphasis as if shooing chickens, eager to return to his letter.

From the ground, Dámaso could see he would share that corner of the wall with two eight-pound cannon and the attendant crew. One cannon aimed northwest, the other at a forty-five degree angle from it. "I see where I'll be. Probably in the thick of the assault. Let's look around while there's still time." Glancing in all directions, he began to see men he knew. "Over there, mounting the stairs to the southwest cannon. It's Toribio Losoya. And there's Andrés Nava standing next to the cannon."

"Of course. I'd recognize him anywhere. He was a *regidor* from time to time and one of our playmates in the old days."

Dámaso pointed toward the inner wall of the compound. "And there's Juan Abamillo over there ordering people about. He must have earned the rank of sergeant."

"There may be many more of us Tejanos here to keep you company, my love. That makes me feel better. Over there! It's José Gregorio Esparza. Looks like he may be manning one of the cannon, too."

"Yes, I see him. I do know that Juan Seguín left with his fifteen men to round up reinforcements. I'll scout around to see if there are any other Tejanos in here. You go on in. I'll meet you in a little while at the convent yard gate."

She patted him on the arm and entered the convent yard, passed the small, two-story hospital building, and entered the church by its side door. It was roofless, but had three cannon on a dirt ramp at the main entrance to the church, protecting the east side of the fort. In a side room, probably once intended to be the sacristy, she found the small crowd of women and children. Screams erupted, and two of the women rushed forward.

"Emilia! It's so good to see you! Why are you here? The main attack could start any minute!" The embrace was smothering.

"Juana!" Emilia was surprised by the warmth.

Juana Navarro Veramendi, her old nemesis, deigned to speak with her for the first time since the siege began. Now married to a Texian, Doctor Horace Alexander Alsbury, she carried a baby in her arms. "This is Alejo, named for my first husband. Horace just couldn't risk leaving us out there with all those Mexican soldiers."

"I see. But it must be—"

Emilia's reply was interrupted by Juana's younger sister, Gertrudis Navarro Veramendi, whose embrace was somewhat cooler. "Hello, Emilia. I'm sorry you've been caught in the middle of this mess. I'm here to nurse my brother-in-law, James Bowie."

"Gertrudis, if you need any help, please call on me. I've had some nursing experience and will probably stay the night somewhere nearby."

The reply sounded formal. "Thank you, Emilia, I certainly will if I need you."

A group of women stood a little apart. Emilia turned to see who they were, and recognized them as Toribio Losoya's mother Concepción, who ducked shyly behind Ana Salazar Castro Esparza, Gregorio Esparza's wife. Hiding behind her or in her skirts were three sons, Enrique, Francisco and Manuel, while elder daughter María Castro stood close by but not too close. Emilia embraced each one. Aloof from the others, Susanna Dickinson stood with her baby girl, Angelina.

Emilia approached to speak with her. "You always keep to yourself, Señora, and now more than ever you seem to feel very much alone. Why don't you join the others?"

The woman tried to strike a commanding pose, but failed. Her trembling betrayed her. She spoke a passable Spanish. "I-I just can't imagine how we are going to survive this situation. I fear the worst."

Emilia tipped her head to one side with a faint smile. "And so do I, Señora." She continued to make the most of her slight training in nursing. "I am a nurse, and if you need me, please call on me. I'll be here all night."

Mrs. Dickinson laid a hand on Emilia's arm. "Why, thank you, Ma'am. I'll remember that and call upon you if I need to."

As Emilia moved to leave the stuffy little room, a tight group of five women with a child joined her. One of them introduced herself in a breathless voice. "Excuse me. I heard you're a nurse. Maybe you can escort us to the gate. I'm Juana Milton, Toribio's sister, and here with me are Petra Gonzales, Mrs. Cadbury and her sister Victoriana Salinas and her little girl, and this is Trinidad Saucedo. We've decided we'd be safer in than up here when the bombardment begins. I hope we're not imposing too much...?"

Emilia from the beginning had felt cold terror lurking in the pit of her stomach, as if the Angel of Death hovered over her but was biding his time. Outwardly, she remained calm. "Of course I'll guide you to the gate. I agree, you'll be far safer away from direct cannon and gunfire. From what we saw on our way up here, we suspect that *General* Santa Anna will begin his attack very soon, probably at first daylight, so be sure to be as far from here as possible when that begins."

She led them to the gate, and accosted the tall, wiry guard. "These ladies are noncombatants. They wish to spend the night elsewhere. Please allow them to leave."

Although she spoke in Spanish, he understood. "You bet, Ma'am, I'll let 'em out. Less mouths to feed." He opened the door to the east of the gate fortification, and the ladies hurried out, only Juana Milton remembering to thank her.

Emilia turned her back to the entrance and looked for Dámaso. He was not at the door into the convent yard, but she walked over and waited. She could see the cannon atop the north corner emplacement, but no one was there. She'd be patient, although her anxiety and that cold terror deep inside forced her to move continuously, walking in a tight circle, clasping and unclasping her hands.

He appeared at last, surprising her when she'd almost given him up. "I saw some other Tejanos. Juan Badillo from Nacogdoches and Antonio Fuentes. They said Guadalupe Rodríguez and Carlos Espalier are here, too, but I didn't see them. So I'm not the only damn fool to think it's worth putting our lives on the line to delay Santa Anna and try for Texan independence."

She wrapped her arm around his waist. "Let's go find a quiet place to sleep or at least to be by ourselves for a while. It may be our last chance."

She'd seen a haystack in one of the rooms in the chapel. She led him there, and they nested in a corner, her skirts providing them some protection from the prickles. They lay in each other's arms and gently kissed. She whispered, "No matter what happens, I will love you forever."

He stroked her hair. "No matter what happens, I'll be with you your whole life long."

Chapter Eighteen
Battle

*S*hortly before five the next morning, someone outside the fort, very close to the walls, shouted "*¡Viva Santa Anna!*"

The planned surprise attack spoiled, a bugler sounded the call for the assault. Other bugles took up the call, on all sides of the Alamo.

Dámaso leapt to his feet, shaking off fragments of hay. Emilia clung to him, too electrified to kiss him, only pressing her body against him. "We two are as one," she whispered in his ear, "and will ever be so."

"Amen," he told her, "but I must go." She loosened her encircling arms and for a second saw his silhouette, black in the arched entrance against the faint light of predawn. Then nothing.

Seconds ticked by as she stood still, listening. From outside the walls came cries of "*¡Viva la República!*" and "*¡Viva Santa Anna!*" and from within, the shouts of Captain John Baugh, the duty officer, crying "The Mexicans are coming!"

Now the rooms and open spaces around her became hives of frantic activity. The hundred-eighty men inside the old mission rushed to the battlements to defend the Alamo until death.

A rocket fired somewhere outside the walls gave everything a momentary ghastly red glare, then came the thunder of running feet. She entered the courtyard, confused, not knowing what to do. A tall figure brushed past her, then turned and grabbed her arm.

"What the hell're you doing out here, woman?"

She didn't understand his words, but recognized the man who had opened the main gate for her and Dámaso and for the women only yesterday. She stuttered, uncertain what to say. "I...I—

"You said you were a nurse." He began half guiding, half dragging her toward a building next to the front gate. "Then get inside and help the doc. There's sick men and men wounded in the siege in there."

He jerked open the door to a room, its stone walls enclosing an area about twenty feet by eighteen. Shoving her into semi-darkness, he slammed the door behind her. She heard his bootfalls fading as he ran. A single lamp glowed several feet from her, and in its wavering light a bearded man in a bloody apron leaned over a bed, working frantically, it seemed, to save a life. She moved toward him and could now see five army cots crammed into this small space, each holding a sick or wounded Texian. The bearded man called to her in a hoarse voice. "Come here! Give him more whisky. He keeps jerking out of my hands." He nodded toward a bottle standing on an upended crate. She understood enough to know he needed help and what the bottle contained. She took it up at once and prepared to dose the patient. "*Contra el dolor*," she told the wounded man.

He opened his eyes and mouth at the same time. He nodded, whispering, "*Contra*... against. *dolor*... pain." Then aloud, "Yes. Please."

The doctor, a Texian, raised a bloody left hand, thumb and finger parted by two inches. "*Poquito*," he rasped.

She dribbled a swallow onto the patient's tongue, and when he gulped, another swallow. Then he let his head fall back.

The doctor issued an order. "Hold the lamp closer."

She raised the lamp and held it near the patient's side. She could now see that the doctor had been trying to clamp a severed blood vessel, an artery, it seemed. As he changed his hand position, the vessel slipped out of his grasp, spraying them both with blood. He grabbed it again. "Set that lamp down. Pinch just below my hand. Stop the bleeding."

She quickly obeyed, pinching the artery with all her strength, her fingers becoming slippery like the doctor's. He made a loop of silken thread, dropped it over the end of the vessel and drew it tight, making a knot. Releasing the vessel, he waited to see if there was leakage. There was. He added another silken tie, then, satisfied, began to close the wound. She wiped her hands on her dress, covering the bodice with blood.

He stared at her. "Who are you, and why are you here?"

She shook her head. "*¿Habla Usted Español?*"

"*Sí. Un poco.*" He continued in Spanish. "*¿Quién eres?* Just who are you?"

Emilia explained. "I had experience during the cholera epidemic. I'm here to help."

"Good. There's a barrel of water in the corner. Bandages and clean cloths and tin pans are on the shelf beside it. Check the bandages on each wounded man and check on the sick ones. If the bandages need changing, do that. There's another bottle of whisky on the shelf. Wash their wounds with that, especially if you smell putrefaction. I'm trying to stop gangrene. Most of the wounded have been here a while. This fellow was slashed in a knife fight." He jerked his chin toward the man lying before them. "Stupid waste of an able-bodied fighter!"

His last words were lost in a roar of gunfire, the booms of cannon. They froze, listening to the onset of battle. Emilia heard the screams of the Mexican soldados as they ran to scale the Alamo's walls. Unearthly screams, like hunting panthers, either dying or attacking. She shuddered, then remembered where she was and what she needed to do. She approached the first cot, occupied by a scraggly-bearded man, pale, gaunt, seeming on the point of death.

His bandages, on his left leg and around his chest at the level of his navel, were pink with bloody lymph and yellow with pus, especially from the leg.

She turned to the shelf the doctor had pointed out. As she moved away, a bullet penetrated the wooden shutter over the south-facing window at the head of the patient's bed and smacked against the opposite wall. It would have struck her had she remained standing at the foot of the cot. She kept moving, filled a pan with water, took a cloth and carried that and the whisky bottle back to the patient. The chest wound was superficial; the bullet had merely scored the lateral muscle but had not penetrated the ribs, and was beginning to form a scab around the edges. She sponged the wound, then pressed a pad soaked in whisky to it for a few moments and replaced the bandage. The leg wound was another matter. As she loosened the bandage, she could smell putrefaction. She dropped the soiled dressing on the floor and examined the wound.

The patient groaned and pressed his head into the pillow.

The doctor also smelled rotting flesh and came to her side. "We need blowflies in here. The maggots could have prevented this—and might've saved this man's life."

"Ugh! How do you know that?"

"I saw it in the War of 1812. I'm Dr. Bill Howell. At least one other doctor, Amos Pollard, is in the old convent building. Maybe John Reynolds made it up there, too—I don't know. There're more sick and wounded up there on the second floor. I'm doing the best I can here."

Emilia repeated what she'd done for the chest wound, but saw telltale red streaks running up the leg from the wound. "How can we stop that?" She pointed at the redness.

"Under other circumstances, I'd amputate the leg. We just don't have the time. Wash it with more whisky and go on to the next patient."

They had to put their heads close together and almost shout their words to one another. Whenever the twelve-pound cannon mounted on the apse of the church fired, both jumped and grimaced. She began to distinguish the rattle of musket and rifle fire from the main gate and the cannon emplacement on the southwest corner next to them from the more distant noise from the north wall. That was where Dámaso was fighting. She felt reassured when she heard the almost simultaneous reports of two cannon from the north side. She couldn't be sure whether they were from the northwest corner or the center, but at least they were still in friendly hands.

She noticed a door at the west side of the room and nodded in that direction. "What's in there?"

The doctor looked up from replacing stitches that had torn loose from a deep wound. "That's *Colonel* Bowie's room. Señorita Gertrudis was nursing him overnight. I can't say if anyone's with him now. Perhaps not. He's desperately ill. Won't make it 'til dark, I think."

"Should I go in there?"

"No, I wouldn't. No one knows what he's got. It might be highly contagious."

The roar of the twelve-pounder cut their words short, while they continued cleaning wounds and giving whisky to those in acute pain. Cannonballs shot by the Mexican army fell in the main plaza, sometimes scattering shrapnel that impacted their building and its heavy wooden door with various thuds and crashes, while small arms fire continued, now in a fury of simultaneous reports, now with a series of single shots. To Emilia, it seemed that an hour had passed, when the noise from outside changed.

It came from the north wall. *¡Viva el Presidente! ¡Viva el General Santa Anna!* A confusion of shouts, orders from Mexican officers, cries from *soldados* mingled with shouts of the defenders in an English she could only occasionally understand. Running feet. Rifle and musket shots, pistol reports and the clang of sabers filled the main plaza space outside. Louder noise came closer, ever closer, with screams of wounded men, groans of the dying. Someone pawed at the door and begged to get in, then cried out in agony. Along with a continuous barrage of rifle and musket fire, the loudest noise of hand-to-hand combat moved away to their right, into the church courtyard and then perhaps into the convent buildings and the church itself. And then noise increased again before the door.

Rifle butts slammed into the wood, and after repeated attempts the frame splintered and buckled. Emilia backed against the wall to the side of the door as soldados rushed in, bayonets fixed. Three of the wounded leveled their pistols and fired at them, felling the men they shot at. They were swiftly run through with bayonets or slashed with sabers, not once but several times. The doctor was first shot, then bayonetted. Emilia screamed, drawing attention to herself. A soldado grabbed her collar and slammed her against the wall, bruising the back of her head. Her attention was instead fixed on the long knife between her attacker's teeth. As he grasped the handle, another soldado threw an arm around his neck and pulled him away.

"¡El Jefe nos dijo no matar a mujeres y niños! The chief said not to kill women and children!"

With unnatural clarity, Emilia watched every move the soldados made. They kicked in the door in the west wall, and immediately two shots in quick succession came from within. Two men fell, one dead, one wounded. But others rushed the room and, howling, bayonetted the man on the cot. She could hear them shouting and stabbing with their bayonets, not able to see the scene, but imagining it. She became nauseated, increasingly dizzy, knowing she was the only living soul left among the defenders in the room. Dámaso! Where was he? He had to be dead; the soldados had made their first entry over his wall. The thought took her last vestige of strength. She crumpled unconscious to the floor.

At the northwest corner of the wall, the defenders had fought off attackers and climbers for, it seemed, an eternity. One cannon was out of action, its crew shot. Dámaso handed the last cannonball to the remaining cannon crew. He then grabbed his father's rifle and reloaded. Santa Anna's troops were numberless, an ocean coming in waves. They climbed the wall over heaps of fallen comrades and fired, stabbed and fired, their ammunition inexhaustible. The cannoneer aimed, fired the last cannonball and then gave a strangled cry. He was shot through the head, dead still standing. Dámaso shuddered as he saw the man fall, face down, draped like a rag over the cannon barrel. He smelled burnt cloth and the odor of cooking flesh. The barrel was red hot. *Dear God, don't let him feel any of that. Let him be truly dead.* Dámaso looked up just in time to see a figure in a sergeant's uniform face him from the top of a ladder newly placed against the wall.

He raised his rifle. His mouth opened in surprise. "Sergeant Padilla! I can't shoot you!"

Padilla's bullet struck him just below the heart and knocked him on his back. He felt the sergeant's boot crush his hand as he bayonetted the second cannoneer. Footsteps of more men followed, passing him by and thudding down the ramp. No resistance remained as more ladders were placed against the wall. Hordes of soldiers poured over the silent cannon emplacement.

Hand to hand combat, pistol and rifle fire, sabre against bayonet against bowie knife raged in the compound, where the Texians struggled to reach the fortified long barracks and convent buildings. Once there, they began a withering fire on the Mexican soldiers already in the main plaza.

The Mexican soldiers had seized the cannon at the gate of the courtyard, turned it around and were now firing against the convent and church walls. A portion of the convent wall collapsed and soldados began to pour in upon the defenders. Thanks to their sheer numbers, they overwhelmed the desperate courage and skill of the Texians. Even after all were slain, the soldados continued to slash and fire at anything that moved. It took minutes of vain shouting for the officers to stop the men from killing each other.

Silence descended, punctuated from time to time with lone musket or rifle shots.

Chapter Nineteen

Aftermath

anta Anna had won a glorious victory, at the cost of at least 400 lives of his own men, sacrificed to kill the 182 Texian and Tejano defenders.

The general, accompanied by several of his officers, his bodyguard, and the young *Alcalde*, José Francisco Ruíz, arrived to inspect the Alamo, awash in the blood of attacker as well as defender. Ruíz was no ally of Santa Anna's Centralist cause, to rid Texas of all Anglo settlers. Like his father, he was a republican partisan of the Constitution of 1824, abrogated by the man beside him. Santa Anna had forced Ruíz to accompany him to inspect the damage and identify the bodies of Travis, Bowie, and Crockett.

The concentrated stench of blood and gunpowder assaulted them as they passed through the gate and entered the main plaza of the Alamo. Both men halted, the general's escort almost stepping on their heels. The space before them was littered with bodies, mainly soldados, with a few of the Texians fallen in pools of blood here and there.

Santa Anna looked toward the courtyard and the chapel. "I was told there were women and children here."

"*Sí, Excelencia.*"

"Find them. If any one was injured, I'll find and punish the man who did that. I ordered non-combatants to be spared."

They moved a few feet farther into the open space, avoiding corpses. As they neared the stone building next to the gate, a member of the bodyguard called, "There's a woman in here, Your Excellency."

The group paused, and a guard dragged a limp body into the early morning sunlight.

Ruíz gasped and ran forward. "*¡Dios Mío!* ¡Emilia!" He knelt beside her and lifting her wrist, felt for a pulse.

"She's still warm. I think I feel a heartbeat. Is there any water anywhere?"

A member of the escort had scanned the interior of the rooms. "There's a barrel of water. And there's someone important in the little side room."

Santa Anna immediately entered the building, passing by Emilia's body as the guard dashed a pan of water into her face.

The general's voice came from within the second room. "Do you know who this man was, Ruíz?"

Francisco rose and entered the building. He regarded the corpse with pity and sorrow. It was riddled with bullets and bayonet wounds. "*Sí, Excelencia.* That was James Bowie. I heard he was ill during the fighting, but, look! he still holds a pistol in his right hand. Another's lying on the floor on his left side."

"He shot at least one of my soldados." Santa Anna pointed to a body lying near the inner door. "That corpse was across the door when I came in."

They returned outside. Emilia was sitting up, bewildered, looking at the circle of soldados around her. José Francisco hurried to her side. "Emilia! Are you hurt?"

"*Ah, Señor Ruíz!* Thank God you're here. Help me up, please."

Ruíz lifted her, heedless of soiling his own clothes. "You're all bloody! Are you wounded?"

"No, I don't think so. I was helping care for the wounded men in there." She nodded at the stone building. "You must help me find Dámaso! But... why are you here?" She wrung her hands.

Ruíz turned slightly toward Santa Anna, who had taken a few steps farther into the plaza. "*El General* demanded that I witness his total victory. I had no choice."

At that moment, Ramón Músquiz hurried up to the group. "Sorry, Francisco, I was held up." He glanced at the general with apprehension.

Su Excelencia sniffed, gave him a nod, then turned and began impatiently tapping his boot shank with his cane. "Where are Crockett and Travis? I must see them. And who is this woman?"

Emilia's chin came up. "*Soy Emilia Altamirano, enfermera.* My husband is Dámaso Jiménez, a rifleman at the northwest corner cannon emplacement. I must know if he lived or died."

Santa Anna slanted his head, looking Emilia up and down. "Washed and dressed properly, you'd be a beauty. Well, Ruíz, we'll go in that direction. After all, that's where the battle was won, when my reserves came up and forced the common soldiers over the wall."

Two officers near her gave each other sour glances.

Santa Anna continued. "We'll inspect the Alamo going clockwise." He strode off and the entourage followed. "Small chance even a flea survived up there, but let the woman see. Then we'll round up the other women, get someone to take them and the children out of here."

José Francisco placed Emilia's arm over his and they followed in the direction of the northwest cannon emplacement. As they neared it, they could see one body draped over a cannon barrel. Emilia's heart stopped. No! It couldn't be Dámaso! She and Ruíz mounted the ramp slowly and as they reached the top, Emilia moaned aloud.

The Texians lay where they had fallen, in various tortured positions. One man lay with the ramrod still gripped in one hand. Both he and the man looped over the cannon had been bayonetted as well as shot.

Dámaso! He lay on his back, throat exposed, in a pool of blood, shot in the chest and stabbed. Emilia fell to her knees, leaning in, ear against his pale lips. His body was faintly warm, but there was no breath, no movement, no pulse.

She lowered her head as close to him as she could, her unbound hair falling around his face. "I am with you always, my beloved...." She took her husband in a fierce embrace. "Yes, we two are one, and it will ever be so." She held him for a long moment, then stood, realizing that her arms and the front of her dress were sticky with more blood—the blood of the men she'd tried to help, but most of all with Dámaso's life blood, drenching his clothing and pooling around him as he lay.

He seemed peaceful now. She paused for a last look that she hoped would remain engraved in her memory and descended the rough log ramp into the land of the dead. Ruíz, wordless, followed her. An eerie silence had fallen. They walked among the dead bodies, the fallen enemy and corpses of those who had fought shoulder to shoulder, the Tejano patriots who fought for Texas's self-determination as one of the United States of Mexico, and those who had wished to take Texas from Mexico for themselves. She covered her face and moaned.

She stumbled and leaned on Francisco for support as they rejoined Santa Anna's group proceeding to the central cannon emplacement on the north wall. Ruíz stared toward the base of the ramp leading up to the cannons. He thought he recognized a corpse sitting there.

"¡Excelencia! That looks like *Colonel* Travis." He strode closer. "Yes, it is he. Seems he was killed by a bullet in the brain... but look! He's grasping a bloody saber! He must have gone down fighting."

"At least we were not fighting cowards." Santa Anna stood staring for a long minute as if memorizing the scene.

They had rounded the northeast corner of the plaza when a tall, imposing officer met them, leading two more officers and a group of five prisoners taken alive and under guard.

"That's *General* Castrillón," Ruíz told Emilia.

One of the prisoners, the tallest, who carried himself with dignity, struck her as familiar. She whispered, "Is that David Crockett? Alive?"

Ruíz nodded and brought his finger to his lips. Castrillón was speaking, asking for mercy for the prisoners. "I promised them clemency and told them they would be escorted to Mexico City as prisoners."

Santa Anna's face became more flushed by the second. "Damn you, Manuel! I gave an order that none of these dogs should be spared and I stand by that order." He turned to the men around him. "Execute these prisoners at once!"

Several of the officers voiced objections, but Santa Anna wouldn't hear them. "My order stands! Execute them! Now!" He turned on his heel and stalked away.

In the moment of hesitation that followed, Francisco grabbed Emilia's arm and pulled her in the direction of the main gate. "You mustn't see what's going to happen now! Don't look back!"

Behind them, orders, protests and exclamations in Spanish, then the clash of swords and sabers, cries and groans, but not one plea for pity from the men being butchered without mercy. Emilia took giant steps to keep up with Ruíz, but, horrified at the general's barbaric and infamous brutality, she pressed her face against the sleeve of Ruíz's jacket.

Once through the gate, the two took deep breaths of relatively fresh air. Inside the Alamo plaza, the air was increasingly unbreathable. Some soldados had piled severed limbs, torn uniforms and even dead bodies in heaps and set them burning. Some of the bodies were naked, since destitute soldados had stolen less disreputable uniforms. The stench was nauseating; the sight something out of religious depictions of Hell.

Hurrying footsteps issuing from the gate behind them startled them both. They turned to see Ramón Músquiz, who had trailed the group with Santa Anna inspecting the fallen Alamo. "I wish to God I'd never stayed to see that atrocity. You were right to take Emilia out of there. That sight will haunt my nightmares and torture me forever."

José Francisco laid a hand on Ramón's shoulder. "I wanted to avoid just that, and I knew Emilia had already been tortured beyond human endurance. Can you escort her home? I must get back in there or Santa Anna will find some way to punish my absence—probably take it out on my family."

"I will, gladly. They already know that the women and children should be taken to my house. We'll find food and drink for them, I'll see to that."

"*Mil gracias, amigo.*" Ruíz turned back and reentered the hell the Alamo had become.

Ramón took Emilia's arm. "Lean on me, my dear. I'll get you home soon. Or would you prefer going to my place? The other women will be there before long."

Emilia managed a faint smile. "*No, gracias, Señor Músquiz.* I need to get clean and change clothes. That's what I need most."

Santa Anna remained in Béxar until the end of March, when he departed with all but a thousand soldiers left behind under the command of *General* Juan José Andrade. Somewhere around a hundred-fifty wounded men remained alive with only twenty men to attend to them.

Emilia went through the motions of living, but felt that her soul was dead along with so many in the battle. The dead Texians and the Tejanos who had fought with them, including Dámaso, were cremated on two long funeral pyres on either side of the row of cottonwood trees east and a little south of the Alamo. Poor José Francisco Ruíz was tasked with the disposal of the four-hundred-odd soldados and their officers slain in combat. He buried around a hundred officers and men in San Fernando graveyard, but having run out of space, he obeyed Santa Anna's order and cast the other bodies into the San Antonio River, running swift and deep. Unfortunately, some bodies clogged the river from mid-city to a mile below. The stench of death hung like a pall over Béxar, and Santa Anna blamed Ruíz for not burying more of his dead men. Ultimately, enough helpers were dragooned into service to push the bodies away from the shores where they had lodged and send them on down the river to be devoured by buzzards and coyotes.

The dying did not cease. Those men who had been wounded continued to die, since Santa Anna had not thought to bring doctors, hospital equipment and medicines to care for what he'd expected to be a small number of casualties. There were hardly any medical provisions in Béxar. Even those with slight wounds died of gangrene, abetted by the poor diet of corn and occasional meat with no green vegetables to provide proper nutrition.

The population of Béxar dropped to a mere fifty original Tejanos as families and individuals fled the huge army's continued presence and the stench and constant presence of death. Santa Anna and the bulk of the army left the town over three weeks later, on March 31, to win, as the general thought, more glorious victories. *General* Andrade, now in command, desperately sought medical assistance.

After fourteen days of near paralysis, weeping, sleeping too much, forgetting to eat what poor food she could find, Emilia would have starved if José Francisco Ruíz and occasionally Ramón Músquiz had not seen to it that she eat a decent meal at least every other day.

I feel numb. Nothing is important; nothing has meaning. My soul must have joined Dámaso's and flew away with his. Without a soul

I, like the rest of the physical universe, am meaningless. Without him everything is gray. All gray.

When the period of deepest mourning was past, she began, a little at a time, to offer her services as a nurse.

On April 20, six weeks after the battle, Drs. Joseph Henry Barnard and Jack Shackleford had survived the massacre at La Bahía and arrived as prisoners from Goliad. Shocked by the condition of the wounded soldados so long after the battle, they hoped to set to work at once. But first, Dr. Shackleford had undertaken a small duty. He sought out José Francisco Ruíz. "Señor Ruíz, I have here a letter from a colleague, Dr. Charles McCray, addressed to a Señorita Emilia Altamirano. Do you know of such a person?"

Francisco pondered the sender's name. "Hmmm. 'Dr. Charles McCray.' That has a familiar ring. Oh, yes! He helped with the cholera epidemic a couple of years back. Emilia lost her mother during that scourge, while she was nursing.... Yes, yes, I know Emilia. I can get the letter to her. Just follow me. She'll be with the worst wounded."

The two doctors with their armed guard followed Ruíz to the Veramendi palace, set up as a sick ward for soldiers with compound fractures, many of whom had already died of lack of proper medical attention. They found Emilia changing bandages.

Dr. Shakleford, assuming she was the person addressed on the envelope, spoke first. "Are you Emilia Altamirano? He looked in shock at the patients on the beds surrounding her. "Just what are you doing for these men?"

She turned, her face nearly devoid of emotion, a length of bandage in one hand, scissors in the other. She answered in the English she had learned in the intervening weeks. "Yes, I am Emilia Altamirano. I am here to ease the dying of these wounded men left here without medical attention. The only disinfectant I have is whisky. I sponge their wounds with it and re-bandage them."

"I see." He introduced himself and Dr. Barnard. "We will help you in any way we can. But first, I have a letter for you."

"For me?" Emilia was amazed that anyone outside Béxar would know her. She examined the envelope. "Ah! From Dr. Charles Mc-Cray in Victoria!" She tore open the envelope and read:

My dear Emilia,   20th April, 1826

We here in Victoria have heard of the hideous defeat and massacre at the Alamo. Santa Anna's troops have passed north of us and burned Harrisburgh, but we have remained in relative safety. I know that you have been without caring relatives since your dear mother died. Because Béxar is in such dire straits at the moment, we intend to pass by and take you home with us to Victoria to give you some time away from such a dire scene. We will come to you as soon as it is safe to travel.

With my warm affection and love,

Your Charles

She wondered who "we" could be. Probably Charles had married by now. She did look forward to seeing visitors from somewhere far away from this scene of death and dying. Whether she would leave Béxar for a short time, a respite, she would decide later. She folded the letter as Dr. Barnard rejoined her and the group around her after examining those patients with fresh bandages. He nodded to her. "You're doing a competent job. I trust that you will assist us as we operate on the men who require it."

She gave a ghost curtsy. "I'd be happy to."

Since the men had struck up a conversation among themselves, she nodded to them and continued re-bandaging the soldados.

Afterwards, she acted as chief nurse to both doctors as they attended to the Alamo wounded, also to a new contingent of wounded from the Battle of San Jacinto when they arrived after May 6.

Only then did the Bexareños learn of General Houston's victory and the capture and imprisonment of Santa Anna. The wounded soldados told horror tales of surprise attack, bloody vengeance, and mass slaughter, and how the attacking forces kept shouting "Remember the Alamo! Remember Goliad and La Bahía!"

The utter defeat of the Mexican Army and lack of clear orders left Andrade in confusion until, on May 19, an order from *General* Vicente Filisola arrived, commanding him to leave Béxar and join the rest of the army retreating to Matamoros. Andrade had a couple of tasks to complete before leaving: the destruction of the Alamo as a fortress and disposal of the cannon. His troops dismantled the walls and most buildings of the Alamo compound, filled the trenches in and around it, and, since he considered the Texian cannon of inferior quality, he had them spiked and thrown into the river. He led his army out of Béxar on May 24. He surrendered Béxar to the Tejanos in the person of Juan Seguín, who became the latest *Alcalde*.

That night, the Ruíz, Músquiz families, the two doctors and Emilia met in the Músquiz house to enjoy a meager celebratory meal and to drink some of the whisky left over from the hospital dispensary.

Emilia, pleased to be included, watched the interaction between the Anglo doctors and the host families. The Músquiz women hastened to serve the doctors as if they were nobility, but Francisco leaned back in his chair, much more relaxed. "Like me," she thought, "he's seen enough—the heights of heroism and the depths of depravity—and he's not easily impressed."

Ruíz surprised her by raising the first glass. "Here's to the departure of the Mexican Army. I have correspondence from my father confirming that we've lost Texas in any case. As you all know, on March 2, even before the battle of the Alamo, the Texians met in Washington-on-the Brazos, wrote a Declaration of Independence and declared Texas an independent republic. My father and José

Antonio Navarro, your beloved mentor, Emilia, signed it. We even have a new constitution. We are now under Anglo domination.

"Thanks to the actions of that bloody dictator, Santa Anna, Mexico has lost our state to the Texians who now officially govern us. We all, including you, Drs. Shackleford and Barnard, are now citizens of a new nation." He drank off his whisky, leaving the other guests around the table in doubt as to whether to follow his lead or not.

Emilia heard a thunderous knock on the front door. Señora Músquiz admitted the visitor, Juan Seguín. As he joined the group in the dining room, all stood to honor their new *alcalde*.

He thanked them and asked them to take their seats. "The saddest thing. Odd, too," he began. "I just learned that when Ángel Navarro heard the news of the victory at San Jacinto, he went out into the street in front of his house and began to dance until he fell down dead. He must have had a heart attack. And we always thought his sympathies lay rather with the Centralist cause. Juana and Gertrudis have decided that his funeral mass will be tomorrow. We all need to honor him—he did much for Béxar in times of great stress."

Ruíz shook his head. "No, he was no Centralist. He despised Santa Anna. He knew how to temporize with him enough to prevent more damage to our town, but he hated him. He probably felt that the monster had finally received what he so richly deserved. Here's to Ángel Navarro. We'll give him a proper burial. May he rest in peace." He drank off a second glass of whisky, and this time, all joined him.

Emilia poured another finger of whiskey into her glass. She spoke, her voice strong and clear, past caring what others might think. "I drink also to the rank and file soldados, the men I've been caring for until the army left today. They are those who, like my beloved Dámaso for three years, had no choice of whom to shoot at. I've heard from survivors of San Jacinto how many hundreds—

a thousand, maybe—have been wantonly killed as vengeance for the Alamo slaughter. Thanks to that *cabrón*, Santa Anna, there are hundreds of new widows, thousands of orphans. And no one to care for them—certainly not the central government." She raised the glass. "To *all* innocent victims!"

Most of the guests lowered their eyes; there were sharp intakes of breath, then silence. Seguín broke it. "Emilia's right. Here's to those victims of war—all of them—forced to suffer and die for a cause most of them didn't even understand."

The guests talked until late that night, whereupon most of them, except for Emilia, dispersed to their homes or temporary residences.

The next morning, an important arrival: José Antonio Navarro appeared at the door, still splattered with mud from the last night's rain.

He greeted Señora Músquiz, who had answered the door. "I hear that you were hostess to some distinguished ladies of Béxar, the only survivors of the battle."

"Welcome, Señor José Antonio!" Yes, that's right. Santa Anna spared them."

"And that Emilia Altamirano was among them and is still here."

"Yes, she stayed the night."

At his point, Emilia, who could recognize her Tío's voice anywhere, rushed to the door and into Antonio's arms. "Ah, Tío, my most faithful friend! I've missed you so dreadfully!"

He embraced her for a long moment, then, his arm still around her shoulders, entered the house. Breakfast was still on the table, so Antonio helped himself, and then heard what everyone had to say about the siege and battle—everything that had happened in his absence.

For Emilia, the climax of Tío's account of his own activities was this: "Perhaps my most important function while I was away was to discourage a consistent tendency in the writers of the new constitution for the Republic of Texas. It's still in draft form, of course. They've written a clause making slavery legal in Texas, of course, but what truly makes me angry is that several of them want to include a clause depriving 'all Spanish-speaking inhabitants' of the right to vote. I intend to fight to the death, if need be, to prevent that clause from sneaking in and to preserve our rights as citizens."

The breakfast might well have lasted until mid-afternoon, but was interrupted by another thunderous knock on the door. Emilia politely offered to open to the newcomers. Before the door stood a tall, blond man, a slightly darker-haired young female companion at his side.

"*¡Dios mío!* Dr. McCray! Welcome!" She turned to the young woman and took her hand in both of hers. "And I suppose you must be Señora McCray?"

The doctor laid his hand on her shoulder. "No, Emilia, may I present my sister, Christina McCray? Christina, this is Emilia Altamirano, about whom I've told you much."

"Pleased to meet you, Emilia!"

"Likewise." She was delighted that both brother and sister had, from the beginning, spoken in fluent Spanish. "You've come just at the right moment. The Mexican army left yesterday with only a few of the severely wounded left behind."

Christina replied. "Yes, we knew that. We stayed outside in one of the nearby ranches until we were sure that all was clear."

Emilia smiled up at Charles. "I received your letter of April 20th even before we heard of the victory at San Jacinto. I've been thinking about your offer..."

"That's why we're here." Charles' intense look almost frightened her. "We've come to take you away to live with us in Victoria."

Startled, Emilia covered her mouth with one hand. "'To give me some time away from such a dire scene' is what you said. A respite, you meant, surely."

Charles cocked his head to one side. "A respite is a good beginning."

Emilia turned and beckoned them over her shoulder. "Well then, you'd better come into the parlor; we'll have to discuss such an outlandish proposal!" In itself, their proposal seemed logical and even necessary for her general health. What she feared, however, was to be totally immersed, all of a sudden, in Anglo life.

Two days later, the trio left Béxar in the carriage. Emilia had said good-bye to her tío, now on his way back to join the Texian legislators, and to the few friends left in Béxar. She fully intended to find Andrés and Carmen when she arrived in Victoria, where they had taken refuge with relatives. She took next-to-no luggage, but in her reticule she carried two carefully wrapped wolf carvings.

1848, *Twelve Years Later*

E milia stared out the window of the salon in her comfortable home, surveying the small town of Victoria. A white clapboard building two blocks away drew her attention. Someone approached the entrance, apparently unaware that it was Saturday when school was not in session. She, a teacher of the lower grades, supervised most of the school's curriculum and kept track of needed supplies. The stranger turned away after trying the door, and Emilia shifted her attention to the unsteady footfalls of the toddler behind her, Daniel, two years old. Before she could turn, she heard a thud, and a piping voice saying, "Oh-oh!"

"Dani! What was that?"

Vase and flowers lay on the floor, water dripping off the table and darkening the rug.

Dani pointed. "Dani dwop it."

"So I see. But it fell on the rug, so it didn't break. Lucky boy!"

She swept the child into her arms, bounced him a little and brushed his mid-brown hair out of his hazel eyes. "Let's go get a rag to sop up the water, then we'll give the flowers another drink. All right?"

"*Ahri*, Mama."

For the moment, she and Daniel were alone in the house; Dr. McCray and their first born, Carlos, seven last month, were out to see a patient. Emilia, who acted as his nurse when Charles needed her, such as during the cholera epidemic two years ago, was pregnant with a third child, a girl this time, they hoped. Carlos, named for his father Charles, was growing to be a handsome lad, with dark, almost black hair and intense blue eyes.

Emilia, at last, was happy. It had taken her four years to cease having nightmares and days of deep depression, still reliving the battle, still in mourning for her mother María and for her eternally loved husband, Dámaso. But Charles's steady love, gentle care and understanding had conquered her fears, and she was at peace. They had married early in 1840.

She now wore modest but elegant dresses and never spoke about her presence in the Alamo during that horrendous battle. She hadn't told Carlos, since children cannot help but talk. She'd tell him and Daniel when they were grown, since they had a right to know that part of the family history. Nor would she tell anyone else. She didn't want to become a circus attraction like Susanna Dickinson and her daughter Angelina.

Emilia had been accepted by the community of Victoria, despite her Mexican heritage—after all, she was their beloved town doctor's protégée and then wife, who had proven her worth in many ways. She had nursed the wounded and destitute after the devastating Comanche raid of August 1840 and the desperately ill during the recent cholera epidemic. Only a few Tejanos had returned to the town in the last few years after having been driven out en masse after the Battle of San Jacinto. Outside this tiny tolerated group, however, rank prejudice reigned, and anyone who looked or spoke like a Mexican was treated as inferior, a traitor, or both.

Yes, she was happy. But her world, her real world, had been submerged in the Anglo-American flood. She now spoke English most of the time, wore Anglo fashions, lived in an American house, taught an Anglo curriculum and her children would be brought up Anglo. All positions of importance and influence in government, commerce, even education were now dominated by that—to her—foreign culture. A small vestige of her world remained: a tiny Hispanic Catholic church, to which she belonged. This provided an anchor where she clung.

She remembered her mother's words, years ago now, referring to *General* Joaquín de Arredondo and the Battle of the Medina River in 1813: "Interesting, isn't it, how that massacre back then has determined the whole history of Texas from then on—including mine and yours, Emilia."

Appendix

A Brief History of Béxar de San Antonio

Béxar had existed for nearly a century when the story, *Before the Alamo, A Tejana's Story* begins". In 1718, Franciscan friars established the first of the missions, San Antonio de Valero (later "the Alamo") with its accompanying presidio, the fort that was to protect the mission. Craftsmen and families of the soldiers came, and their initial mud and wattle, thatched-roof huts (*jacales*) were the first buildings of what would become the village of Béxar. In 1731, the number of missions increased to five, and despite occasional Apache or Comanche raids, they prospered and converted a large number of Indians. Also in 1731, a group of Canary Island families arrived, who set to work turning the clump of *jacales* into a true village and then a town. The missions had accomplished their work by 1793 and began to be secularized, their lands distributed to the citizens of Béxar.

Spain's rule over "New Spain," as Mexico was then called, was heavy-handed and inefficient. Any important decision had to be referred to the viceroy in Mexico City and thence by ship to Madrid in Spain. A response could be delayed for months.

Béxar, the largest town in Texas, became the capital of the province, with a governor, an *alcalde* (mayor), and an *ayuntamiento* (city council). The *alcalde* also acted as juez de campo (chief judge) with the *ayuntamiento* as jury. This governmental plan worked efficiently until 1836.

A strict hierarchy ruled social life in all of New Spain. Spanish-born settlers were deemed superior to everybody else and held all important positions in government, in the military, the Roman Catholic Church, and in politics. Their New World-born offspring, a step down, though also of pure Spanish extraction, were called creoles and were considered second-class. Third came those of mixed parentage, native and Spanish, the mestizos. Then came the coyotes, a mixture of native, Spanish, and African. Last came Native Americans and at the bottom, Africans. The harsh rule of the Spanish, their exploitation and cruelty, earned them the pejorative name *gachupines* and ultimately, in 1810, fomented rebellion in the Mexican War of Independence.

Father Miguel Hidalgo, a creole, began it with a sermon against the tyranny of the king of Spain and the injustices of the status quo. He raised an army mainly of creoles along with untrained and undisciplined natives. The element of surprise gained them initial successes. However, the Royalist Army of trained, disciplined cavalry and foot soldiers defeated the insurgents and captured Hidalgo and his associates. They beheaded him and his close allies, displaying their heads at the corners of the Alhóndiga de Granaditas in Guanajuato—this to help put down the insurrection. It continued, however, in one form or another until 1821.

Texas joined the rebellion with an army of 1,800 raw recruits, many of them from contiguous states of the United States of America. Perhaps the most savage Royalist *general*, Joaquín de Arredondo, a Spaniard, engaged the Texan army at the Medina River in 1813 with a force of 2,000. His previous policy had been to take no prisoners, slaughtering insurgents and their families, and burning villages to ashes. At the Medina River, his tactical acumen easily carried the day. He trapped the rebel soldiers in a pincer movement and massacred them down to the last man. Leaving their corpses to rot, he moved into Béxar and executed any rebel sympathizer he could root out. Many had fled to Louisiana. Arredondo continued his "rebel cleansing" all over Texas until he had reduced the Hispanic population by half (some 6,000 to 3,000). Texas became a realm of widows. Since so few Tejano men were left, the remaining population of women and children was unable to grow. Arredondo, his Royalist troops and surrogate governors continued to occupy Béxar until 1821. He left Texas vulnerable to the Comanche, whose empire could now move back eastward, raiding for goods, weapons and horses, and slaughtering defenseless ranchers and the populations of small towns.

In 1821, the government in Mexico City declared Mexican independence from Spain. That same year, Stephen F. Austin obtained permission from Mexican central authorities and from Béxar to settle 300 Anglo-American families in Texas. Béxar saw them as an added barrier against Comanche expansion. The settlers wanted to grow cotton, a highly lucrative crop, and East Texas had a similar climate to the U.S. Deep South. The problem was labor: only African slaves could withstand the backbreaking labor of cotton-growing, the stifling heat and humidity. But when the young Mexican nation drew up its constitution in 1824, slavery was outlawed. Texas got around that stricture by passing an amendment allowing immigrants to bring in "indentured servants." Documents were then drawn up calling the slaves indentured servants, and in they came.

The federal Constitution of 1824 conferred statehood on the erstwhile Mexican provinces, each with a governor, legislature, judiciary, and militia—and its own constitution, governing its particular interests but in harmony with the federal Constitution of 1824. The Congress in Mexico City combined Texas—since it had so few citizens—with Coahuila to form the State of Coahuila y Texas. Now, Coahuila had ports on the Gulf, and the combined state had enough population. The amalgamation was finalized over Béxar's fierce opposition.

Anglo-American immigration into Texas increased at a feverish rate until by 1830 there were at least 20,000 Anglo settlers. Some came legally by means of land grants; others simply came, squatted, and were called "filibusters." Mexico City, alarmed at the rate of anglification, angry at the ruse that allowed slavery to continue unabated in Texas and fearing a takeover by the United States, prohibited further Anglo settlement. It also levied fees and taxes on imported goods, which caused resentment among Anglo-Americans against Mexico. Reluctant to learn Spanish, adopt the state religion (Catholicism), and abide by the laws of their new country, the Anglos frightened Mexico City and caused friction with the native Tejano population.

Antonio López de Santa Anna, former lieutenant under Arredondo and politician, posed as a Federalist and a liberal. He was elected president of Mexico in 1833. The previous president's program of extreme liberal reform had aroused conservative resistance among older, well-established politicians, military powers and clergy elites. Santa Anna, seeing power shift to the conservative, Centralist side, abolished the national congress and declared himself dictator and leader of the Centralist forces. He further abolished the Constitution of 1824 and led the army in brutal suppression of Federalist states, notably Zacatecas.

Texas was a hot-bed of resistance, led by Tejano partisans of the Constitution of 1824 and by Anglo-American settlers bent on forming an independent Republic of Texas. Both groups were passionately opposed to Santa Anna's dictatorial, Centralist policy.

After subduing Zacatecas, Santa Anna felt he must destroy Tejano Federalism and drive the Anglo settlers from Mexican soil. In late 1835, he and his army marched north. Their first goal was the suppression of Béxar and its Alamo fort. The Battle took place on March 6, 1836, where Santa Anna won a costly victory. He then marched eastward, destroying Anglo settlements as he went. Anglo settlers fled before the advancing army in what is known as the Runaway Scrape.

After the Battle of San Jacinto on April 21 and the unexpected but total victory by the Texian Army, the new Republic of Texas was fully established (declared even before the Alamo battle, on March 2, 1836). Raucous and unruly, it lasted to February 19, 1846, nearly ten years. It was annexed at the end of December 1845 by the United States, which had been hovering for decades over Texan land and resources. The Mexican War began four months later, and ended in 1848. The United States gained 525,000 square miles of territory (California, Arizona, New Mexico, Texas, and parts of Colorado, Utah, and Nevada). President Polk had achieved his ambition, however unjustly, to preside over a nation that stretched "from sea to shining sea."

List of Characters

(The "f" after names means "fictional"; the "h" means "historical")

Main Characters

Altamirano, Emilia – (f)
Altamirano, María – Her mother – (f)
Altamirano, Juan Andrés – Her father, (f)
Altamirano, Carmen Losoya – Juan Andrés' wife (f)
Jiménez, Dámaso – Emilia's beloved (h)
Miguel Jiménez – his father (f)
Luisa Jiménez – his sister (f)
Pedro Jiménez – his brother (f)
Navarro, José Antonio – Emilia's mentor, prominent Bexareño citizen, *Regidor*, *Alcalde*, state legislator (Coahuila y Texas), signer of the Texas Declaration of Independence (h)

Minor Characters – Bexareños
(in order of mention)

Navarro, José Ángel – Loyalist, prominent Bexareño, *Regidor*, *Alcalde*, half-owner of the mercantile store (h)

Zambrano, José Darío – Priest of San Fernando Church (1811-1820) (h)

Rosita – Owner of the fonda (cafe) on Main Plaza (Plaza de las Islas) (f)

Minor Characters – Bexareños (Cont.)

Ruíz, Francisco – (the elder), Prominent Bexareño citizen, *Regidor* (city council member), *Alcalde*, educator (h)

Veramendi, José Martín de – Prominent Bexareño, *Regidor*, state legislator and Governor of Coahuila y Tejas, half-owner of Béxar mercantile store (h)

Veramendi, Josefa Navarro de – Wife of José Martín (h)

Navarro, Concepción – Wife of José Ángel (h)

Navarro/Veramendi, Juana– Daughter of Concepción, adopted by the Veramendis (h)

Navarro/Veramendi, Gertrudis– Daughter of Concepción, adopted by the Veramendis (h)

Navarro/Escalera, Chipita – Daughter of Concepción (?) adopted by Luz Escalera (h)

Escalera, Luz – Adoptive mother of Chipita (h)

Baron de Bastrop, Dutch, prominent citizen of Béxar, *Regidor*, state legislator of Coahuila Texas – and impostor (h)

Erasmo Seguín, Spanish, prominent citizen of Béxar, *Regidor*, *Alcalde*, delegate to the central government in Mexico City, state legislator (Coahuila y Texas) (h)

Seguín, Juan Nepomuceno – Son of Erasmo, prominent citizen of Béxar, military leader who participated at the Alamo battle, fought at San Jacinto, *Alcalde* (h)

Gabriela – Rosita's daughter, heiress to the fonda on Main Plaza (f)

Arciniega, José Miguel de – Prominent citizen of Béxar, Regidor (h)

de la Garza, Refugio– Priest of San Fernando Church (1820-1840), delegate to the central government in Mexico City (h)

Nava, Andrés – Regidor, died in the Alamo battle (h)

Ruíz, José Francisco Antonio – Son of Francisco Ruíz, *Alcalde* of Béxar during the siege and Battle of the Alamo (h)

Músquiz, Ramón – Wealthy merchant, influential Bexareño (h)

Historical Persons of Importance

Austin, Stephen F. – Empresario of the first Anglo colony (300 families) in Texas (h)

Bustamante, Anastasio – First President of Mexico under the Constitution of 1824, deposed by Santa Anna (h)

Domínguez, Cristóbal – Governor of Texas (1813-1814); Arredondo appointee (h)

Hidalgo-Costilla, Miguel Gregorio – Instigated the rebellion against Spanish supremacy over Mexico (h)

Martínez, Antonio María– Governor of Texas (1817-1822) (h)

Salinas, Francisco García – Governor of Zacatecas; General who fought for the Federalist Constitution of 1824 and lost (h)

Anglo Characters not in the Battle of the Alamo

Bobbs, George H. – Merchant in Béxar (h)

Crow, Jedediah – Settler ("filibuster") (f)

Crow, Kathleen, his wife,

Crow, Bonnie , his daughter

McCray, Charles – Physician from Stephen Austin's colony (f)

McCray, Christina – Dr. Charles McCray's sister (f)

McCray, Daniel and Carlos – Charles McCray's/Emilia's sons (f)

Texians in the Effort against Santa Anna
(in order of mention)

Travis, William B. – Commander of the Alamo defenders (h)

Baugh, John – Captain, Texian Alamo defender (h)

Crockett, David – U.S. Senator, defender of the Alamo (h)

Bowie, James – Pioneer, talented military commander, husband of Ursula Veramendi, died in the Battle of the Alamo (h)

Fannin, James Walker, Jr. – General of the Texian army in La Bahia/Goliad (h)

Houston, Sam – Commander of the Texian army, Statesman, First President of the Republic of Texas (h)

Texians in the Effort against Santa Anna (Cont.)

Howell, William – Doctor in the Alamo. Other doctors: Amos Pollard, John Reynolds (h)
Doctors pressed into service to care for wounded Mexican soldiers in Béxar – Joseph Henry Barnard and Jack Shackleford, prisoners from La Bahía (h)

Tejanos in the Battle of the Alamo

Herrera, Blas – Tejano scout under Juan Seguín's command (h)
Members of Juan Seguín's Militia – Manuel Flores, Ambrosio Rodríguez, Antonio Menchaca, Eduardo Ramírez, Antonio Cruz, and Silvero (h)
Died in Battle – Toribio Losoya, Juan Abamillo, Gregorio Esparza, Juan Badillo, Antonio Fuentes, Guadalupe Rodríguez, Carlos Espalier, Andrés Nava, and Dámaso Jiménez, [recorded as Damasio] all officially listed among the historical Tejano defenders of the Alamo

Women in the Alamo

Alsbury, Juana Navarro/Veramendi – Wife of Doctor Horace Alexander Alsbury and widow of Alejo Pérez – Juana's baby son by a first marriage (h)
Dickinson, Susanna – Wife of Almaron Dickinson, who died in the Battle of the Alamo and Angelina, their daughter (h)
Esparza, Ana Salazar Castro – Gregorio Esparza's wife; sons Enrique, Francisco and Manuel, older step-daughter María Castro (h)
Losoya, Concepción – Toribio Losoya's mother (h)
Navarro/Veramendi, Gertrudis – Juana's younger sister (h)

Other women who left the Alamo before the battle – Juana Milton, Toribio's sister, Petra Gonzales, Mrs. Cadbury, her sister Victoriana Salinas, her daughter, and Trinidad Saucedo (h)

Characters in the Mexican Army (in order of mention)

Arredondo, *General* Joaquín de – Royalist general, winner of the Battle (and massacre) of the Medina River (1813) (h)

Urrea, José de – General under Santa Anna's command; never defeated in battle (h)

Padilla, *Sargento* – Mexican army (f)

Teniente Francisco de Castañeda – Mexican army, known for having lost the Battle of Gonzalez (h)

Farrier – Mexican army (f)

Ugartechea, Domingo de – Commander of Alamo Presidio in 1835; Mexican army (h)

Cos, Martín Perfecto de – General, Mexican army, occupied Béxar from October 9-December 9, defeated in the Siege of Béxar by Benjamin R. Milam, commanding the Texian attack force (h)

Officers in Santa Anna's army – Juan Nepomuceno Almonte Manuel Fernández Castrillón, José Miñón, José Batres, Antonio Gaona, Francisco Duque, Vicente Filisola (h)

Andrade, Juan José – General left in charge of Béxar after Santa Anna's departure (h)